# PRAISE FOR DENISE HUNTER

"Denise Hunter's newest novel, *Sweetbriar Cottage*, is a story to fall in love with. True-to-life characters, high stakes, and powerful chemistry blend to tell an emotional story of reconciliation. Readers will sympathize with Josephine's tragic past and root for her happy ending as old wounds give way to new beginnings."

— BRENDA NOVAK, *New York Times* BESTSELLING AUTHOR

"*Sweetbriar Cottage* is a wonderful story, full of emotional tension and evocative prose. You'll feel involved in these characters' lives and carried along by their story as tension ratchets up to a climactic and satisfying conclusion. Terrific read. I thoroughly enjoyed it."

—FRANCINE RIVERS, *New York Times* BESTSELLING AUTHOR OF *Redeeming Love*

"From start to finish, *Sweetbriar Cottage* is a winner! Heartache, intrigue, and complex character issues all wrapped in Denise Hunter's signature style of romance make this a must read for lovers of this genre."

—TAMERA ALEXANDER, *USA Today* BESTSELLING AUTHOR
OF *To Whisper Her Name* AND *The Inheritance*

"Warning: sleep deprivation, palpitations, and acute soul-searching may occur . . . and you will devour every single moment! A powerful novel of second chances, *Sweetbriar Cottage* is a haunting love story that will take you from the depths of divorce to the breathless heights of a marriage transformed."

—JULIE LESSMAN, AWARD-WINNING AUTHOR OF THE DAUGHTERS OF
BOSTON, WINDS OF CHANGE, AND ISLE OF HOPE SERIES

"Hunter has a wonderful way of sweeping readers into a delightful romance without leaving behind the complications of true love and true life. *Sweetbriar Cottage* is Hunter at the top of her game—a rich emotional romance that will leave readers yearning for more."

—KATHERINE REAY, AWARD-WINNING AUTHOR OF *Dear
Mr. Knightley* AND *A Portrait of Emily Price*

"In *Sweetbriar Cottage*, Denise Hunter has written one of the best stories about emotional healing and forgiveness that I've read in ages. I couldn't turn the pages fast enough to reach the resolution. Suspenseful, heartbreaking, and ultimately sigh-worthy, you don't want to miss this one."

—ROBIN LEE HATCHER, RITA AND CHRISTY AWARD WINNING AUTHOR OF *You'll Think of Me* AND *You're Gonna Love Me*

"With cameos of favorite characters from previous novels set in rural Summer Harbor, Maine, Hunter delivers what her audience expects: sweet romance and intriguing mystery involving seriously likeable characters."

—*Publishers Weekly* ON *The Goodbye Bride*

"Can romance be any more complicated than a bride who doesn't remember running away from her groom? Denise Hunter's take on a woman's attempt to find her way back to happily ever after again is sweetly endearing. Readers will keep turning pages, wanting to know how true love ever went so wrong . . . and if *The Goodbye Bride* gets her chance to say 'I do.'"

—BETH K. VOGT, 2015 RITA FINALIST AND AUTHOR OF *Crazy Little Thing Called Love*

"I've been a long-time fan of Denise Hunter's, and *The Goodbye Bride* has everything I've come to love about her romances: a plucky heroine with lots of backstory, a yummy hero, and a terrific setting. Her fine attention to detail and the emotional punch of the story made me want to reread it immediately. Highly recommended!"

—COLLEEN COBLE, *USA Today* BESTSELLING AUTHOR OF *Mermaid Moon* AND THE HOPE BEACH SERIES

"Denise Hunter has done it once again, placing herself solidly on my must-read list! *The Goodbye Bride* is a tender, thoughtful look at the role memories play in a romance. The clever plot kept me up way past my bedtime—and happy to be so!"

—DEBORAH RANEY, AWARD-WINNING AUTHOR OF THE CHICORY INN NOVELS

"*The Goodbye Bride* is one heart-stopping, page-turning romance that will leave the pickiest romance reader delighted and asking for just a few more pages."

—CARA C. PUTMAN, AWARD-WINNING AUTHOR OF *Where Treetops Glisten* AND *Shadowed by Grace*

"Hunter's fans will want this one."

—*Library Journal* ON *Falling Like Snowflakes*

"With her usual deft touch, snappy dialogue, and knack for romantic tension, inspirational romance veteran Hunter will continue to delight romance fans with this first Summer Harbor release."

—*Publishers Weekly* ON *Falling Like Snowflakes*

"Hunter is a master romance storyteller. *Falling Like Snowflakes* is charming and fun with a twist of mystery and intrigue. A story that's sure to endure as a classic reader favorite."

—RACHEL HAUCK, AUTHOR OF *The Wedding Dress* AND THE ROYAL WEDDING SERIES

"A handful of authors dominate my must-read list, and Denise Hunter is right at the top. *Falling Like Snowflakes* is a taut romantic thriller that will warm you to the core."

—JULIE LESSMAN, AWARD-WINNING AUTHOR OF THE DAUGHTERS OF BOSTON, WINDS OF CHANGE, AND HEART OF SAN FRANCISCO SERIES

"[*Married 'til Monday*] . . . leaves one knowing that love is worth fighting for."

—*RT Book Reviews*, 4-STAR REVIEW

"A beautiful story—poignant and heartwarming, filled with delightful characters and intense emotion. Chapel Springs is a place anyone would love to call home."

—RAEANNE THAYNE, *New York Times* BESTSELLING AUTHOR ON *The Wishing Season*

". . . skillfully combines elements of romance, family stories, and kitchen disasters. Fans of Colleen Coble and Robin Lee Hatcher will enjoy this winter-themed novel."

—*Library Journal* ON *The Wishing Season*

"This is an emotional tale of overcoming the fear of loss to love again and God's love, made manifest through people, healing all wounds. The heroine's doubts, fears, and eventual acceptance of the gift God has given her are told in a sympathetic and heartwarming way. The hero's steadfastness is poignantly presented as well."

—*Romantic Times*, 4 STARS ON *Dancing with Fireflies*

"Romance lovers will . . . fall for this gentleman who places his beloved's needs before his own as faith guides him."

—*Booklist* ON *Dancing with Fireflies*

"Hunter's latest Chapel Springs Romance is a lovely story of lost and found, with a heroine struggling to accept that trusting God doesn't make life perfect—without loss or sorrow—but can bring great joy. The hero's love for her and willingness to lose her to save her is quite moving."

—*Romantic Times*, 4 STARS ON *Barefoot Summer*

"Jane Austen fans will appreciate the subtle yet delightful Austen vibe that flavors this contemporary cowboy romance—and not just because *Pride & Prejudice* is protagonist Annie's favorite book. *The Trouble with Cowboys* is a fast, fun, and touching read with the added draw of a first kiss that is sure to make my Top 5 Fictional Kisses of 2012. So saddle up, ladies: We have a winner!"

—USATODAY.COM

# Sweetbriar Cottage

# OTHER NOVELS BY DENISE HUNTER

# Sweetbriar Cottage

## DENISE HUNTER

THOMAS NELSON
*Since 1798*

*Sweetbriar Cottage*

© 2017 by Denise Hunter

Published in Nashville, Tennessee, by Thomas Nelson. Thomas Nelson is a registered trademark of HarperCollins Christian Publishing, Inc.

Thomas Nelson, Inc., titles may be purchased in bulk for educational, business, fund-raising, or sales promotional use. For information, please e-mail SpecialMarkets@ThomasNelson.com.

Scripture quotations are taken from the New King James Version®. © 1982 by Thomas Nelson. Used by permission. All rights reserved.

Publisher's Note: This novel is a work of fiction. Names, characters, places, and incidents are either products of the author's imagination or used fictitiously. All characters are fictional, and any similarity to people living or dead is purely coincidental.

### Library of Congress Cataloging-in-Publication Data

Names: Hunter, Denise, 1968- author.
Title: Sweetbriar Cottage / Denise Hunter.
Description: Nashville, Tennessee: Thomas Nelson, 2017.
Identifiers: LCCN 2016055698 | ISBN 9780718090487 (softcover)
Subjects: LCSH: Married people--Fiction. | Reconciliation--Fiction. | GSAFD: Christian fiction. | Love stories.
Classification: LCC PS3608.U5925 S94 2017 | DDC 813/.6--dc23 LC record available at https://lccn.loc.gov/2016055698

*Printed in the United States of America*

17 18 19 20 21 LSC 5 4 3 2 1

# Chapter 1

*Copper Creek, Georgia*

*Present day*

There was nothing like a letter from the IRS to stop a man in his tracks. Noah Mitchell came to a halt outside the Copper Creek post office, an uneasy dread leaking into his veins as he stared at the envelope.

He should've known better than to come down off the mountain and ruin a perfectly good Saturday. Granted, this wasn't the way he'd feared it would be ruined, but it was still a kick in the pants.

He sank onto a nearby bench, dumping the bundle of mail beside him. A cold breeze blew across the valley, but heat prickled beneath his jacket. Though March had arrived in northern Georgia, Mother Nature hadn't gotten the memo. The grass lay brown and dull against the semi-thawed earth, and the branches of the skeletal trees clacked together in the wind.

He pulled a finger through the envelope's seal, sending a plea heavenward. He supposed he was due. He was thirty-one and had never experienced the joy of an audit. Unfortunately, he'd filed for himself last year.

Noah unfolded the paper as the sun broke through the clouds, its reflection nearly blinding on the white paper. He scanned the paragraphs, squinting against the light, his eyes stopping on a key sentence in the second paragraph.

He reread the sentence, blinking in disbelief. *Of all the idiotic . . .*

Noah was as patriotic as they came. He'd served overseas for a tour, for crying out loud. Stars and stripes, baseball, apple pie, all that. But sometimes the ineptitude of the American government left him scratching his head.

"Well, look who's come off the mountain."

Noah looked up to find his best friend, Jack McReady— "Pastor Jack" to most of the town—ambling toward him. Even though it was a Saturday morning, he wore khakis and a button-down. His lips stretched into the smile that had half the single females in his church swooning. He was oblivious to it all.

"Hey, Jack." Noah rose, grasping his friend's hand and pulling him in for a shoulder bump. "Good to see you, buddy."

"I was starting to think I was going to have to come up there and drag you down."

"The ranch is keeping me busy."

"Even horses sleep. How are you? Make it through the winter okay?"

"Lost a foal back in January. Other than that, it's going well. I'm finishing the attic in the cottage. How are things here in town?"

"Oh, you know, the usual. Rumors, Facebook drama, town council tiffs. Let's grab a bite. I was just heading over to the Rusty Nail."

Noah thought of the letter, now burning a hole in his coat pocket. "I'd like to, but I have a few errands. Have to be back to the ranch by three. Let's do it soon though."

Jack's blue eyes fastened on Noah's, doing that thing where he seemed to look right into his soul. "Everything okay?"

Nothing had been okay for a long time. Not since the divorce. But Jack already knew that. "Yeah. Just . . . life . . . you know."

"Sure." Jack nodded, his eyes still piercing. "Sure."

They parted ways a few minutes later, promising to touch base in the next couple weeks.

Noah gathered his mail and started the short walk toward Walt Levenger's office. He tugged down his cap and lowered his head—against the wind, he told himself. After all, her shop was on the other side of town and no doubt bursting at the seams on a Saturday morning. Chances of running into her were slim.

The downtown of Copper Creek was straight out of a movie set. Diagonal parking along Main Street. Two-story shops with colorful awnings, proudly facing the street, their *Open* flags fluttering in the wind. You could walk from one end to the other in fifteen minutes, and a few minutes later Noah was most grateful for that.

When he stepped into the CPA's office, the phone was ringing. Two people waited by the front desk where a harried teenager shouldered a phone and jotted on a yellow Post-it.

He took his place in line, his mind going back to that one jarring sentence in the letter. Walt was a family friend. He'd tell him how to straighten this out. Then Noah would just put this behind him.

But somehow the letter had stirred up all kinds of things he thought he'd already put behind him. Memories—the best of his life, the worst of his life—swirled together in a confounding cocktail of joy and pain. A vise tightened around his heart, squeezing until his breath stuttered.

"Can I help you?" The teenaged girl peered at him through a pair of thick-framed glasses.

He eased forward. "Hi, I'm here to see Walt."

The phone pealed. "Do you have an appointment?"

"No, but it's a pressing matter. He's a friend of the family."

"Name?"

"Noah Mitchell."

"Have a seat, please."

She answered the phone while he joined the others in the waiting room. The letter crinkled in his pocket as he settled against the curved plastic chair.

He took out his phone and made a list of items he needed from the Piggly Wiggly. He could hit Buddy's Hardware while he was in town too. He needed mud and sanding paper for the attic. Might as well get the paint too. Save him a trip back to town. Maybe he'd hunt down his brother and grab a cup of coffee if he had time.

"Noah, you can go on back."

He followed the short hall to the first open door on the left and tapped on the frame.

Walt stood up behind a cluttered desk and extended his hand. "Noah, come on in."

Noah shook his hand. "Good to see you, sir."

Walt was winning the weight war that often accompanied a desk job, but he was losing the battle with his hairline.

"Thanks for seeing me on such short notice. I'm sure you're swamped with the tax season."

Walt pulled off his bifocals. "I have some help this year.

Young sprig, fresh out of college. He's going to be the death of me."

Noah's lips tugged northward.

"You look more like your daddy every time I see you," Walt said. "Good-looking son of a gun. Have a seat, why don't you. How are your folks?"

"Enjoying retirement. They're in Las Vegas this week. Last week they were hiking the Sierra Nevadas. Next week, who knows?"

"Good for them. They've been looking forward to this a long time."

"They have. How's your family?"

"Fine and dandy. Here's my new grandbaby." He handed Noah a framed photo of a newborn, swaddled and pink-skinned. "Lori Ann, after my wife."

"Congratulations. She's a beauty."

"That she is." Walt settled the photo back in place. "Well, what can I do for you, Noah? Needing some help with your taxes this year?"

"Not exactly." He pulled the letter from his pocket and handed it over the desk. "Got this in the mail today. Was hoping you could advise me on how to go forward."

Walt settled his readers in place. A frown creased his brow as he read.

It seemed like an hour passed before the older man's eyes finally lifted, meeting Noah's gaze over the straight rim of his glasses. "When was your divorce finalized, Noah?"

*Divorce.* Would he ever get used to the word? "Before January of the tax year in question."

"You were right to file single then, of course." His gaze fell to the letter.

"How can I fix this?"

"Well, if it's in error, you just send them a copy of your final divorce decree. In a month or two you'll receive a letter stating that the matter's been resolved."

"What do you mean '*if* it's in error'?"

Walt handed back the letter. "Well, you might just check with your attorney and be sure things got tied up nice and proper."

Noah blinked. "Of course they did."

"Well, sure. You just send a copy of that final decree, then, and that'll be the end of it."

The end of it. The divorce had been uncontested, as simple as the act could be, he supposed. But there was nothing simple when it came to separating one flesh. If there was anything he'd learned in all this, that was it.

The phone pealed again in the front office, shaking Noah from his stupor. "All right then. Much obliged, sir. I won't take any more of your time." He stood, his legs quaking beneath him.

"Good luck, Noah. You say hello to your folks the next time you hear from them."

"Will do."

Noah's heart raced as he strode down the hall, his mind spinning.

The final decree. He had those papers. He'd signed them, and Josephine had sent him a copy. He remembered that much, even if those grief-laden months were as foggy as the valley on a warm spring morning. Facing Josephine across that old scarred table. Feeling like strangers, despite their nearly two-year marriage, her porcelain skin pale against her red lipstick. Working in a daze, forgetting to eat. Lying in his empty bed night after night, a concrete block on his chest.

The divorce decree. He couldn't say where it was just now, but he knew he had it.

It was all just a mistake. But there was no sense going all the way back up the mountain when he could drive across town and make absolutely sure. He'd get a copy from the attorney and mail it while he was still in town. Get it behind him. Lickety-split.

He turned left at the sidewalk and worked his way back to his Silverado. Traffic in town was heavy, everybody out running errands like he was. When he reached the Connelly Law Offices he turned into the space and headed inside.

The jingling bell announced Noah's arrival, and Joe Connelly came out of his office.

"Noah, good to see you."

"I wasn't sure you'd be open."

The men shook hands. Joe's partner, Vernon, had represented both Noah and Josephine in the divorce. But a serious heart attack soon had the man retiring to Colorado where he could enjoy his son and grandkids.

"A man's got to be open on Saturdays anymore if he wants to stay in business. My secretary's out sick with the flu. Have a seat. Can I get you a cup of coffee or a glass of tea?"

"Coffee sounds great."

Joe poured a cup and handed it to him. "Come on back. I'm just working on a deposition, nothing that can't wait."

As Noah followed, he drew a deep breath, trying to steady his nerves. Was it just him, or did the building actually smell like a place where marriages came to die?

He took a seat across from Joe's desk—a direct contrast from Walt's. Other than a tidy stack of papers and a canister of pens it was all glossy mahogany.

Joe folded his hands on the desk. "What can I do for you, Noah?"

For the second time this morning he withdrew the letter from his pocket and explained the situation.

Joe listened intently, his hawk-like eyes fixed on Noah. "I see," he said when Noah was finished. "Well, hopefully the IRS is mistaken—it wouldn't be the first time. Do you remember signing the divorce decree?"

"I do. I have a copy at home." He probably hadn't been as attentive as he should've been through the process. He had been reeling, and there was an intense desire to push all the details onto Josephine. She'd had it coming, after all.

"A divorce is finalized when the decree is signed by both parties, then by the judge."

"The judge?" Noah palmed the side of his neck, feeling like an immense idiot. "I don't remember seeing a judge's signature, but I wasn't really looking for it either."

"Well, the courthouse is closed, but we can certainly check our files." Joe stood and walked over to a wall of filing cabinets. "I just can't imagine Vernon letting this slip through the cracks."

"Things were winding down in the process when he had his heart attack."

Joe's fingers walked along the top of the files. "He came back to the office to tie up loose ends before he moved. I suppose it's possible the decree was overlooked." Joe pulled a file and shut the drawer. "Let's see what we have here."

Noah's heart pummeled his ribs as Joe flipped through the papers. *Please, God.* He'd just come to town to run his errands. How could this be happening?

Joe pulled a packet from the envelope. "Well, here's a copy of the decree."

Noah's lungs emptied. "Thank God."

"Well . . . hold your horses," the lawyer said after he flipped to the last page. "It's not been signed by the judge."

Noah sank into his seat.

"There's a note stating he gave a copy to Josephine on September 28. Once the judge signs, copies are sent to both parties, and we retain a copy for our records. Since there's no such copy here, it was never submitted to the judge. You can check with the courthouse on Monday to be certain, but it looks as though your divorce was never finalized, Noah."

A nervous laugh slipped out. "I can't believe this is happening."

Joe set his hand on Noah's shoulder. "I know it seems bad, but this is easily rectified. The divorce is probably still pending. It happens more often than you'd think. Just be glad neither of you has remarried. And yes, that actually happens."

*Easily rectified.*

The words bounced through Noah's head as he left the office. Easy for Joe to say. *He* hadn't been unknowingly married for the past eighteen months to the woman who'd wrecked his world. He hadn't been completely failed—twice now—by the woman he'd once loved more than life.

*Josephine. You're still married to her. She's still your wife.*

His traitorous heart gave an extra heavy thud, followed by a quick stutter. Longing surged, strong and unrelenting, making his chest tight, his breathing laborious.

The innate reaction made his blood boil. That she still had that power over him . . . Would it never end? What kind of idiot was he?

This was all her fault. She'd promised to handle this. And here they were. Eighteen months later and still married.

He'd somehow kept a lid on his emotions through the endless process of their divorce. Had somehow bottled it up, clamped his teeth together, locked his lips. If she knew he was shattered it wasn't because he'd fallen apart in front of her. If she knew about the anger churning inside him it wasn't because he'd raged at her.

But the emotions roiling now begged for release. And his feet, now striding purposely down the sidewalk, seemed helpless against the force. This time she was going to know exactly how he felt.

# Chapter 2

Josephine Mitchell dragged a comb through Abel Crane's newly trimmed hair. Her nimble fingers tugged here and there on the coarse strands, covering a cowlick, taming a wave. Abel was in his sixties with a thick head of gray hair that grew as fast as a June lawn.

The Saturday-morning crowd filled Josephine's Barbershop with the familiar sounds of chatter, the buzz of a razor, and the splash of water in the bowls. She caught the nutty scent of shaving cream and heard the scrape of a blade as her friend and fellow stylist, Callie, drew it deftly across her customer's cheek.

Josephine whipped the cape from Abel's shoulders. "Ta-da! Handsome as ever, Mr. Crane."

"Much obliged, dear."

Abel lived in the foothills in a mobile home that had seen better days. Two years ago, after a back injury at the gravel pit, he'd had to file for disability. His wife stayed home with their grown daughter, who had severe cerebral palsy and was confined to a wheelchair.

The bell over the door tinkled behind the partition wall as Josephine replaced her tools. Her four stylists were busy with their own customers.

"Be right with y'all," she called.

On Abel's way to the lobby he fished his wallet from his pocket in a routine as familiar as the smell of shampoo.

Josephine stopped him. "Now, sugar, you know your money's no good here. Go buy that wife of yours a Danish, and tell her I said hey."

Abel's round cheeks flushed. "Aw, you don't have to do that, Josephine. Things is better now that our boy's out on his own."

She gave his arm a light swat. "Now you get on, Abel Crane. I'll see you next month. And tell Lizzie to stop in and see me."

"Will do," he said, exiting the shop. "Much obliged, Josephine."

She turned, seeking the new arrival. "Just give me a second to sweep up and—"

Her eyes connected with the waiting customer. But it wasn't just any customer. It was Noah. Standing tall and confident in the corner of her little lobby, making her chest ache on sight. That's how it was with Noah. He walked through her door, and just like that the past eighteen months fluttered away on a breeze.

"Noah." His name escaped on a breath.

His hair was wind-tousled, his jaw all sharp angles and scruffy bristle. His amber-colored eyes snapped with fire. "We need to talk."

Her mouth opened, but her brain was a jumble. She couldn't think why on earth he'd be here, why he'd be angry with her. She hadn't laid eyes on him since the deposition.

She crossed her arms, a flimsy barrier at best, and pasted a smile on her lips. "All right. What is it?"

A shadow passed over his jaw. "What is it? I'll tell you what it is, *Josephine*."

That stung. She didn't expect to hear "baby girl" in that low gravelly voice, but Josephine? He'd called her Josie from the start.

He leaned closer, and the full effect of his masculine smell made her woozy. "I need to see a copy of our divorce decree."

She blinked, her eyes fluttering around the lobby, grateful it was empty. Still, the partition wasn't made of steel. A wave of heat flooded up her neck and into her cheeks.

"Lower your voice, please."

"The decree, Josephine. Go get it."

"Fine. It's upstairs. I'll fetch it." She hated the way her voice wobbled. She turned and headed toward the back of her shop. The smile fixed to her lips faltered when she caught sight of Noah in the mirror, following her.

Well, this would surely be all over town by lunch. Josephine DuPree Mitchell entertaining her ex-husband in her apartment in broad daylight.

She slipped through the back door into the short hall that led to her apartment stairs. When she reached the landing, she saw Noah lagging behind at the bottom of the stairs, thick biceps crossed over his chest.

"Aren't you coming?"

He nailed her with stormy eyes that flickered with distrust. "I think I'll just stay put."

The heat in her cheeks intensified as she made her way up the remaining stairs, knees wobbling like a three-legged table as her brain tried to digest the past surreal minute. Noah here. In her shop.

She tried to forget the flinty look on his face. So different from the way he used to look at her, his lion eyes soft with adoration, his beautiful lips curved with contentment as they lay noodle-limbed in their bed. It had always been easiest to push back the fear in those satiated minutes before sleep dragged her under.

*Well, you have no one to blame but yourself, Josephine.* The familiar stab of guilt twisted hard in her chest, and she let herself feel its impact for a long, self-indulgent moment.

She couldn't think on that now. Focus. Where had she put those papers?

Her eyes scanned her cluttered apartment. She had no real file cabinet, but everything of importance wound up on her desk. She fluttered past the bills and dived to the bottom of the stack. Not there. She moved on.

Her fingers trembled, clumsy. A pile of papers drifted to the hardwood floor, and she stooped down to gather them, coupons mostly and ads she hadn't had time to sort through. She wavered as she stood back up. Where was it?

She moved to the drawers, rifling through them. Mercy, what a mess. She needed to get organized. One never knew when one's ex-husband would be waiting, arms crossed, temper flaring, at the bottom of one's stairs.

The clock was ticking, and the temper—she had a notion— was getting worse with each passing moment. She found the decree in the bottom of the last drawer and pulled it out with a heartfelt sigh.

She took an extra moment to steady her breath, her eyes catching the mirror by the front door. The adrenaline flowing through her system had left her cheeks flushed and her forehead dewy. She blotted her skin with a tissue and resisted the urge to freshen her lipstick and fluff her hair.

Funny how she still wanted to look nice for him. Some things never changed, she supposed.

Clutching the packet, she left her apartment and took the stairs slowly, drawing deliberate deep breaths. Noah waited at the bottom, silent and dangerous—but only to her emotional well-being.

She scrounged up a smile as she surrendered the envelope. "Here you are. I can make you a copy if you've lost yours."

He spared her a stony look as he pulled the document from the envelope.

She shifted on unsteady legs. "I agreed to all your terms, Noah. I can't imagine what's got you all riled up." Her laugh sounded nervous, choked off as it was by the tightness of her throat.

He opened the stapled document and folded it back, then held it in front of her. "What's this, Josephine? What do you see here?"

She backed away until the print on the page sharpened. Their names, typed out nice and neat. Their signatures on the corresponding lines.

And a line below that for the judge. An empty line.

"So . . . I-I guess we forgot to get the judge's signature?"

"*We* didn't forget. *You* did."

She took the packet from his steely grip. "The attorneys probably have the signed copy."

He gave a laugh, not the humorous kind. "Oh, I assure you, they don't." He took the papers and leaned in until she caught sight of the flecks of brown in his eyes that used to mesmerize her.

"We're not divorced, Josephine. The papers were never signed by the judge."

Her heart skipped a beat. "What—what are you talking about?"

"You didn't finish the process! It never got finalized." He leveled her with a look. "We're still married, Josephine!"

"That—that can't be true," she squeezed out. A niggling voice at the back of her mind gave a mocking laugh.

"You said you'd take care of this. 'I'll handle everything, Noah. Don't you worry about a single thing, Noah.' And now look!" He turned around to face the wall. His shoulders rose and fell, and she'd swear the temperature had risen by ten degrees.

"I'll fix it. We'll get it signed and turn it in."

He clasped his hands at the back of his neck, his biceps bulging. His shoulders sank, some of the fight leaking from his body. "It's not that simple. The papers are dated. Joe doesn't know if the divorce is still pending or if it was dismissed altogether."

"I'm so sorry . . . I don't know how this happened. Vernon dropped off the papers, we signed, I made copies and sent one to you and one to him. I thought that was that."

"Well, it wasn't."

"I'll take care of it right away."

He turned around, his eyes cold as a mountain spring. "Oh no, you won't. I'll take care of it this time. I'll call the courthouse on Monday and find out what we have to do to straighten this out."

"Of course. Whatever you want."

"I want this handled. And I want it done quickly."

He couldn't wait to be rid of her. Just like last time. Her

insides shriveled up tight as heat poured into her cheeks. "You have my complete cooperation."

And just as quickly as Noah had reentered her life, he was gone. Leaving her both stirred up and depleted all at the same time. Just like the first time he'd walked through her doors.

# Chapter 3

*Copper Creek, Georgia*

*Three and a half years ago*

Josephine draped the new black cape around the young man's shoulders. He looked to be barely legal, but she felt his eyes fixed on her in the mirror. She met his gaze as she settled her hands on shoulders that were still warm from the hot and muggy June day.

"What can I do for you today, hon?"

"Just a trim." He had a nice smile going for him and puppy-dog eyes that probably made all the young girls swoon.

The bell on the door jingled, and a blast of hot, humid air blew around the temporary partition. Another customer, she hoped. "Be with y'all shortly."

"Take your time," a deep voice called.

Josephine plugged in the clippers and went to work. Her first weeks had been slow, but business was picking up. Word of mouth, she reckoned. Men were better at that than most people supposed. She sure hadn't had any extra money for advertising.

Getting the space into working order had cost more than she'd figured, and she only had one bowl, one chair. Improvements on her dingy upstairs apartment would have to wait. It would take the rest of her inheritance to fix up the place, add more stations, more stylists. But it had to be done and soon. She could hardly make a living this way. The bid she'd received from the contractor who'd done the preliminary work was out of her ballpark.

"What's your name, sweetheart?" the kid asked a few minutes into the trim, a flirtatious smile curving his lips.

Her eyes flickered off his in the mirror. Word traveled fast in a small town. No one knew that better than she.

She gave him a saucy smile. "Why you asking?"

"A man ought to know the name of his future wife."

Wasn't this one bold. And so young. "You don't know me yet, handsome. Maybe I'm not the kind of gal you take home to meet your mama."

His neck went blotchy red, and Josephine suffered a ping of guilt for being so blunt. She suspected he was more untried than he let on. He'd been in the chair five minutes and hadn't once gone for the "accidental" body graze.

"My mama's gone," he said. "But my daddy'd like you."

She chuckled. "I'll just bet he would, sugar."

He kept on, trying his best to impress her, but Josephine toned it down. Even if he caught her—which was never going to happen—she suspected he wouldn't quite know what to do with her.

She chatted him up as she trimmed his golden-brown hair.

He hardly even needed a trim, but she'd had a couple of those this week. Curiosity, she supposed. All the single men checking her out. As long as it kept customers in her chair, Josephine was just fine with that. And if a little flirting kept them coming back, she was happy to oblige.

In the barbershop lobby Noah flipped blindly through the pages of *Blue Ridge Country*, his ears tuned to the conversation beyond the trifold partition. Even if he hadn't recognized the blue Ford truck out front he'd have known Bryce Collins's voice. He was a good kid, nearly ten years Noah's junior, but he was giving it his best shot with the new gal in town.

*Good luck with that*, he thought, shifting on the old church pew that served as waiting-room seating. He'd yet to lay eyes on Copper Creek's newest resident, but he'd heard she was quite the looker. And, if she was twenty-six as rumored, closer to his own age than Bryce's. The boy's mama would roll over in her grave at his forwardness.

As for Noah, he was only looking for a trim. He already had his share of dates, and he wasn't ready to settle down, much to *his* mother's dismay. He was just glad not to have to drive to Ellijay for a haircut anymore.

He ran a hand over his hair. He was recently returned from a short stint in the marines, but his "high and tight" had long since grown out. Nothing much had changed around here while he'd been gone, but he kind of liked that. He'd needed the time away to grow up and decide if Copper Creek and the family business was really what he wanted. He'd come home more certain than ever that it was.

The conversation continued in the next room, and Noah found himself drawn by the woman's low, sultry voice. He wasn't sure about her styling skills, but she sure had the womanly wiles thing going for her. Poor kid didn't stand a chance.

Though her manner was Southern flirtatious, he detected an edge of cynicism in her laughter, in her quick responses. Cynicism was a protective mechanism—he knew this firsthand from his granny. Tell yourself people can't be trusted, then you won't be disappointed when they let you down.

His curiosity about the new gal was growing. What had put that jaded note in her tone, he wondered.

It wasn't a mystery why she'd gone into the barber business. He had yet to test her styling ability, but it didn't matter much. As long as she didn't leave her customers bald, she'd keep a full clientele with those people skills alone.

The buzz of the clippers stopped, followed by the ripping sound of Velcro. "There you go, hon."

"Looks great, Josephine. I'll definitely be back."

"You tell your friends to come on by now. I give 10 percent off for referrals."

"I'll keep that in mind."

Bryce came around the partition, a silly grin on his face, fishing his wallet from his back pocket. His eyes locked on Noah, and his ears went instantly red. "What's going on, Noah?"

"Not much. Just finished up for the day. How's your daddy doing? Haven't seen him in a few weeks."

"Aw, he's good enough. Busy with work mostly."

The boy kept talking, but just then the new stylist came around the partition. She fixed her blue eyes—twin pools of heaven—on Noah, and he went blind and deaf to everything else.

Her red lips curved into a lazy smile. "Be right with you, hon."

"No hurry," Noah croaked, his throat suddenly dry. His eyes swept down her slender curves before she disappeared behind the counter.

He couldn't take his eyes off her as she rang up Bryce. She had shoulder-length blond hair that was tousled artfully around her pretty face.

Though *pretty* didn't do her justice. Her creamy skin was almost pale against her lush lips. She hadn't given in to the tanning craze that the rest of the country had taken to, and it suited her. Long, dark lashes fanned against her cheeks as she reached into the drawer.

No wonder poor Bryce was smitten. She was a bombshell. A siren. Even her movements—the knowing toss of her chin, the confident sway of her hips—exuded raw sexuality. But it was her eyes that stopped him cold. A pale ice-blue, they some-how seemed years older than the rest of her. There were secrets behind those eyes, and suddenly he wanted to know them all.

Josephine aimed another smile his way. "I'll be right quick. Just give me a minute to sweep up."

Noah realized Bryce had left. The glass door was still fall-ing shut beside him, and the jingling bells over the door played back in his memory. He couldn't even recall if he'd given the boy a proper good-bye.

He tried to remember everything he'd heard about her. Paul Truvy was her father, and he'd left her his estate when he passed away last fall. She'd come up in the early spring from Cartersville, where she'd worked in a salon, to open her own barbershop.

She'd given Beamus Jenkins, the town drunk, a free haircut

after hours on her first Saturday open, and he'd shown up in church the next morning for the first time in twenty years. There was probably more going around, but Noah wasn't one to gossip.

His family's construction company had bid on phase one of the small renovation project that got her business up and running. His brother, Seth, had quoted the project; he remembered the file lying around the office. A competitor got the job though.

He looked around the lobby. The place still needed a lot of work, from what he could see from here. The original wood floors needed refurbishing, and the trifold partition that separated the lobby wasn't enough. She was losing air through the front door. It would be a major problem once the sweltering summer weather arrived.

He'd put up a pony wall that went up about three-quarters of the way to the ceiling. And he'd sand the floor just enough to remove the old stain, but leave the scars and character of the wood. An espresso color would be a nice contrast with the old brick wall to his right.

Josephine reappeared around the trifold. "Come on back, hon."

His dopey heart leaped in his chest at the endearment. He got up and followed her to the chair, racking his brain for something to say. But he felt like he'd been clobbered in the head with a two-by-four.

His eyes were working just fine though. Josephine was petite, he noticed, now that he was on his feet. At least nine inches under his own six-foot-one frame. Square shoulders, slender waist. Curves like a mountain road.

He took a seat in the chair and met her eyes in the mirror.

His voice seemed lodged in his throat. What the heck was

wrong with him? Maybe he wasn't a smooth-talking devil, but he never got tongue-tied. Noah mentally gave Bryce credit for keeping it together. It was more than he was doing.

"I'm Josephine Dupree." She swung the black cape around him.

"Noah Mitchell."

"Pleased to meet you, Noah." She set her hands on his shoulders, and he felt the touch clear down to his toes. "What are you looking for today?"

He jerked his eyes from her reflection and stared at his own. "Need about an inch and a half off." His voice cracked like he was seventeen. Heat crawled up in his neck as he cleared his throat. "It's been awhile."

She swiveled his chair around, and he suddenly remembered that he'd signed in for a wash too. He regretted it now. Especially when she lowered the back of his chair and leaned over him, putting her generous curves up close and personal.

His heart beat up into his swollen throat as he closed his eyes. And that's when he became aware of her smell. Sweet, with a hint of spice. Intoxicating.

The water came on, and her fingers threaded through his hair, followed by a rush of warm water. His pulse jumped, and he worked to steady his breath. His body was humming like a tuning fork.

*Get a grip, Mitchell.*

"You have real nice hair," she said in that smoky voice. "Lot of men would kill for a thick head of hair like yours."

His mouth worked. What was he supposed to say to that? Thanks? You too? While he pondered his response, the seconds ticked away until it was too late to say anything at all. She probably thought he was addle-brained.

She raked her fingers through his hair as she wet it. His heart pummeled his rib cage, and a shiver passed down the back of his neck. *Jeez O' Pete. You'd think you'd never been touched by a woman before.*

He shifted in the chair.

"Too hot?"

He cleared his throat. "Um, no. It's fine." *Four words. You're on a roll, buddy.*

The water shut off, and her fingers began working the shampoo into his hair.

He kept his eyes closed, letting her smell assault his senses. He could feel the heat from her as she leaned close to reach the back of his head. Her breath brushed the hair at his temples, making every soapy cell follicle sit up straight.

The water finally kicked on again, and she began rinsing away the suds. Almost done. He realized his hands were balled into fists. He relaxed them, wiping his sweaty palms down his thighs.

When she turned off the water, he waited for the towel, needing some space. But instead her fingers began working through his hair again, and a pleasant musky smell mingled with her perfume.

"Doesn't this stuff smell like heaven? It's my favorite. It'll leave your hair feeling like silk too."

"Smells great."

"How'd you hear about my shop?"

"Uh, word of mouth, I guess. You'd just bought the place when I returned from serving overseas."

"Well, thank you for your service, Noah. Which branch?"

"Marines. Actually, my family's company bid on your renovation. Mitchell Home Improvement."

She worked her fingers at the base of his neck in a mini-massage that was just about the best thing he'd ever felt. He swallowed hard, wanting to lean into her touch and scramble from the chair all at the same time.

"Oh, sorry 'bout that. Sawyers was a little lower, and I'm having to watch every penny."

"They're a good company. Good folks."

"I'm taking bids on the next phase. One of your guys is working up an estimate for me. Billy, I think his name was. I'm on a pretty tight budget, what with just getting started up."

She turned on the water and began rinsing out the conditioner.

He suddenly wanted that job more than he wanted his next breath. These days he mostly handled the bigger projects. They had several capable crews, and there was always a lot to do in the office too. But he was tempted to take a hands-on approach with this one—so to speak.

"I'll take a look at the bid. See what I can do."

"Well, aren't you nice. I'm looking to get started as soon as possible. One chair isn't going to keep me in business long."

"You're wanting to expand?"

"Yes, sir. I got some secondhand chairs and sinks from a shop that went out of business in Atlanta. Plus the floor needs some work, and I need a wall or two put up."

"Looks like the ceiling up front sprang a leak at some point."

"That's from my bathroom upstairs. The leak's fixed, but the ceiling needs repaired."

"You're living up there?" That apartment had been closed up for years. He couldn't imagine what kind of condition it was in.

"For the time being." She shut off the water and blotted

his hair with a towel before sitting him up in the chair. "To be honest, based on the one bid I already got, I'm probably going to have to work out some kind of deal."

Vivid visions of moonlight kisses flashed in his mind. He blinked them away. "What kind of deal?"

She pumped up the chair, then ruffled his head with the towel, soaking up the rest of the water. Moving to his side, she dragged a comb through his hair. "I was thinking I could lend a hand. You know, during the evenings and on my day off."

"You mean . . . with the construction?"

She paused, her eyes locked on his, glinting with amusement. "I'm good for more than just standing here looking pretty, you know."

Heat flooded into his cheeks. "I didn't mean . . ."

Her chuckle was low and sultry, and her eyes arched into half-moons. "Relax, sugar. I'm no handyman, but I know a flathead from a Phillips. And I'm a quick study. I was hoping an extra set of hands might help offset the cost a bit."

She leaned closer as she gathered up his bangs, bringing her intoxicating scent with her. "You think you might be open to something like that?"

He'd like to meet the man that wouldn't be.

Still, from a business perspective, he'd be a fool to agree. All manner of things could go wrong. She'd probably end up slowing him down. No doubt she'd be as distracting as all get out. And that didn't even address the issue of insurance.

But he looked into her guarded eyes as she snipped his hair, focusing on her task. There was more to her than met the eye. He wanted to know everything there was to know about Josephine Dupree, and he couldn't think of a better way to learn. If that made him a fool, so be it.

"I'd definitely consider that," he said. *And your smile will do for a down payment.*

"Glad to hear it."

Noah took advantage of her focus on her work to examine her at leisure. Even up close her porcelain skin was flawless. Her dark lashes were ridiculously long and curled. Delicate eyebrows arched mischievously over almond-shaped eyes. His gaze dropped to her full red lips. Perfection itself.

Oh yeah. Come hell or high water, he was getting this job.

# Chapter 4

*Sweetbriar Ranch*

*Present day*

Noah opened Rango's stall and led him toward the grooming area. The horse's breath fogged the air, though it was almost midday. A bank of clouds obscured the sunlight, and the scent of pine hung heavily in the air.

Rango nickered softly. Brushing ranked right up there with eating where this horse was concerned. Noah led the paint into the stall and released the lead. "Stand."

All the horses at Sweetbriar Ranch were trained to ground-tie. Rango was fairly new though, and still had a tendency to wander.

He began brushing the horse's black-and-white coat. "Got yourself into some burrs, huh? Sometimes I think you do it on purpose, big fella."

Rango sighed. The rest of the horses, eleven of them, were

already fed, checked, and in the pasture. If it got much colder, he'd have to put their coats on.

His phone buzzed in his pocket, and he checked the screen. Finally. He'd called the courthouse at ten on the dot this morning and had been waiting for them to check their records and get back with him.

"Mitchell here."

"Hi, Mr. Mitchell, this is Cheryl from the courthouse."

"Hi, Cheryl. Thanks for getting back to me so fast. What'd you find out?"

"Well, I did a record search and found out you're exactly right—your divorce never went through. I'm afraid you're still married."

His pulse jumped. "Still married," he muttered to himself. No matter how many times he had the thought it didn't seem to sink in all the way.

"Afraid so. It's still pending though, so that's good. Just a matter of getting freshly dated papers and signatures. Your next step would be to contact your attorney."

"Will do. Thanks so much, Cheryl."

"You're welcome. Have a good day, now."

Noah wasted no time. He got hold of Joe, who promised him a freshly printed divorce decree by the end of the day. Noah thanked him and hung up.

Tomorrow he'd go into town and pick up the papers, sign them, have Josephine sign them, and drop them back off.

No, not tomorrow, he thought as he mentally reviewed his schedule. He was meeting with a potential boarder in the afternoon, then the chiropractor was coming to work on a couple of the horses.

And Wednesday afternoon he was meeting with Mary

Beth to go over the summer camp schedule. Plus, there was cold rain and wind coming in from a big storm system sweeping over the area. He'd need to get the horses stabled before it hit. He wouldn't have time to drive all the way into town. His sigh came from deep inside. Thursday, provided the weather cooperated, he had two trail-riding groups in the afternoon.

He wouldn't be able to get down the mountain until Friday. A complicated mix of emotions washed over him. It was so bizarre to think he and Josephine were still married.

Not for long though. By next week, if the judge were merciful, all this would be over. Except for the taxes. He'd have to refile those, and he'd need Walt's help. This was just getting better and better.

He looked up the number for Josephine's Barbershop on his phone and dialed, hoping she was too busy to answer. For once things worked in his favor. Her low drawl came on the line, giving instructions to leave a message, and his mind went back to Saturday when he'd gone to confront her at her shop.

She hadn't changed a lick, in looks or manner. Still flirted her way through life, trampling hearts along the way. Some small part of him—the part that remembered her tender heart for the needy and the raw vulnerability she hid so well—protested the thought. But he quieted that voice. He didn't want to like Josephine anymore.

A beep sounded in his ear, and his abrupt tone came naturally. "It's me. Just got off the phone with the courthouse and everything's still . . . pending. Joe's drawing up the papers today. I can't come into town till Friday afternoon, so you need to get over there and sign them sometime this week." He hung up, not bothering with a good-bye.

Rango turned and nudged him with his nose, and Noah picked up the brush, drawing it over the horse's withers. He wondered how many men Josephine had been out with since they'd parted ways. Since they'd thought they were divorced. He told himself it didn't matter. She wasn't his anymore, even if the law said otherwise.

But he couldn't deny she hadn't been far from his thoughts since Saturday. The memories—so good, so bad—were closer to the surface than he'd realized. This had stirred up the past. And the past was definitely best buried.

He looked up to the barn rafters as if he could gaze straight through to heaven.

*What kind of cruel trick is this?*

Josephine played the message for the third time in a row. Outside her shop night had fallen. The *Closed* sign was turned, the door locked. Noah spoke through her phone speaker, his voice hard. Cold.

She'd seen his call come in between customers. She'd had nothing better to do than sweep the dusty corners, but she couldn't bring herself to answer. Instead she froze, the broom gripped in her clutches as he spilled the facts. Just the facts, ma'am, and nothing but.

The message finished again, ending with his curt order to go sign the papers.

Still married. The thought played cruelly at the edges of her mind, taunting her. Married, divorced, what did it matter? She lived like a eunuch anyway. Not that the people of Copper Creek would believe it. She'd finally learned her lesson.

Should've learned it years ago. Why on earth she'd ever let Noah convince her otherwise was anybody's guess.

She'd hurt him, and for what? Shame, familiar and deserving, washed over her, and she welcomed it. Maybe she wasn't a "bad seed," as her stepfather had called her, but even after a year of therapy she didn't trust herself with another relationship. She wasn't inflicting herself on anyone else. Not ever again.

She wished for the hundredth time she could go back in time and hire Sawyer's Construction instead of Noah. Would've saved them both a whole heap of trouble.

Trying to shake the thoughts, she turned down the air, then made her way up to her quiet apartment. Once there she flipped on the radio to fill the lonely corners.

She needed to put Noah from her mind, but he was like a burr caught in a snarl of hair. She pulled out her schedule for Saturday. Residents from the Hope House Girls Home were coming in for some well-deserved pampering. The high school's spring fling was Saturday night, and she was bringing in all her stylists to provide free updos and makeup. She'd found two manicurists from the surrounding counties willing to donate their time. She could hardly wait to see the girls all dolled up and confident.

The planning kept her busy until her eyes grew tired. She readied for bed and crawled under the sheet, willing a cool breeze to drift through the window. It was a vision of Noah's face that drifted by instead. Those cold eyes fixed on her. His jaw twitching with anger.

His voice on the machine played back in her head, his tone so full of disgust it made her ache inside. He'd be coming to town Friday, he said. Though it was obvious he wanted this over yesterday.

Maybe she couldn't turn back time and do things differently.

Maybe she couldn't make them magically divorced. But she could save him a trip down the mountain and speed up the process by a few days. For Noah's sake. Maybe for hers too. Wednesday after she closed up, she'd deliver the papers to him herself. It was the least she could do.

# Chapter 5

*J*osephine turned over the key of her Ford Focus, her mind already on the evening ahead. The car's engine faltered, as it often did. It needed work, but she'd been putting it off.

She tried again. "Come on, baby. You can do it." She had to get this over with. She could hardly concentrate on a thing for thoughts of Noah Mitchell.

The engine turned over, and she gave a heartfelt sigh. The packet of papers from the lawyer's office resting in her passenger seat, she pulled from the curb and exited town. Noah now lived at Sweetbriar Ranch, a good thirty minutes over the mountain.

The sun was on the horizon, and she already dreaded the drive back through the winding mountain roads after dark. But not as much as she dreaded seeing Noah again.

Her heart gave an extra thump. *Dreaded* was too simple a word for the complex emotions he stirred. At least he'd be glad to see her. Not because he wanted her company, of course, but because she was expediting the divorce process. She didn't for a moment think the good deed would balance out her colossal failures.

Rain started shortly after she entered the mountains, and she turned on the wipers, slowing to accommodate the twists and turns. It was beautiful up here. Full of pine and mountain views, and the kind of quiet that made your thoughts loud.

She wondered if Noah was sitting down for supper. For the first time, she wondered if he was alone. She'd heard rumors in town about him and his equine instructor, Mary Beth Maynor. What if Josephine was interrupting a quiet night or a romantic supper for two?

Her palms grew sweaty on the steering wheel. Mary Beth was a sweet church girl with a good, proper upbringing. She was pretty in a girl-next-door kind of way, with her straight dark hair and easy smile. She'd be good for Noah.

The thought was like a fist around Josephine's heart.

No wonder he'd been so riled up by their situation. If he was seeing Mary Beth, he was unintentionally cheating, and there was no one more loyal than Noah.

The road wound on, twisting north and south, east and west, until her stomach grew queasy. The sun had dipped under the horizon now, and rain fell steadily, pattering against the roof of her car.

She slowed as she neared Old Hollow Road, a gravel lane that shot off to the right down a steep slope. A sign at the juncture pointed toward Sweetbriar Ranch. The road went on before finally opening to a broad area of rolling hills lined by a white ranch rail fence. A sign out front confirmed her arrival.

Gravel popped under her tires as she made her way down the long drive. The landscape was monochromatic in the waning light, but she imagined the rolling hills green and dotted with the horses she'd seen once before, during happier times.

She crossed a wooden bridge over a creek that meandered through the pasture.

Growing up, Noah had worked at the ranch as a stable boy when his family's construction business was slow. It had surprised her when she heard he'd bought the place. As much as he loved horses, construction was part of his DNA. She couldn't even imagine him giving it up. Somehow she'd taken on the guilt for that too.

She topped a hill, bringing a small cottage into view. A light burned through the window, and a curl of smoke wound from the chimney. She braked in front of the house and grabbed the packet, then dashed through the cold rain for the shelter of the porch.

Three knocks later her stomach had sunk to her toes. Surely she hadn't come all this way for nothing. What if he'd found a break in his schedule and gone into town for the papers? He'd be fit to be tied if he went all that way and found her gone.

She scanned the property in the waning light and spied the shadow of a barn in the rear of the property. A faint light glowed. Of course.

She dashed back to her car, fighting the engine and winning after the second try. She pulled down the visor and winced at her reflection: wilted hair, rain-slicked face, and thin ivory cardigan, speckled with water. Oh well. He wasn't likely to be impressed no matter how she looked.

She followed the drive back to the barn and spotted his truck beside it. As she got out she heard a loud whinny from inside the barn, followed by Noah's deep voice. She dashed toward the shelter and stopped just inside the door.

Noah was leading a brown horse into a stall. He wore a dark slicker, the hood raised, and his face was wet with rain. A black horse stood in the aisle, waiting. His ears pricked in her direction, and he gave a soft nicker she could barely hear.

At the sound, Noah turned and spotted her by the opening. Something flared in his eyes, surprise maybe and something else, before they narrowed into slits.

His jaw knotted as his gaze raked over her. "What are you doing here?"

"I-I brought the papers."

His gaze dropped to the packet in her hand.

"I thought it would expedite the process if I brought them over."

The glow of light did nothing to soften his harsh features. "You should've called. I have to get the horses in."

She fished in her purse for a pen. "If you just sign them, I'll be on my way. I can get them back to Joe first thing in the morning."

He gave a wry laugh. "If you think I'm signing without reading, you're plumb crazy."

Heat crawled into her face. "They're the same papers we agreed to before. I just picked them up."

He backed out of the stall and shut the gate. "Just the same, I'll look them over."

She shifted, clutching the packet to her middle. "Right. Well, I suppose I'll just sign them and leave them with you then." He could return them at his leisure. So much for her trip up the mountain.

He retrieved the black horse's lead, a frown puckering his brow.

Josephine waited patiently while he led the horse into the stall, apparently deep in thought.

Feeling dismissed, she uncapped her pen and flipped to the

last page. She set the packet on a nearby Rubbermaid bin and signed her name on the line, her hand shaking.

*No big deal, Josephine. You thought it was already over anyway. Just a formality.* Inside though, a jumble of emotions threatened to spill over.

She finished, straightening. "Okay. I'll just leave it right here." When he didn't respond she turned to go. The rain had picked up, and she crossed her arms and ducked her head in preparation for the onslaught.

"Wait."

Josephine turned while Noah finished removing the coat from the black horse, working quickly.

When he finished he turned his dark gaze on her and heaved a sigh. "I don't want to drive back into town. If you can wait a bit, I'll be finished here in twenty or thirty minutes."

She had nowhere better to be. "I'll wait in the car."

He opened his mouth, and she wondered if he was about to invite her to his house. But if he was, he reconsidered. "Fine."

She left the pen beside the papers and dashed back to the warmth of the car. She watched through the rivulets as Noah disappeared into the darkness of the pasture. Awhile later he appeared with three more horses.

While he was inside the barn, the sound of the rain turned to pings, and Josephine realized the downpour was turning to sleet. She thought of the curvy mountain roads and mentally urged Noah to hurry.

A few minutes later the sleet still continued steadily, and Noah was still in the barn. If she had any hope of getting safely back to town, it was now or never. She dashed back into the barn, shivering now from the cold and wet.

Noah was removing a coat from a chestnut-colored horse.

"Noah . . . I think I'd best just leave the papers."

"I'm almost finished."

"The rain's turned to sleet. If I don't leave now . . ." She let him draw his own conclusions.

He speared her with a look, not a friendly one, his hands working in quick, efficient motions. "Fine. Go on then."

Nice. So much for her efforts. Feeling a little spark of irritation, she turned on her heel and headed for her car. The wind whipped her wet hair around her face, and it clung to her cheeks. She was wet to the skin and shivering from the inside out. And all for nothing. It would be a slow, dark drive down the mountain.

She turned the key over, her gut clenching when it failed to start on the first try. And the second. A blur of motion in her peripheral vision caught her eye—Noah, striding back toward the pasture, oblivious to her rising concern.

"Come on, baby, you can do it." She tried again. This time the engine only gave a quiet click. Her heart stuttered. "No. No, no, no." This was a new sound, and not a good one, she supposed. She hit the steering wheel with her palm.

After a few more efforts she sat back in the seat, giving up. Her eyes scanned the darkened pasture for Noah, but by the time he returned, leading two horses, twenty minutes had passed.

Sleet stung her skin as she hurried toward him. She huddled against the wind, blinking. In her rush she slid on the icy ground, catching her balance just before she fell.

She saw the moment he noticed her. His spine lengthened, and his brows drew tight. "What are you still doing here?" he yelled over the wind.

"My car won't start."

He walked over, the horses trailing, and held out his hands for the keys.

Clamping her lips shut, she handed them over.

He led the horses into their stalls, working fast while she waited, shivering in a shadowed corner of the barn.

Did he really think she wasn't capable of turning a key? Or maybe he thought she was lying. Maybe he thought this was some ploy to work her way back into his good graces. Ha.

He strode past her into the pounding sleet. When he reached her car, he opened the door and got in, probably banging his knee on the steering wheel. One foot remained planted on the ground.

She watched and waited from under the barn's overhang, but he didn't even put the keys in the ignition. He just sat there, staring out the front windshield. Even from here she could see the sharp rise and fall of his chest.

The interior light shone on his face, highlighting the sharp angles of his cheekbones and the sleek line of his nose.

She hunched over and darted across the yard, stopping at the open car door. "What are you doing?"

He said nothing as his jaw knotted.

"Aren't you going to give it a go?" She'd once been good at reading his mind. But that's when he was looking at her, his emotions naked on his face. Now there was nothing but dead eyes and a blank slate.

"It's too late," he said flatly.

She barely heard him over the wind and the ping of ice. "What do you mean?"

"Look at the windshield. There's a coat of ice on everything."

He was right, she thought, realization settling over her. There was no way she'd make it up those hills with her balding tires, even if her car magically started. Even the ground beneath her was turning slick.

The wind gusted, driving the pellets into her cheeks. She ducked her head. "I'm sorry. I guess you'll have to take me in your truck then. It's four-wheel drive, isn't it?"

He turned slowly, nailing her with a lethal look. "That won't do us any good in this ice, Josephine."

His meaning began sinking in. Good and deep. Oh no. No way. "Well—well, it'll have to do."

"Don't be ridiculous. We wouldn't even make it up to the road."

"Well, I'm not staying here."

"You don't have much choice."

"I'll—I'll stay in my car then."

"It's thirty-four degrees, Josephine."

"I don't care." She backed away. She wasn't imposing on him. She knew when she wasn't wanted. Noah would rather chop off an arm than spend an hour with her, and she wasn't too crazy about the idea either.

"You'd freeze to death out here."

She thought of the little house on the hill, the glow of light, the cozy fire burning in the fireplace. Just her and Noah and an avalanche of warm memories. A cold shiver of fear washed over her.

"Get me a blanket. I'll be just fine."

He stepped out of the car and shut the door.

When she reached for the keys, he pointed them at the car and pressed a button. The locks clicked into place, and he pocketed the keys.

A red heat fired up inside that somehow made her shiver harder. "Give me my keys!"

But Noah was already halfway to his truck.

She scrambled after him, slipping once on her way. "Noah!"

She caught up with him as he opened the passenger door. His face was as hard as a block of ice. "Get in."

"Give me my keys!"

"Get in, Josephine, or I'll put you in myself."

She darted a hand into his coat pocket, but before she found the keys, he'd scooped her up into his arms. He took a step, dumped her unceremoniously into the truck, and shut the door beside her.

By the time she sat up and reached for the handle, Noah had slid into the driver's seat, and the locks clicked into place.

Josephine popped the lock on her door, but before she could reach the handle, Noah grabbed her arm. "Settle down! You're being ridiculous."

"Well, you're being a bully! You can't just kidnap me. I don't want to stay here."

"Then you shouldn't have come!"

That smarted. She worked to control her tongue. "I was trying to do you a favor."

He gave a wry laugh as he started the truck and whipped it around.

She grabbed the dash to keep from falling on him. The truck gave a little slip, and he slowed as he took the next curve.

Josephine's eyes locked on the cottage hunched on the distant hill. All the anger drained away, replaced by the kind of terror that seeped slowly into the veins. This was really happening. She was with Noah. She was spending the night with Noah. All alone. Just the two of them.

She closed her eyes, making the house evaporate for one sweet moment of denial. She drew in a deep breath, and the familiar masculine scent of him, musk and wood, filled her nostrils.

She couldn't escape this. Couldn't escape him.

He was right. It was too cold to spend the night in her car, and she was soaked to the skin. Her teeth chattered, and her body vibrated with the kind of cold that went bone-deep. How could this be happening? She was such an idiot. Why had she come out here? Why hadn't she checked the forecast?

She opened her eyes and focused on the cottage growing ever closer. It was so little. As small as their bungalow on Katydid Lane. She remembered snuggling up on cold winter nights on their lumpy couch, an afghan wrapped around them. Making supper together in the tight kitchen, his hand finding the curve of her waist, his lips the slope of her neck. Abandoning skillets on the stovetop, dinner congealing, as he walked her backward to their bedroom.

The memories flashed through her mind like falling stars, leaving a trail of despair. Her pulse leaped in her throat. Her chest went tight, and the backs of her eyes burned.

He pulled up alongside the cottage and shut off the engine. She stared out the window, past the melting rivulets to the house beyond, and wondered how she was going to make it through the night.

# Chapter 6

A howl of wind joined the quiet chinking of sleet against the roof of Noah's truck. He turned to Josephine, who stared out the fogging passenger window, quiet.

The fight seemed to have drained from her on the short drive from the barn, and she'd gone inward. She did that sometimes. Noah preferred her riled up, sparks shooting out her blue eyes. Anger he could fight. This quiet stoicism rendered him helpless. And he didn't like feeling helpless.

Much of his own anger had burnt off too. Enough that he felt guilty about the way he'd dumped her into his cab. He'd never been anything but gentle with her, even when he'd been provoked. He wondered if that was why her shoulders were now hunched up tight, her knees tucked away from him.

"It might change to rain and melt off in an hour or two," he said.

When she didn't respond he got out of the truck and headed for the house, relieved when he heard her footsteps behind him. At least he wasn't going to have to resort to force again. Fool woman. She wouldn't make it three hours out here. She got chilled when the thermometer dipped below seventy.

He opened the front door and ushered her in, then closed it against the howling wind. Shadow, his black Lab, came to greet him, tail swashing a wide path. Noah ruffled his fur, but the traitor, recognizing Josephine's scent, gave a soft whine as he nuzzled her open palm.

She knelt down, and Shadow licked the water off her face. For the first time since she'd arrived a little smile curved her lips. "Hey there, baby," she cooed. "Oh, I missed you. You're such a good boy, yes, you are."

He gave them a moment, feeling a twinge of guilt for keeping them apart. True, Shadow had been his dog, but there was no denying the special bond between Josephine and the Lab.

She finally stood shivering on his rug, looking like a bedraggled wet kitten. Her hands shook as she pulled off her flimsy pair of flats. Her white sweater was so thin and wet he could see the pale-blue shirt under it.

"You need a warm shower." He pointed down the hall. "Bathroom's that way."

She glanced at the wood planking, pushing a strand of wet hair behind her ear. "I don't want to drip all over your floor."

"It'll clean up."

He waited until the shower kicked on, then headed back out. Mary Beth kept extra clothes in the barn. He hadn't thought to get them before. The wind was nasty, whipping the ice at his face as he dashed to the truck.

He'd expected wind and rain. Lots of rain. The storm front was massive. But the temperature wasn't supposed to drop low enough for sleet. Now that it had, he wondered what else was coming. Maybe the sleet would turn back to rain, and he could drive Josephine back to town later tonight. He'd call a tow for her car, and she'd be out of his hair for good.

In the barn he took a moment to soothe Kismet. The bay thoroughbred was new to his stable and apprehensive. He'd sat in the pen with the horse for forty-five minutes yesterday while it paced, emitting tremulous high-pitched neighs, ears flicking back and forth.

Now Noah spoke in low tones and stroked Kismet's withers when he was invited with a nudge. After a few minutes the horse settled, and Noah collected Mary Beth's T-shirt and faded jeans. He grabbed the divorce papers from the tub and snatched Mary Beth's work coat from the hook on his way out. As an afterthought he grabbed her boots as well.

He couldn't see Josephine in these rugged clothes. Mary Beth was about the same height and size, but she was all straight lines and angles, coltish. Whereas Josephine . . . wasn't.

When he entered the warmth of his house, he was surprised to hear the shower already shut off. He used to tease her about her long showers, but she'd either reformed her ways or was being considerate.

The door clicked open as he finished pulling off his boots. "Noah?" There was an edge of panic to her voice, and he wondered how many times she'd called for him.

"Just a second." He took the bundle of clothing to her. Steam rolled through the crack in the door as he slid the clothes through. He averted his gaze and tried not to think about what she was wearing—or not—on the other side.

"Thanks." The door snapped shut.

He shucked his coat and sweatshirt, leaving only his black T-shirt and damp jeans. Figure out supper first. Then he'd shower and check the weather. He'd only begun surveying his pantry when he heard her behind him.

Shadow left his side to greet her, tail wagging, tongue lolling.

"Do you have a dryer I can put these in?"

"Back there." He gestured with a nod of his head.

He watched her go, her bare feet padding across his kitchen floor. The jeans were the right length, but they were tight in the seat and gathered at the waist by a belt she must've had on before.

He turned back to the pantry, trying to vanquish the image of her heart-shaped derriere from his mind. Was it lust if they were still married?

He banged his head on the pantry door once. Twice. Idiot. He'd been blinded once. Never again. Feed her and get her out of here.

He scanned the selection of canned goods and boxed food. Noah didn't bother cooking for himself, and his pantry reflected his simplistic culinary skills. He'd planned to grab a few things from the Piggly Wiggly on Saturday, but he'd been sidetracked by his ill-fated stop at the post office.

He was still trying to work out a plan when the dryer kicked on. He felt Josephine's presence at his back a moment later.

"Why don't you grab a warm shower while I get supper on," she said.

"There's not much food-wise." He glanced over his shoulder. "I'm overdue for a visit to, ah . . ."

The Farnam logo on her heather-gray T-shirt stretched tight across her chest. If Mary Beth had ever worn that shirt, he sure didn't remember it.

He jerked his eyes from the logo and blinked. "The, ah, grocery. There might be something in the freezer."

"I'll work something out."

The kitchen had shrunk two sizes. Something metal clinked repetitively in the dryer drum.

Her damp hair was tousled, and her face was makeup-free, making her eyes stand out, though they'd yet to lift as high as his face. He'd always preferred her this way. Natural. She didn't need lipstick and mascara. Though in true Southern-gal fashion, she never left home without it. There was something vulnerable about her without that makeup mask.

*There's not a vulnerable bone in her body, Mitchell.*

His heart rallied behind the notion, but his brain knew better. As much as she tried to hide it—from him, from everyone—there was a broken little girl in there somewhere.

But that particular puzzle was no longer his concern. He turned toward the bathroom. "I'll leave you to it."

Josephine sagged against the wall as soon as the bathroom door closed. The shower had warmed her up, but the adrenaline from this untenable situation had left her noodle-kneed.

Shadow slid his muzzle under her hand, begging for attention and getting it. He stared up at her with sparkling brown eyes, one pointy ear perked, the other flopping forward. Noah had always teased that it was broken, but Josephine argued it was just part of his charm.

"All right, girl," she mumbled to herself. "Get it together." She turned to the pantry, pushing cans aside, scanning the labels, but she soon gave up at the mishmash of goods. The freezer turned up some ground beef and frozen broccoli.

She'd defrosted the beef and had patties sizzling in the skillet by the time she heard Noah stoking the fire in the next room. A dart of grease splattered on the T-shirt as she flipped a burger, but she couldn't bring herself to care.

When he said he would find her some dry clothes, she'd expected one of his shirts and a pair of sweats. But these duds had "Mary Beth Maynor" written all over them. She tried not to ruminate on the reason Mary Beth left clothes at Noah's house. Tried to shove all the rumors into the corners of her mind. But they crept from the shadows, taunting her.

*It's none of your worry, Josephine. He's not yours anymore. Never you mind the papers.*

She finished up the burgers, put them between slices of white bread with a generous dollop of mustard, and placed two on Noah's plate. She dished out the steaming broccoli and set the plates on the dinette that used to belong to his granny.

"It's ready," she called.

Noah entered the room, smelling clean and dressed in a fresh T-shirt and jeans.

He sat across from her and bowed his head, excluding her from his silent prayer. He was probably begging God for a heat wave.

He used to hold her hand at this very table and pray for both of them, giving her hand a gentle squeeze after the amen. Josephine wasn't much for praying. It had never done her any good. But she'd taken comfort in their nightly ritual. In his faith.

She looked at his hands now, rolled into fists on either side of his plate. She'd always liked his strong, masculine hands. A man's hands, rough with calluses, but gentle in touch. A faint sprinkling of dark hair covered his forearms, leading to her favorite part of his anatomy—his biceps, sculpted and hardened from hours of physical labor. His occupation had changed, but not those arms.

Her gaze swept up to his unguarded face. Dark brows slashed

over his closed eyes. His lashes were wet and spiked against his olive skin, and a generous sprinkling of stubble coated his jaw. Two days' growth, she guessed.

She used to shave him sometimes on lazy Saturday mornings. He could never keep still or keep his hands to himself. He often ended up half-shaved and back under the cool sheets with her, the laughter in his eyes turning serious soon enough.

His eyes opened and fastened on hers. She was a deer caught in the headlights. She wondered if he could read her thoughts, and heat washed into her cheeks. They'd never had trouble in the chemistry department.

Her eyes fell to her plate, and she picked up her burger with trembling hands.

She had to stop thinking like that. See what he did to her? She couldn't even be near him without wanting him again. She'd told herself those feelings were dead, but clearly they'd merely been dormant. Threatening to push toward the surface at just a hint of warmth.

"Still a praying man, I see." She was pleased to find her voice strong and indifferent.

"It's gotten me through." He bit into his burger, and Josephine let the silence fall around them.

Why'd she go and say that? She didn't want to talk about faith. It was one of the many perplexing facets of her life. The emotional conversion when she was just a child, the absence of God when she'd needed Him most, the conflicting needs for absolution and penance. She couldn't make sense of it. She'd stopped trying.

When she'd first moved to town, her quiet confessions to Pastor Jack had offered temporary solace. But once she realized the Lutheran minister was a good friend of Noah's, she'd discontinued her sessions with him. As far as she knew, he'd kept her appointments—and her secrets—to himself.

They ate in silence, the meal dragging on till Josephine was about to go stir-crazy.

Finally Noah stood and took his plate to the sink. "I'm going to check the weather." He disappeared into the next room.

Josephine finished eating, then took her time washing the dishes by hand. When she entered the living room, she found Noah staring at his laptop, the glow of the screen harsh on his features.

She stopped on the threshold, hesitant to enter the too-small room with its crackling fire and familiar couch. The room looked cozy with its soft lighting, stone fireplace, and low-beamed ceiling. A large braided rug hugged the wood floor, inviting guests to kick off their shoes.

Frowning at the screen, Noah didn't seem to notice her arrival.

She folded her arms over her chest. "What's the weather saying?"

His gaze flickered toward her, then back to the screen. "More of the same for the next few hours. The temperatures were supposed to stay above freezing, but they're expected to hover right on the line for a while."

"More sleet."

"Looks like."

She shifted on her feet. It looked like she was here for the night. From the scowl on his face, Noah was even less happy about that than she was.

This little favor she'd planned—what a bust. "I guess you're stuck with me for the night."

Noah's nostrils flared and his eyes tightened at the corners, though he didn't look at her or respond.

"Do you have a spare room?"

"Nope."

She'd passed the master bedroom, its king-size bed filling the space. But she'd also noted a narrow flight of steps at the end of the hall. "What's upstairs?"

"It's unfinished."

Oh. Well, there was no way she was taking his bed. "I'll take the couch then."

A log shifted in the fireplace and sparks sizzled.

A vein pulsed in Noah's forehead. "You can have the bed."

"I don't mind the couch."

He nailed her with a stony look.

She shrank at the intensity but found a little spark in her tone. "Fine."

"Fine."

Her eyes darted to the mantel clock. It was too early for bed. Way too early, but that was too bad. She wasn't staying out here where she wasn't wanted for another moment.

Her eyes moved back to Noah, and she noticed the packet of papers on the table beside him, folded open to the last page, his signature line still blank.

"At least you'll have time to read that over now," she offered.

His eyes cut to hers, his lips flattening.

"I-I guess I'll turn in." When he failed to respond she turned toward the hall. "Good night," she said, but he didn't respond to that either.

Entering the bedroom, she glanced around. The bed was unmade, a few articles of clothing strung here and there, but mostly picked up. She didn't recognize the navy quilt or gray sheets, but the oak headboard and nightstand had graced their home on Katydid.

She slipped off the jeans, leaving the small bedside lamp on, and got under the covers. What was she going to do for the next couple hours? A quick scan of the room turned up a paperback, open and cover side up on the nightstand—a Tony Dungy biography. Not exactly her normal fare, but beggars and choosers and all that. She picked it up, dog-earring the marked page, and turned to chapter one.

She wasn't sure how much time had passed when her eyes began getting heavy. She was setting the book on the nightstand when a tap sounded on the door.

She pulled the sheet to her chest, her pulse skittering foolishly. "Come in."

The door opened and Noah appeared, looking more haggard than he had a couple hours ago. "Your clothes . . ." He stepped inside and set the short stack on the nightstand, keeping a wide gap between them.

She drew up her knees under the sheets. "Thanks."

"I need to get some things for morning. And I didn't get you anything to sleep in." He moved across the room to the tall oak chest in the corner. The drawer squawked as he opened it and pulled out a blue T-shirt and a pair of sweats. He tossed them to her.

"Thanks."

He pulled a few more things from the drawer and headed out. "Good night."

"Night."

The door was nearly shut when he flipped off the light switch.

She bolted upright. *"Don't."*

Noah's shadow stopped on the threshold.

Her heart scraped across her chest like shattered glass, and she barely stopped herself from scrambling from the bed. "I-I mean . . . leave it on, please." She hated the panic in her voice.

The lamp came back on, its golden light leaving her raw and exposed. In front of Noah. Heat crawled into her cheeks as she dragged her eyes from him. She worked to steady her breathing, calmly adjusting the blankets as if she hadn't just completely lost it.

"Thank you." Her body was flushed with heat. She sank against the pillows, trying for casual, and closed her eyes. The thudding of her heart made the mattress quake. "Good night."

It seemed like ten minutes that he stood in the threshold, the weight of his gaze on her. Finally the door clicked shut, and a deep breath whooshed from her body.

# Chapter 7

*Cartersville, Georgia*

*Sixteen years ago*

Josephine's mother died the summer she turned twelve. It happened on July sixth. It was easy to remember the date, because Josephine had gotten her period the day before and wanted to tell her, but Mama wasn't speaking to her because Josephine was in trouble for wearing eye shadow to Shelby Green's Fourth of July party.

The wreck on 985 killed her mother instantly. The next few days passed in a foggy blur. Mostly Josephine just tried to stay out of her stepdad's way.

Eddie was nice, mostly. He cajoled her mom out of dark moods and took them for ice cream on Friday nights. But sometimes he drank beer, and he wasn't so nice then. He frowned a lot and snapped at her. After her mom died, she saw a lot of Ugly Eddie.

Saturday nights became poker night in their doublewide

trailer—something Mama had forbidden. Josephine didn't like Eddie's friends. They were loud, and they chewed with their mouths open and filled the trailer with cigarette smoke. So she stayed in her room, listening to the radio or talking to Shelby on the phone.

"Jo!" Eddie called to her. "Why aren't these dishes done yet?" His voice was loud and sloppy, and she didn't want to test his temper by ignoring him. He'd embarrass her in front of his friends.

"Coming!" She was already dressed for bed in her black shorts and favorite pink cami with butterflies on it.

Bits of dirt clung to her feet as she padded down the hall. She needed to sweep, but between homework and getting supper on the table, there never seemed to be a spare moment.

In the kitchen she slid quietly past the table to the sink, where a couple days' dishes were piled.

As she had hoped, the four men were too fixed on their game to pay her any mind. Empty brown bottles littered the table and countertop, and the smell of cigarette smoke hung in the air. The window air conditioner hummed in the next room, working futilely to cool the space.

She could hear the men plainly even over the rush of water in the sink and the quiet *clank* of the dishes as she washed them.

"That's it," Eddie said, his cards slapping the table. "I'm done. Let's call it a night."

"It's only eleven o'clock."

"Yeah, Eddie. I need a chance to win my money back from Shark over there. Meg's going to kill me if I come home without the rent."

"You shouldn't have lost it." Where the rest of the voices

were sloppy and loose, Shark's was low and controlled. He had little black eyes that reminded Josephine of hard pebbles, and his scruffy neck was thick with veins. She thought the others were a little afraid of him.

"Come on. One more round. I'd rather be dead in a ditch than go home without rent money. Meg'll nag me into next year."

"I ain't got nothing left," her stepfather whined. "He just took my grocery money, and I don't get paid till next Friday."

"You gotta have something of worth around here."

Josephine scrubbed the pan from last night's supper as a moment of silence ensued.

"All right, fine. Ain't nothing 'round here I can't do without. 'Cept the TV. You can't have that!"

"Winner takes his pick then." Shark's voice rumbled through the room.

"All right, now we're talking. Deal 'em."

A bottle top popped open as another round of poker got underway.

Josephine scrubbed and scrubbed at the pan. She hated the mess eggs made. The skillet had long since lost its shiny surface. She wondered what they were going to eat this week if Eddie didn't win this round. There were only a few cans in the cupboard, and they were out of meat.

Maybe she could babysit for the Crays this week. She liked the toddlers, but sometimes the Crays forgot to pay her. There were always the apple trees in the neighboring lot. But Eddie got tired of apples, and he'd soon enough forget he'd been the one to cause this trouble.

She finished washing the stack of dishes and shut off the water, grabbing the towel from the stove handle.

"Let's supersize it," Shark said. The silence was broken by the sound of something sliding across the table.

Eddie swore.

"He's bluffing," one of them said.

"Maybe," Shark said. "Maybe not."

"I wouldn't feed these cards to my dog." Cards slapped the table. "I'm out."

"Me too. Dang it, Shark, you're merciless. Meg's going to kill me."

"And then there were two."

"How 'bout it, Eddie?" Shark said.

A long silence sounded, followed by the *pop* of another bottle top.

"Time to separate the men from the boys," Eddie said.

Josephine set down the dried pan and started on the glasses.

"Nice hand," Shark said, pausing for a purposeful moment. "Almost as nice as this one."

A series of groans sounded behind her, followed by laughter.

"Sonova . . . ," Eddie swore. "You got the dangedest streak of luck I ever saw."

"Thanks for playing, ladies," Shark said.

Josephine put away the last glasses and began gathering the empty bottles from the table. Eddie didn't like clutter, and she didn't want the place reeking of beer tomorrow. It was already going to stink of smoke.

"Whatcha gonna take, Shark?"

"Yeah, Shark."

"Shut up, losers," Eddie said. "I'll tell Meg whatcha said about her, then we'll see who's gloating over someone else's misfortune."

Shark's chair creaked as he leaned back, a satisfied smirk on his face.

Josephine reached for the bottle nearest him, and his eyes locked onto hers. Their dark intensity held her captive a long, stifling moment before they raked down her body.

A trail of chills raced down her arms, raising the hairs. She tore her eyes away, wishing her pajamas covered more of her.

"You said he'd have his pick. Whatcha gonna take, Shark?"

The bottles clinked as Josephine cradled them to her chest, turning away from the table.

"Oh, I have my eye on something." His voice scraped across his throat.

"Not my TV! You heard me, boys. I said it was off limits."

"He don't want that thing! Have you seen his AV setup?"

Josephine dropped the bottles in the trash can and scurried back to her room. At least the game was over. They'd be gone soon. She shut her door and turned off her light, then scooted between the covers, curling up on her side.

The window was open, a hot breeze barely moving the air. Only a slit of light beneath the door broke up the darkness.

She wished she could erase the image of Shark's beady eyes from her memory. Mama had said she was an early bloomer. She'd said it like it was a good thing, but Josephine didn't like the way boys looked at her now. And she especially didn't like the way Shark looked at her.

She turned away from the door and closed her eyes. She'd almost drifted off when a glow of light from the hall made her eyelids flutter open. Darkness fell over her room once again, and her door clicked shut.

Her ears pricked. She felt a presence in the room. She lay still on the mattress, eyes wide in the suffocating darkness.

The sound of footsteps on the carpet made her blood freeze. Quietly, so quietly, she rolled over, her heart thudding against her ribs. A black shadow hulked over her, and a cold shiver of fear passed through her. Her throat tightened against a scream, and a hand covered her mouth, hard and smothering.

# Chapter 8

*Sweetbriar Ranch*

*Present day*

*N*oah sat up on the couch and stretched, his aching muscles extending painfully. His sofa wasn't meant for sleeping on, that much he'd learned last night.

Not that he'd done much sleeping. He'd been fretting in the dark for hours waiting for the sun to come up. Sometime around five the plinking of the sleet against the windows had stopped. With any luck the temperature would rise with the sun and melt the ice.

Now that a bit of daylight was slipping silently through the curtains, he could see what was going on outside, then tend to the horses.

He jumped up from the sofa and pushed the curtains aside. A thin blanket of white covered the hills, the trees, his truck. No.

No, no, no.

Snow was still falling at a steep angle, gusts of wind making it swirl in vicious circles.

*You've got to be kidding me.* He let the curtains fall back over the window and drove his palm into the frame.

He grabbed his laptop, took it to the couch, and opened it to weather.com. The cold front had dipped farther south than predicted. He stared with disbelief at the day's forecast.

Four inches of snow by nightfall.

His breath left his body. Josephine would be stuck in his house for another night at least. He didn't let himself think any further than that or remember how long it sometimes took the plows to get around to the mountain roads.

He palmed his jaw before sliding his hand to his neck, where a bundle of tension had gathered.

*Really, God? You're really fixing to do this?*

Shadow came over and nuzzled his hand, sensing his agitation. Noah rubbed behind the dog's ears.

His eyes caught on the divorce document lying on the end table. He didn't even want to think on that right now.

He closed his laptop and got up. The horses needed tending, and he needed something to keep his mind off of Josephine. Off the fact that she was lying in the next room, in his bed.

A few minutes later he was ducking from his truck to the barn. It was a good thing he'd brought the horses in the night before. Looked like they'd be staying put today too.

Inside the barn the wind howled. Kismet gave a tremulous high-pitched neigh. His ears flicked back and forth, and his eyes roved the stable. He'd been pastured since his arrival. Noah knew last night would be hard on him. He should've taken some time with the horse, but he'd been distracted by Josephine.

"Hey, buddy," he said, approaching the stall slowly. "It's all right. Everything's gonna be just fine." He held out his hand, but the horse stepped back.

Noah reached into his coat pocket, where he stashed sugar cubes. It took a few minutes of sweet talk, but Kismet eventually stepped forward and took them from his palm.

"Attaboy."

In a nearby stall Rango nickered, eager for his feed. A couple of the other horses followed his lead. "All right, all right. I know you're all hungry. You'll get your turn."

After calming Kismet Noah began feeding them. He added a little valerian to Kismet's feed since he'd be stalled for the day. He took a little time with each horse, offering affection and brushing down a couple of them in the grooming area.

Outside the wind howled, whistling through the eaves. He thought of Josephine curled up in his bed, her hair probably scenting his pillow. She wouldn't be any happier about the weather forecast than he was. Maybe she'd sleep until noon.

He moved to Digger's withers, brushing in long, slow strokes. The horse sighed as his muscles relaxed.

Noah's thoughts moved back to Josephine, remembering her panic the night before. He'd realized his mistake the moment he'd flipped off the light. She'd always been afraid of the dark. Something from her childhood, he guessed. She'd always been fine as long as he was with her. But the moment she was alone in the darkness, she panicked. He fought the protective feelings that rose inside him just as he'd done the night before. Not his responsibility.

He finished tending the horses and drove back to the house. The snow was still coming down, the wind causing whiteout conditions. The sky had brightened as much as it was going to, given the thick gray abyss overhead. If only he could stay in the barn all day.

The house was quiet when he entered, arms loaded with firewood. He shed his winter gear and stoked the fire, his thoughts heavy. How was he going to spend a full day and another night alone with Josephine? Just being near her messed with his head. A cloud of dread swelled inside until his lungs felt constricted by it.

He heard a noise in the hall. So Sleeping Beauty had awakened. And it wasn't even nine o'clock. The shower kicked on a few minutes later.

He tossed the last log on with more force than necessary, then started on breakfast. He peered into the fridge, spying the carton of eggs. *Scrambled, salt and pepper, a bit of cheese.* He recalled her preferences much too easily.

Awhile later he headed toward the bathroom to let Josephine know breakfast was ready. The door opened just as he raised his hand to knock. Steam rolled out, and Josephine jumped back.

Her hair was dry and tousled around her face. Her creamy skin bare of makeup. Beautiful, in other words.

She pressed a hand to her chest. "You gave me a fright."

"Breakfast is ready."

"I was going to grab something from the coffee shop." She maneuvered around him, and he gave her a wide path. "Are you ready to go? I just need to get my shoes on."

Obviously she hadn't looked outside yet. The bedroom window was covered in opaque plastic, being old and single-paned. The bathroom didn't even have one.

"Noah? I have appointments today. The sooner I get back, the better."

He gathered his wits, cleared his throat. "You may as well not bother with your shoes."

She eyed him for a long moment. "Why is that?"

Somehow saying it out loud would make it real. He pressed his lips together and nodded in the direction of the living room.

After a long scrutinizing look, she crossed to the window and reached for the drapes.

As she parted them, a little squeak escaped her throat.

It looked even worse than it had before—and that was saying something. It was a sea of white. He could barely see past the porch.

Her fingers clutched the drape as she stared, and her shoulders rose and fell.

He let her take it in. He didn't know what to say anyway.

A moment later she turned and collapsed onto the sofa, giving him the stink eye. "It wasn't supposed to snow."

"Well, it did."

Her eyes flashed. "Thank you ever so much, Einstein."

He lifted his hands. "Hey, it's not my fault. I'm not the one who decided to barge in without warning."

"I was trying to help."

She glared at him across the space, and he glared back.

Like this was his fault. If she'd just finalized the divorce in the first place like she promised, this wouldn't be happening. And he wasn't the one who'd traipsed across the mountain without so much as a phone call.

She crossed her arms. She was wearing the white sweater she'd worn the day before. "How long till it stops? I have a business to run."

"You might want to call someone to fill in. It's not supposed to let up for a while."

Her stormy gaze clashed with his. "How long?"

He looked over her shoulder to the wintry scene outside. The wind blasted just then, whistling down the chimney. The fire snapped, and a log shifted.

"All day."

Her lips parted, and her shoulders sank as a breath left her body. "Are you kidding me?"

"Unfortunately not."

"I have a whole boatload of things to do today. Not only the appointments. I have a big event at the shop this weekend. I have a lot of planning yet to do."

"I don't know what to tell you."

"Tell me you're kidding!"

He pressed his lips together. Did she think he liked this? It was his worst flipping nightmare.

"There's scrambled eggs in the kitchen if you're hungry."

# Chapter 9

The front door shut behind Noah, and a week's worth of tension drained from Josephine. He'd left, supposedly to check on the horses, but she figured it had more to do with a desperate desire to escape her. He hadn't spoken one word since he'd offered her breakfast. Even now the eggs sat congealing in her stomach.

Have mercy, how was she going to make it through this day?

She was going to stay busy, that's what. She retrieved her phone from the bedroom and dialed. Callie answered on the fifth ring, her voice still groggy with sleep.

Josephine got down to business. "I'm afraid I can't make it in this morning. I know this is your day off, but could you spell me?"

Callie cleared her throat. "Why, of course I can."

"My first appointment is at eleven, and I have a few more this afternoon. Ellen will be in at three."

"No problem. Is everything all right?"

Josephine gave a huff. "Depends on your definition of *all right*. I'm stuck in the mountains until this storm lets up."

"Where on earth are you?"

Josephine closed her eyes. Since coming to work at the shop Callie had become her best friend. The woman knew a bit about her history with Noah. Of course, who in town didn't?

"At Sweetbriar Ranch."

A long pause followed.

"Callie?"

"Noah's ranch, you mean?"

"That'd be the one."

"Oh. You didn't tell me—"

"No. It's nothing like that. I just came up to get the divorce papers signed and . . . got stranded."

"Oh my. What possessed you to do that? I thought he was signing them on Friday."

"Well, I got it in my head I'd save him the trip."

"Hoo-boy."

"You can say that again." Josephine palmed her forehead. "I can't believe this is happening."

"Is there anything I can do?"

"Actually, there is."

She instructed Callie to scan some of the documents on her desk for the Hope House pampering party, then check the stock room for adequate supplies. Josephine would have to get a final list of the girls' names and work out a schedule for hair, makeup, and nails. She could also confirm times with the stylists by phone today.

"All right then, anything else?"

Josephine thought of Noah, returning soon to the cozy

little cottage with too little space and not enough distractions. Not nearly enough.

"Yeah. You could pray for the snow to stop."

"Will do, friend."

After hanging up, Josephine turned on the TV and made some other calls. After she was finished she shut off her phone to conserve battery power.

To kill time she wiped down the counters and washed the skillet, wondering what was taking Noah so long. Not that she wanted him to return, but the conditions outside were bad. The wind howled, blowing up so hard that the screens rattled in their frames.

Was it possible to get lost between the house and barn, like those old stories of settlers on the prairie? She went to the front door and lit up the outside like a Christmas tree. Then she scolded herself, because Noah was terribly competent and was surely only trying to avoid her.

She gave a wry grin. That might be a first. A man who didn't want to be alone with her. Sometimes she missed the old Josephine.

The front door opened, and she spun around, suddenly aware she was standing in the middle of the room like a befuddled idiot.

Noah closed the door against the wind and snow and started removing his outer gear.

"Everything all right?" she asked.

He tossed a snowy boot to the side. "Fine."

"It still looks awful bad out there."

The other boot came off and joined the first with a *clunk*.

"I was wondering what kind of phone you have," she said.

He spared her a glance.

"I'll need to charge mine later, and obviously I didn't bring a cord."

He named the latest iPhone model—reluctance in the tightened corners of his eyes.

Different type. "Guess I'll just have to conserve power then."

The room fell quiet as he walked to the fireplace and began adding more logs. One of those gabby talk shows played on the TV, the kind where the women sat around a table and talked a subject to death.

"If it's not too much bother, could I use your laptop to check my e-mail and print some documents?"

Without looking, he gestured to the laptop on the end table.

Tension had rolled into the room with him. Already her shoulders were tight, and a headache throbbed at the base of her skull. Is this what they were going to do all day? Ignore each other? She didn't think she could tolerate ten more minutes.

She tucked her hands into her back pockets. "Noah . . . how 'bout we call some kind of truce or something?"

"I really don't have anything to say to you, Josephine."

Once again she flinched at his use of her full name. "I know you're cross with me, Noah—"

His flinty look choked off her words.

She felt the impact of those fiery eyes clear down to her painted toenails. "And you have every right to be. But we're stuck here for the day, and this'll be painful enough without—"

"I know we're stuck together—I can't help that. But I don't have to like it. And I'm not going to pretend everything's all right when it isn't."

He headed toward the bathroom.

"So you're just going to give me the cold shoulder all the livelong day?"

His only answer was the *click* of the bathroom door as it closed between them.

Noah leaned against the bathroom counter, his head hanging low between his shoulders. He could almost feel the adrenaline racing through his veins, flushing his body, quickening his pulse. Fight or flight.

He'd wisely chosen the second option, and that was his official plan for the remainder of this nightmarish day.

He raised his head and met his gaze in the mirror. A vein pulsed in his forehead, and his brows crouched low over his eyes, two grooves separating them. His whole face bore the grimness of someone fighting for his life.

Or his sanity.

He pushed off the counter, turned on the shower, and shucked his clothes. The hot water felt good on his tight muscles, so he lingered under the spray until his skin was red, the pads of his fingers wrinkled.

When he entered the living room awhile later, Josephine didn't even glance up from the laptop. Her fingers danced over the keys, clicking and clacking. Her eyes were narrowed on the screen—her focused look.

She'd taken the same corner of the sofa that had always been her spot. Noah suddenly realized he never sat there. As if he were saving the seat for her, as if she might walk through the door any moment and make herself comfortable.

*Lame, Mitchell. Real lame.*

He settled at the kitchen table—as far away from her as he could get—and did his bills. He usually didn't do them until midmonth, but his plan was to stay busy.

After the bills he rescheduled this week's trail rides, then checked on the horses again, taking Shadow with him. He stalled for time, brushing Digger and Rango and taking extra time with Kismet.

When he came back, Josephine was in the kitchen. A few minutes later she announced that lunch was ready.

He sat opposite her at the table in front of a plate of buttered toast, peas, and potato chips. He flicked a glance at her.

The corners of her lips were tilted up in a sardonic look he'd seen a hundred times before. "You really need to get to the grocery more often."

Her attempt at levity fell flat, and he sensed rather than saw the curling in of her body.

He closed his eyes and pretended to pray for a long moment before he actually began thanking God for his food. Sad state of affairs when prayer became a temporary reprieve.

They ate in silence, their forks scraping their plates. The refrigerator humming. Time was like a long tightrope, stretching into infinity, skinny and treacherous.

"It's supposed to stop snowing later on tonight, right?"

He followed her gaze to the kitchen window. A miniature white snow devil danced a few feet away.

"Yes."

He wasn't lying. It was supposed to stop. What he failed to mention was that after a few hours of lull it might kick up again. The second part of the system.

He closed his eyes briefly. *Please, God. A little mercy here.*

"How long will it take to clear the roads?"

"Depends how much help they get."

He finished his toast in peace, making a mental schedule for the rest of the day. While the tension hanging in the air was punishing him as much as it was her, he couldn't bring himself to do anything about it. He didn't have it in him to be nice to her. Or maybe he was afraid of what that might lead to.

He strangled the thought until it was limp and gasping for air.

He grabbed his plate and put it in the dishwasher, along with the pan she'd used to heat the peas. He was leaving the kitchen when she spoke.

"Noah . . ."

He stopped in the middle of the living room.

"I'm—I'm real sorry."

Sorry? Heat flushed his neck. He turned and faced her. Look at her, sitting so innocently at his table, her shoulders hunched, her eyes wide and vulnerable.

"About what, Josephine? About the fact that we're still married? About getting yourself stuck up here? Or about what you did—" His jaw clamped down hard, and he turned away. "I don't want to talk about this. Any of it."

He threw his schedule out the virtual window. He couldn't be trapped in here another second. He shoved his boots back onto his feet and thrust his arms into his coat sleeves.

"Come on, Shadow."

He ushered the dog out the door and somehow managed to close it softly behind him.

He couldn't say he'd gone into this relationship blindly. He'd been warned. He'd just been too stupid to listen.

# Chapter 10

*Copper Creek*

*Three and a half years ago*

The savory smell of barbecue and the familiar commotion of a rowdy Saturday-night crowd welcomed Noah into the Rusty Nail. He made his way to the back.

The place did have a certain charm, with its beamed ceilings and wavy corrugated metal walls. The back of the bar was tiled with mirrored squares, making the place look double in size—and customers. He nodded to his neighbors as he wound through the clusters of wooden tables.

He greeted Jack and Seth, then pulled out a chair, taking a few minutes to catch up with the two before they ordered.

Seth and Noah ran the family construction business now that their father was easing away from his responsibilities. They were close. Seth was the younger brother who caused all the petty trouble and got away with it. Noah was the one who lived by the rules and got caught the first time he stepped out of line.

And Jack was the voice of reason of the group. Somehow the young Lutheran minister was a good fit with the brothers. When they weren't talking about work or women, they were having spirited debates about their doctrinal differences.

Seth started a story about something that happened on a jobsite, but Noah couldn't bring himself to pay attention. His mind had been elsewhere since last Saturday when he met Josephine Dupree.

He'd commandeered the barbershop's bid sheet as soon as he returned to the office and finished pricing it out. Common sense told him he had to make money on the job, but something even stronger had him slashing prices to his cost. His dad would throw a fit if he knew. But he let Noah handle the finances.

Noah had dropped the bid by the barbershop on Thursday. Josephine—as mesmerizing as the first time he'd met her—was busy with a customer, but she promised to get back with him soon. He'd probably stared at her like a lovesick idiot, but somehow he couldn't help himself.

"Hey." Seth shoved his shoulder. "You're not even paying attention. What's wrong with you? You're all fidgety."

Noah dropped the napkin he'd been shredding to pieces and accepted the Coke from Kendra Stevens. Man, was she really twenty-one? He used to babysit her and her brother.

"Everything okay, buddy?" Jack leaned his elbows on the table, making it rock.

"I met someone."

"Oh boy. My big brother's going down." Seth leaned back in his chair with a smirk. "Who is she? Gotta know who's turned you into a googly-eyed fool."

"She's new to town. It's the woman who opened up the

barbershop. Josephine Dupree." He even loved the sound of her name on his tongue.

Seth's lips fell into a straight line. He rubbed his scruffy jaw. "Dude."

"I know, I know. Out of my league. But I went in for a haircut last week and—I don't know, man. There's just something about her."

Seth huffed a laugh. "It's called lust."

Noah gave him a look. "It's not lust." *Well*, he thought, remembering her generous curves, *not* just *lust*.

Seth leaned forward, planting his elbows on the table. His brother had the kind of intense stare that could rattle a Navy SEAL.

Something in Noah bucked up.

"Look," Seth said. "I know she's . . . striking. Nobody's denying that. But she's got a bit of a reputation, bro."

Noah scowled. "She hasn't been here long enough to have a reputation. She's just friendly."

"She's from Cartersville, right? Buddy of mine runs an auto body shop down there. He told me stuff."

Noah sat back in his chair, crossed his arms. "Since when do you listen to gossip?"

"It's not gossip. My buddy's friend went out with her for a while. She cheated on him."

"There's two sides to every story."

"Maybe so, but according to my friend, she really made the rounds. He went to school with her. She sounds like a real man-eater, Noah."

Noah gave his brother a cold look as something raw and protective surfaced in him fast and furious. "Just the same, I think I'll draw my own conclusions." He looked at Jack, whose brown eyes had grown somber. "You're awful quiet over there. You have something to add?"

Jack's eyes fell to the table. He flicked away a few grains of salt, then clasped his hands on the table. "What do you know about her spiritual condition?"

"Seriously? I just met her, Jack." His eyes toggled between the men, and he suddenly wished he hadn't brought up Josephine at all. They sure knew how to ruin a man's good mood.

"But I'm planning to get to know her better. I'm going to ask her out."

"Is she going to church anywhere?" Jack asked.

"Not ours," Noah said. "Maybe she's going to yours."

Jack's lips pressed together. "Not that I know of."

"Well, it's a big church. You could've missed her." Though he honestly didn't know how anyone, even a pastor, could miss a woman like Josephine. "Anyway . . . it's just a date. I'm not asking her to marry me, for crying out loud."

Seth turned his hands palm up. "Just don't want you getting hurt, man."

"Yeah, well . . . I can look out for myself."

Noah was relieved when Kendra appeared with their plate of loaded nachos. When she left, Noah changed the subject. Nothing was stopping him from pursuing Josephine Dupree. Not even his well-meaning friend and brother.

# Chapter 11

*Sweetbriar Ranch*

*Present day*

Needing to make a call to the Hope House director, Josephine turned on her phone. Noah had been gone a couple hours. The conditions outside were still nasty. She tried not to let it bother her that he preferred his horses' company to hers.

A new voicemail dinged as her phone came to life. She pulled it up and listened, recognizing the voice of Ava, one of the girls from the Hope House. Ava's mom had passed away, and her dad was in jail. Like the other girls, she'd been anticipating the spring fling for weeks.

Ava's voice was thick with tears as she asked Josephine to return her call. Josephine dialed the number and waited until Ava came on the line.

"Honey, I'm so sorry I missed you. What's the matter?"

Ava's voice crumbled. "I'm not going to the spring fling.

Devon texted me this morning and told me he forgot he'd asked someone else. As if!"

"What? Oh, sugar."

"Maya Pendleton." She spewed the name out as if it were poison. "Brad told Jacob who told Laura that he really just asked her out Saturday night. He's such a liar."

"I'm so sorry, sweetie. You don't deserve that. You deserve someone who respects and appreciates you, and clearly that's not Devon."

"Friday I told him I wouldn't—you know, sleep with him the night of the dance. He only asked Maya because he knows she will! I shouldn't have told him."

Anger flushed Josephine's cheeks. She didn't even know Devon, but she wanted to snatch him bald-headed. Sometimes she really hated the male species.

She barely heard the front door open, barely noticed Noah as he removed his winter gear.

"Honey, listen. You didn't do anything wrong. If that's really all he wanted, then good riddance."

Ava sniffled. "But now I don't have a date for the dance! All my friends have dates, and I'll be sitting at home watching some lame TV show."

The sofa gave a little squeak as Josephine shifted her position. Shadow came over and nuzzled her hand until she petted his damp fur.

Noah stoked the fire and dropped in a log.

"Maybe it's not too late," Josephine said. "Maybe one of your friends can fix you up with someone. Or . . . I know! One of my stylists has a son who goes to Pickens. He's a senior and really nice and cute. Why don't I give her a call and see if he can go with you?"

Ava heaved a sigh. "I don't know. He probably wouldn't want to go out with me."

Her low self-esteem broke Josephine's heart. "You're a beautiful, classy young lady, Ava. He'd be lucky to take you. Let me just give it a try."

A long pause sounded while Josephine encouraged her mentally.

"I suppose so," Ava said on another heavy sigh.

"Good girl. I'll get back with you by tonight with an update. Don't lose hope. And I'll put you on my personal schedule for Saturday. I can't wait to get you all gussied up and see you in your pretty dress."

"Thanks, Josephine. Even if it doesn't work out, I do feel a smidge better. Talking to you always picks me up."

"Right back at you, sweetie pie. I'll call you later."

After she hung up, Josephine called Callie and explained the situation with Ava. Her friend agreed to call her son as soon as he got home from work.

"Is the shop busy?" Josephine asked.

"It's pretty dead what with the weather. The real question is how are you doing?"

"Um. It's all right."

"Why do I have a feeling he's sitting right under your nose?"

"Because that is indeed the case."

"Well, hang in there. The snow has to stop sometime. Hey, gotta run. A customer just walked in."

Josephine ended the call, then looked up to find Noah's eyes on her. She turned off the phone as he put the poker back in the rack and settled in his recliner with his laptop.

She observed him from beneath her lashes, getting a read on him. His cheeks were still flushed from the cold, and bits of melting snow clung to his hair. He seemed less tense than he had when he'd left, thank heavens. His jaw wasn't ticking, and the skin around his eyes wasn't so tight. Whatever he'd done in the barn had burned off some negative energy.

Josephine looked down at the schedule she'd made on the paper and began puzzling out how she'd accommodate Ava on Saturday. If Alex agreed, the girl was going to be a nervous wreck. She'd need lots of positive thoughts.

"Was that about your event this weekend?"

She looked up, surprised he'd addressed her with such a neutral tone. "Yeah."

"I guess it is time for the spring fling. Wouldn't know it by the weather."

"I'm just glad it's hitting now and not Saturday. The girls would be so disappointed."

His eyes flickered to her, then back to the laptop. "You finally got that day-of-pampering thing worked out."

She'd wanted to do this since she'd first heard about the Hope House. But in the early days she'd barely been scraping by.

"This is our first year, and it really mushroomed. Hope Daniels teamed up with me. She did a consignment dress drive, and Oopsy Daisy is providing free boutonnières for the girls to give their dates."

"That's great."

After a moment's silence she went back to the schedule. Just when she thought she had it all worked out, Noah's phone buzzed.

He pulled it from his pocket. "Hey, Mary Beth." The recliner groaned as he leaned back.

A sharp sensation cut through Josephine's middle like

a knife. Her heart gave a heavy thud, and she consciously unclenched her jaw.

He was none of her concern anymore. But that didn't stop her from eavesdropping on his conversation. Wasn't like she could help overhearing anyway.

"Yeah, he was a little spooked last night. Gave him some valerian in his feed and he's better today. Wind's supposed to keep up for a couple more days."

A pause ensued as Mary Beth took her turn.

"I know. How are you holding up? Staying warm enough?"

Noah's deep chuckle ran right through Josephine.

"Well, let me know if it gets any worse. I could run the snow machine over and take a look at it."

A warm flush crawled up Josephine's neck. Super Noah to the rescue. She'd just bet Mary Beth would take him up on that. Heaven knew he was eager enough to escape Josephine.

The phone call went on a few more minutes, moving to more horse talk. By the time he hung up her jaw ached from clenching her teeth.

"That your new girlfriend?" Josephine smirked, blinked innocently, but she wondered if the tightness in her tone gave her away.

Noah fixed her with a stony look. "I don't see what business that is of yours."

"Well, technically you're still my husband." *Hush up, Josephine.*

Noah's eyes tightened and somehow reached a new level of cold. "Technically, you gave up your rights to that claim 'round about a year and a half ago."

She couldn't stop the warmth of shame that flooded her face, but she had many years of practice schooling her features into that I-couldn't-care-less look.

"Mary Beth's a nice girl. She suits you." It about killed her to say it.

His nostrils flared. "I don't need your advice or your approval, Josephine."

She lifted a shoulder. "Just saying. You have a lot in common, with the horses and all."

He pinned her with a deadly look, and she wondered why on earth she was egging him on. It was just that the phone call had set all these emotions roiling inside her, and she could hardly stand to see him sitting there with that secret little smile on his face.

But now he was glowering at the screen, his brows pinched together, a shadow moving as his jaw ticked. Even angry he was handsome. Stop-in-the-street-and-stare kind of handsome, with that jet-black hair and olive skin. She'd known he was trouble from the minute he walked into her shop. But she'd always known just how to handle troublesome men.

At least she always had before. Noah had somehow inched under her defenses with his quiet resolve and unnerving patience.

*No man's ever gonna love a girl like you, Jo.*

The words surfaced from a deep, dark place inside, reaching out with long tentacles and dragging her down.

*You're only good for one thing, and every man within a dozen square miles of you knows it.*

That last part had only been added on in high school after her reputation had been sullied.

She'd somehow convinced herself it would be different with Noah. But in the end, Eddie and her mama had been proven right.

"What?" Noah snapped.

She startled a little. Realized she'd been gawking at him.

"Stop looking at me like that."

The memory had sucked all the wind from her sails, and it took a real effort to school her features. "Like what?"

"I'm not falling for it again, Josephine. That innocent, vulnerable, save-me thing you do. So you can just keep your wiles to yourself."

She fought the sting behind her eyes even as she curled her lips. "I do believe I'll save them for someone they might just work on."

His nostrils flared again. "You do that."

Her body was flushed with heat. "You should go on over to Mary Beth's. Sounded like she needs some help." *What are you doing, you big dope?*

"Itching to be rid of me?"

She gave a careless shrug. "It's obvious you don't want to be here. Or better yet, why don't you just take me back to town on that snow machine of yours?"

"I'd be happy to. Unfortunately we're going to have to wait until the wind dies down unless you want to freeze to death on the way."

A log shifted in the fireplace, sizzling.

Though Josephine's face was a study in indifference, there was a lonely quality to her voice that sucked Noah right in.

*No. She is not lonely. She's a master manipulator. A man-eater.*

And he was a darned fool.

"I could give you a haircut," she said. "It's a little long, and that would help pass the time."

Memories surfaced. Her fingers sifting through his hair, her perfume flooding his senses, her body skimming his shoulders as the scissors snipped quietly. Lazy Saturday mornings. His pulse leaped, and his nerve endings tingled. His body had not forgotten.

"I don't think so."

"You used to like the way I styled your hair."

"I used to like a lot of things. Look, why don't we just try and get through this? You do your thing, I'll do mine. With any luck you'll be headed home tomorrow."

When it came to the weather forecast, he still hadn't told her quite everything. The truth was it would take a lot of luck and a minor miracle besides.

She gave him that smirk he'd come to hate in the last days of their marriage. "Whatever you want, Noah."

They passed the rest of the day in silence. She worked on the laptop and he worked in the attic, putting up sheets of drywall over the batts of insulation. Swinging a hammer was always a welcome release, even if he was making a heap of noise. Even Shadow had deserted him in favor of Josephine.

When she called him for supper he saw that the snow had tapered off to flurries. The weather reports conflicted from one site to the next—some warning of a second system on the heels of the first, others saying rain or a wintry mix starting in the morning. With any luck it would be rain. Tons of it, to melt off the snow.

Supper was a quiet affair. Josephine had retreated to her corner and he to his, and that was just fine. There was nothing but indifference on her face. Sometimes he thought she was made of stone. How she could be in the same room after all they'd shared and feel so little, he hadn't a clue.

When they were finished he cleared their dishes. As he stacked them in the dishwasher, he heard Josephine on the phone with the teenaged girl. Apparently the boy had agreed to the date, but the girl seemed to need some coaxing on the follow-through.

He went outside at dusk to tend to the horses. Even though it was still windy he put them back out to pasture. It took awhile to get their coats on and move them one by one. He cleaned out the stalls, and by the time he was back inside it was going on eight.

Josephine had replenished the wood supply. He heard the sink running in the bathroom as he hung his coat on the tree. With any luck she'd turn in early. If she didn't, he'd work in the attic. It was ready to be taped and mudded. If he finished tonight he could sand tomorrow and start painting. That would keep him busy if Josephine ended up stuck here another day.

He flipped on the TV and stopped on ESPN. He wished March Madness had already begun because the choices were meager tonight. But maybe if he commandeered the TV she'd retreat into the bedroom.

He checked the weather again, feeling a little compulsive. Nothing had changed.

He heard the bathroom door open, and a moment later the bedroom door clicked shut.

His body sank deeper into the recliner. Relief, he told himself. But guilt pricked his conscience. He'd all but driven her to the bedroom with his mandate of silence.

His eyes found the ceiling. *All right, I get it.*

Clearly he had some work to do. He hadn't forgiven her. Was he trying to punish her with his silence? Maybe he hadn't asked for this, but the forced contact was exposing something in him. Something not so pretty.

Something he'd deal with in the morning. He gave a hard sigh and shut off the TV, eager to lose himself in tape and mud.

# Chapter 12

Something pulled Josephine from slumber. Her eyes flew open, and darkness pressed in on all sides. Complete and utter darkness. Suffocating. Her heartbeat thudded, shaking her mattress.

*You're dreaming. You left the light on, remember? This is just an awful nightmare.*

But no. She was wide-awake. And it was so terribly dark.

Suddenly her mind was back in that room, her body flooding with adrenaline. His heavy weight crushing her. One hand clamped painfully over her mouth, another pulling at her pajama bottoms.

No. She wasn't there. She wasn't twelve. She was at Noah's. Safe.

She reached for the tableside lamp, groping in the darkness. Her clumsy hands knocked it over, and it toppled sideways with a clatter. She fumbled for the switch and found it, but twisting it did nothing.

She scrambled backward to the headboard. It clattered against the wall as she huddled against it, drawing her knees in close. Her labored breaths filled the darkness as she searched the room, eyes wide in the suffocating darkness.

*You're at Noah's. Everything's fine.*

But it wasn't. There wasn't so much as a gray shadow to break the inky blackness. And she smelled cigarette smoke and alcohol. Or was that only her imagination?

"Noah." The whisper grated across her throat, not loud enough to stir him even if he'd been sleeping beside her.

She listened intently, but her heartbeat thrashed in her ears, covering any extraneous noises. A sweat broke out on the back of her neck, but she pulled the covers closer.

*You're okay, you're okay, you're okay.*

Noah's eyes opened. A sound had woken him. Lying prone on the couch, he listened. Shadow snored softly on the floor beside him, unbothered. The wind howled outside. Maybe a branch had fallen on the roof. Or maybe he'd left something on the ladder upstairs. Something that might've fallen off.

It felt like the middle of the night, but the sound had him fully alert. He checked the DVR for the time, but the numbers weren't there. He checked his cell phone instead. 2:50.

Another noise sounded, this one loud and clearly coming from his bedroom. He leaped off the sofa, heading that way, banging his shin on the coffee table in his rush.

When he reached the closed door, he tapped twice. "Josephine?"

Hearing nothing, he pushed it open.

Ragged breaths filled the darkness. A nightmare? Where was the light?

He flipped the switch on the wall. Nothing. He remembered the DVR and realized the electricity must've gone out.

He moved into the room, toward the ragged breaths. "Josie, it's me," he said, easing onto the mattress.

A whimper sounded.

"Wake up." He reached out for her but felt only empty bedding. Warm still.

"I—I'm awake." The words trembled, coming from the head of the bed.

His hand moved across the mattress, finding and closing around one of her blanket-clad feet. "You okay?"

"Can you turn on the light?" The desperation in her voice tore at him. "Please?"

He squeezed her foot. "The electricity's out. Where's your phone?" Without turning loose of her he reached for the nightstand, groping in the darkness.

"It's dead."

"I have a flashlight in the laundry room." He eased off the mattress.

She grabbed his arm. "Wait! I'll go with you."

The mattress squeaked as she slid off it. She clutched the back of his T-shirt, following closely behind. He could feel her tremors.

"Watch your step," he said as they moved slowly through the living room.

When they reached the laundry room, he found the large flashlight in the cupboard over the washer. He clicked it on, and a circle of light puddled on the floor, illuminating the room.

He turned toward Josephine, his T-shirt still clutched in her hand. His eyes settled on her. On her pinched face, her terror-stricken eyes, her quivering lip. Her whole body trembled as her shoulders rose and fell with her shallow breaths. There was nothing fake or manipulative about her behavior.

She blinked a few times, then awkwardly let loose of his shirt and stepped away. "Sorry. Sorry . . ."

He extended the flashlight.

She took it, grasping it like a lifeline, and backed toward the door. "I—I'm okay now."

He wasn't sure which one of them she was trying to convince.

"I'll go back to bed."

"It's going to get cold in there. You'd best stay in the living room near the fire."

"Oh."

"I'll add more logs. Go ahead and take the sofa. I'll take the recliner."

She didn't argue—a testament to her state of mind—as he grabbed a second flashlight and made his way into the living room.

His mind spun as he added logs to the fire. Back when they were together he hadn't tried very hard to find out why Josephine was afraid of the dark. Shouldn't a husband know a thing like that? He hadn't even asked a second time, after she'd brushed him off once. Why hadn't he pressed the issue?

But it was too late now. None of his business anymore.

Josephine stirred awake as a cold draft drifted over her. Faint morning light trickled through the slit in the curtains. Her eyes caught on the flashlight gleaming from the table an instant before she became aware of Noah easing his boots off by the door.

"Sorry. Didn't mean to wake you." The low scrape of his voice brought her fully awake.

The night before flooded back, and heat flushed her face. She wished she could pull the covers over her head and pretend the whole thing had never happened. To that end, she clicked off the flashlight, but dawn had already slipped into the room. There was no hiding.

A recently stoked fire crackled in the grate, and the smell of coffee beckoned.

"Is the electricity still out?"

"Yeah. It might be awhile before they get it back on."

"Are the plows out yet?"

"Ah . . . no." His lips thinned, and his gaze fell away as he kicked his boots into the corner and hung up his coat. She noticed the speckles of snow on his hair, on his coat.

She eased up on the sofa. "It's snowing again?"

He ran his hand through his hair, avoiding her eyes. "Yeah . . . about that. It looks like there's a second system coming through."

Her stomach slid down into the crevices of the couch. "What? How bad?"

The corners of his eyes tightened. His glance bounced off hers. "When I checked before bed they were saying another four inches."

"Four inches!"

He heaved a sigh and shelved his hands on his hips. "Look. It's not good, Josephine. I'm not going to lie. It's supposed to snow most of the day. God only knows how long it'll take the plows to get it all cleared off. But if the wind dies down tomorrow I can take you back on the snowmobile if you don't mind freezing half to death."

Tomorrow was her event. Her breath left her body. No. This was not happening.

"We're just going to have to deal with it. I'll get some more wood chopped today. Get some plastic up over the hallway and the kitchen. We need to keep the heat in here as much as possible. Is there anyone you need to call while I still have some battery left? You should probably let someone know we've lost power so they won't worry when they can't reach you."

Her thoughts scrambled with everything this meant. She dragged her mind away from the fact that she was stranded with her ex—with her *husband*—and on to more practical thoughts of work. Callie was going to have to cover for her again today. But the pampering event . . .

"Isn't there any way we can take the snowmobile later today? I have that event at the shop tomorrow, and I'll need to be there early to—"

He was already shaking his head. "It's too dangerous. The wind chill's too low. The wind's supposed to die down sometime tomorrow though."

Her eyes stung in frustration. "I can't believe this." Why, why, why was this happening? She closed her eyes as if she could make it all disappear. But when she opened them nothing had changed. It was still her and Noah—trapped now in one, single, solitary room.

*Think, Josephine.*

She had to figure out her work situation. She'd made the schedule, but now she'd have to find someone to replace her until she could get there. And someone would have to get everything set up tonight.

Just like her life, everything seemed to be getting worse and worse.

# Chapter 13

They had breakfast—toast, cereal, and the last browning banana. Afterward Josephine slipped into the cold bedroom for privacy and called Callie, using Noah's phone.

Callie promised to hold down the fort and set up for the event. "Everything's going to be fine," she said. "I promise. Don't you trust me?"

"Why, of course I trust you. I'm just . . ."

"Frazzled? Befuddled? Still in love with your husband?"

Josephine palmed her forehead, lowering her voice. "This is a nightmare. Someone wake me up."

"Sorry, kiddo. Are things still tense?"

"Well, let's see, I'm trapped in a house with a man who hates me—"

"He doesn't hate you."

"—and I'm missing the event I've been planning for months, and we've lost electricity—"

*"What?"*

"—so now we're basically trapped in one room, relying on a fireplace for warmth."

"Never underestimate the value of body heat."

"You're not helping."

"Hey, you're still married. Desperate measures and all that."

"Ha. Noah will never be that desperate."

"Maybe this is just what the two of you needed. Maybe God's going to use this somehow. That's how I'm going to pray."

"Suit yourself." Josephine didn't want to talk about God. She was confused enough right now. She told Callie she'd work on finding a replacement for tomorrow's event—at least until she could get there—and ended the conversation.

When she entered the living room, Noah was stapling sheets of heavy plastic over the kitchen, shrinking the space in half.

The steady *click-click* of the stapler stopped. He was finished. They were officially trapped in one room.

He set the stapler on the TV stand and faced her as she sank onto the sofa. "I think we need to talk."

Anxiety wormed through her as the memory of last night's terror surfaced. She didn't want to talk about that. Especially not with Noah. Bad enough he'd seen her that way.

She gave him an indifferent smile. "What's up?"

He'd always had an intense kind of stare that made her feel as naked as the day she was born. She resisted the urge to squirm in her seat.

"I know I said yesterday we should keep to ourselves. But given that we're going to be here at least another night—and the house just got a lot smaller—maybe we should, you know, call a truce like you said."

As long as he didn't want to talk about last night. She lifted a shoulder. "Whatever you want, Noah."

"Let's just keep the past off the table, and I think we'll be able to get through this."

Fine by her. Wasn't like she wanted to wallow in that pigpen either. "All right then."

He nodded. "All right. I got some sanding to do upstairs."

"Can I keep your phone a bit longer? I have more calls to make."

"Sure. Just turn it off when you're done."

Two hours later she'd found a stylist from Ellijay who'd just retired. The woman was glad to fill in at the shop the next day. Josephine finished the schedule and borrowed Noah's laptop to e-mail a copy to Callie.

Once it whooshed off into cyberspace, Josephine turned off the laptop, which was almost out of battery power, and went to check on Noah.

It was cold beyond the plastic partition. She crossed her arms against the chill and followed the scratching sound down the hall and up the stairs. Shadow was on her heels, his claws clicking on the wood floor.

Noah's back was to her as he ran the sandpaper over the seams. He stopped to blow the dust away, felt the seam, then continued sanding.

The electric sander sat in the corner, useless. He was either in a big hurry to finish or he was avoiding her. She didn't have to dither long to figure out which.

Her eyes fell over his masculine form. Those broad shoulders tapering down to a trim waist. His no-fuss jeans hugged his derriere and his long, thick legs. He took a step to the right as he smoothed the horizontal seam.

He'd worked for his dad at Mitchell Home Improvement since he was in high school, learning the business from the ground up—as had his brother, Seth. After his dad retired the brothers took over day-to-day operations of the company.

The renovation at the barbershop had been the smallest job he'd taken on personally in a long while—they'd been dating for weeks before he'd confessed that little tidbit.

"Do you miss it?" The words came out before her brain had even engaged.

His hand stilled, the steady scrape of the sanding stopping for an instant before resuming. "Sometimes."

She leaned a shoulder against the doorframe. "How'd you end up here? At the ranch?"

There was a long pause, so long she wondered if he was going to ignore her.

He stopped sanding, felt the seam, and continued. "Needed a change, I guess. Then Sweetbriar came up on the market. Dave and Doreen wanted to retire to Arizona, and they liked the idea of me running the place. So they cut me a great deal."

"How's the family business doing without you?"

"Holding its own. Seth hired someone to replace me—Carl Owens. You might know him."

"He comes into the shop now and then. Was Seth mad when you left?"

Noah huffed. "You could say that. He got over it soon enough though." He folded over the sandpaper. "How's the barbershop doing?"

"Good. It's doing good." She injected some enthusiasm into her voice. It really was doing well. Maybe it just wasn't everything she'd dreamed it would be. The days were long, and the nights in her upstairs apartment were quiet. And long. And maybe a little lonely.

"How's your grandma?" he asked.

"She's all right, I guess."

Eloise Biddle was Josephine's grandma on her father's side, and her only living relative. The woman was the main reason she'd chosen to open her barbershop in Copper Creek when her absentee father had left her with an inheritance.

Unfortunately, she had advanced Alzheimer's. She was at Piney Acres, not too far outside of town. Josephine finally had a grandma, even if the woman didn't remember her from one visit to the next.

Noah looked over his shoulder, and she realized she'd been quiet for too long.

"Her seventieth birthday was last week. You should've seen her with the cupcakes I brought over. She had icing all over her face by the time she was finished. I'd show you the pictures, but my phone's dead."

"She always did like her sweets."

Noah used to go with Josephine to visit Nana on Sunday afternoons. A couple months ago she'd found out from one of the nurses that he still visited her every so often. The discovery had rocked Josephine back on her feet.

She stuffed her cold fingers in her back pockets. "I might could help . . ."

She'd helped him with the sanding at her own shop. Did he remember standing behind her, his hand over hers, showing her how to run the sander over the seam?

He glanced over his shoulder, but his face gave nothing away. "No need for you to get all dusty with only one set of clothes."

"I don't mind. It'll give me something to do."

After a long moment, he gestured toward a package of sanding paper. "You can grab a T-shirt out of my room to throw on if you want."

Josephine found a plain white T-shirt draped over the bureau and slipped it over her clothes. It hung to midthigh, but it would protect her sweater and provide extra warmth. She dragged in a long whiff of his musky fragrance and imagined she still felt the warmth of his skin.

*Get a grip, Josephine.*

Back in the attic she set to work on the adjacent wall. "What are you going to do with this room when it's finished?"

"It'll be an office for now."

"For now?" She had visions of Mary Beth peeking into the room first thing in the morning. A crib set up on the opposite wall, a baby cooing happily from inside. The thought settled like a boulder in her stomach.

"Two bedrooms are better for resale," he said.

"You going somewhere?"

"Just planning for the future. Plus, winters are a little slow. Need something to pass the time."

"You always wanted a little house in the woods."

She bit her lip as soon as the words were out. It was too close to touching on the past—all those long conversations they'd had late into the night as they'd lain in bed, dreaming of their future.

His silence confirmed she'd crossed the line, as did the twitch of his jaw. Last thing she wanted was to ruin the tenuous truce between them. Yesterday's silence had been awfully hard.

"Sorry," she mumbled.

He blew the drywall dust and kept working. "Get everything settled for tomorrow?"

His tone was a little strained, but she was grateful for the subject change. "I did. I surely hope I don't have to miss the whole thing though. I was looking forward to it."

"Those girls won't forget it."

She hoped it was a special night for each of them. She turned the sandpaper in her hand and continued sanding.

"It's a nice thing you're doing."

Her face flushed with the compliment, even though his voice was laced with reluctance. If she were honest, nothing had felt so good in a long time.

"Thanks. I just hope I get to be there to see them all gussied up. Especially Ava—the girl who called yesterday. I hope Callie's son treats her good. She deserves a special night out."

"What's his name?"

"Alex Redding. You know him?"

"Vaguely. My brother hired him to work on a crew last summer. Far as I know Seth never had any complaints."

"Good to know. He seems like a nice kid. I'm just nervous for Ava. Some guy dumped her at the last minute."

The teen years could be so hard. Girls were cruel, and guys could be jerks. She knew that for certain.

"She'll show up at the dance on the arm of a good-looking kid and make that other guy eat his heart out."

"I hope so." But Josephine knew things didn't always turn out so rosy. Sometimes a wonderful evening could take a terrible turn for the worse.

# Chapter 14

*Cartersville, Georgia*

*Thirteen years ago*

Hey, Josephine." Brett Connors leaned against the locker beside hers. His broad frame hulked over her, and his masculine scent tickled her nose.

"Hi, Brett." Her face heated, and she hoped her cheeks weren't turning bright red. Brett was a junior and on the football team. His crowd didn't pay her much mind except for a catcall or whistle here and there. She was only a freshman, after all.

She pulled her English textbook out of her locker and tried to think what else she needed before lunch. It was hard to focus with his green eyes so intent on her.

"I like your sweater," he said. "It matches your eyes."

She glanced down at the baby-blue top she'd gotten at the Goodwill over the weekend. "Thanks."

"So . . ." Brett tilted his head. "The prom's coming up."

"I heard." Her heart was suddenly beating in her chest like a kick drum.

"You planning to go with anyone?"

"Um, no." She gave up on her books and shut her locker, looking up at him. She was sure he could see her pulse fluttering in her neck.

"Wanna go with me?" The corner of his lips turned up in that half smile that had every girl in Bartow County swooning. He had perfect lips. The upper one bowed like the top of a heart, the bottom pleasantly full.

She was staring—at his *lips*! She pulled her eyes away, adjusting her books in her arms.

"Um . . . aren't you going with Shelby?"

The two of them had been going out all year. Shelby, her best friend until last year, when Shelby turned on her over some boy Josephine didn't even like. Ever since then, Shelby and her minions had been her worst nightmare.

"We broke up."

"Sorry to hear that."

"I'm not. You shouldn't be either. She's sure no friend of yours, you know."

Wasn't that the truth. But going out with Brett would only pull off old scabs. And as much as she wanted to go with him, she didn't want any trouble from Shelby.

"So, how about it? We'll have a good time. I'll take you someplace nice to eat beforehand."

"I don't know. I'd like to, but Shelby . . ."

"Hey, listen, she's already moved on. That's why we broke up."

Josephine suddenly wanted this so badly. She'd never gone

out on an actual date. And *Brett Connors*. Every girl at Cartersville High was smitten with him.

She didn't have a fancy dress to wear, but she remembered a pink dress she'd seen in the window at the Goodwill. It had been so soft and beautiful—and only eighteen dollars. She had that much in her babysitting jar.

He raised his brows and gave her a playful look, nudging her shoulder. "So . . . how 'bout it, Josephine Dupree? Be my date?"

Her stomach fluttered wildly. How could a girl say no to that face? "Okay . . . sure."

He walked her to class, carrying her books. She made him late to his own class, but he didn't seem to mind. That week he showed up at her locker at least once a day. He got her phone number and called her twice, firming up plans for Saturday and talking about this and that.

Things had shifted at school as the rumor mill started up. Some of the popular junior crowd acknowledged her in the hallways. Guys who'd hardly paid her any mind at all now gave her long, appreciative looks.

And Shelby gave her the stink eye across the lunchroom. Josephine had thought about approaching her old friend and trying to work things out, but clearly that was off the table now. Josephine didn't know what the big problem was. She'd seen Shelby all week hanging on Everett Smith's arm in the halls and catching rides in his new Mustang after school. What did she care who Brett took to prom?

By Saturday night, Josephine decided she was going to put Shelby and her new friends out of her mind. She was going to enjoy her evening.

She was glad when Eddie left as she was getting ready. Bad

enough Brett was picking her up and would see their crummy trailer. He lived in a nice subdivision on the other side of town. His dad owned a successful car dealership, and his mom was on the town council.

Josephine wasn't going to think like that tonight. Brett Connors had asked her to the prom, and she looked pretty fetching, if she did say so herself. She stared in the speckled mirror on the back of her door. The satiny pink dress made her feel like a princess, and her hair fell in a waterfall of golden waves. Maybe she wasn't good for much, but she knew how to do hair right.

An engine sounded outside the thin walls. Josephine grabbed her bag of clothes for the after-prom and a light sweater, then dashed out the door. No way was she letting him see the inside of this place. The outside was bad enough.

Brett was coming around the front of a shiny Hummer as she exited. He wore a black tux, and when he smiled he looked like he should be on a magazine cover.

His eyes gave a flicker of male appreciation as they raked over her. "Wow. You look awful nice, Josephine."

Her cheeks went warm. "Thank you. So do you."

"You like the car? My dad let me borrow it for the night."

"It's amazing."

He opened her car door, and they were off. She was so nervous, but he put her at ease with a steady stream of conversation. He took her to Antonio's, a nice Italian restaurant in the next town over, where she had a plate of the best pasta she'd ever tasted.

By the time they reached the school, she was flushed with pleasure. They hung around his friends mostly, staying far away from Shelby and Everett and their group. Brett kept a proprietary arm looped around her or a hand on the small of her back. When he danced with her he held her close, looking into her eyes, smiling until his one dimple came out to play. It was without a doubt the best night of her life.

The after-party was in a field at Grant Bradley's place. She'd heard about the bonfire parties and was a little nervous about all the drinking, but Brett stayed close by. She slowly sipped on one can of beer while Brett finished one. Then two. Then three.

It was getting late, and she was growing tired, but she chided herself.

*Relax, Josephine. Just enjoy the night.*

The fire crackled and hissed, sending sparks up into the night sky. The smell of woodsmoke and boisterous chatter filled the air. Josephine shivered.

"You cold?"

"A little."

Brett shrugged out of his jacket and slipped it over her shoulders. "Wanna go for a walk? The creek's right down that path. There's a tire swing and a dock where we swim in the summer. I'll have to bring you here when it warms up."

Josephine returned his smile. "That'd be nice." She was referring to the swimming part, but he took it as an answer to his question about the walk.

She shrugged. Now that she had his jacket, she'd be toasty enough without the bonfire.

He left his beer behind, and Josephine's pulse sped as he grabbed her hand. But as they left the firelight, shadows of the night closed around them, and Josephine's heart stuttered. The suffocating feeling rose up inside, and she worked hard to push it down.

This was Brett, not Shark. He wouldn't hurt her.

Her hand tightened around his. The path through the woods was narrow, so they walked slowly. She was grateful for the full moon that lit the way. Brett held back branches and caught her when she stumbled over a root.

"I got you. We're almost there."

The noise of the party faded about the same time that the trickling of the creek reached her ears. The woods opened to a grassy bank. She was grateful to leave the shadowed woods behind.

He settled her into the tire swing, and she squealed as the tire carried her out over the creek. He laughed and pushed her higher. The wind tugged her hair off her face, and she leaned back, kicking her legs out.

After a while, dizzy with motion, she dragged her feet. "That was so fun. I haven't been on a swing in years," she said as he helped her out of the tire.

She followed Brett down the bank and onto the pier that jutted out into the water, and sank down beside him on the wooden planks.

Moonlight shone off the water, and overhead stars spread across the black sky like a million fireflies. She saw Ursa Minor and Cassiopeia. And there was Andromeda. The familiar sight calmed her.

"It's beautiful," she whispered.

"You're beautiful."

She glanced at him.

The way he was looking at her made her heart pound against her ribs. She'd only been kissed once before, by an older boy at a carnival. His groping hands and ragged breath had reminded her of those awful nights, and she had twisted from his arms and run all the way home. Locked herself in her room.

Brett's hand squeezed her shoulder lightly, and she realized she'd been quiet too long. "Thank you."

He gave her a soft smile. "It's true. You were the most beautiful girl at the whole prom. Every guy there was jealous of me."

She gave a little laugh. "That's not true."

"Sure it is." And there was that sideways smile again.

Her breath stuttered.

"I'm glad you came with me, Josephine."

"Me too."

He hooked a finger under her chin and gently tipped her chin up. His lips were soft and warm. They moved slowly against hers. She willed herself to feel something. He was kissing her exactly right.

His hand slid to cup her jaw as the other came around her waist, pulling her closer. A thread of anxiety wormed through her, but she pushed it back. She wasn't going to give in to fear.

*It's just a kiss, Josephine. For pity's sake.*

And a very gentle one at that. As soon as the thought formed, he deepened the kiss. She told herself to relax. They were only making out. Every girl made out. She was probably the last one in her class to kiss like this.

And with Brett Connors.

Her stomach fluttered, and she told herself it was butterflies, not nerves. Same with the heart palpitations and the perspiration dampening the back of her neck.

He pulled her closer still, groaning. His biceps under her palms were rock hard, and she suddenly remembered everything muscles like that could do.

She clutched at him. But before she could push him away he lowered her back onto the dock. The weight of him pressed into her. Adrenaline flooded through her until she feared her heart would explode.

She pushed at his chest. "Wait. Wait." Her breaths came in gasps.

He was a dark shadow over her. "What's the matter?"

"I-I—" Her throat swelled up, choking out her words.

"Shhh. It's okay. We're just kissing." The white of his teeth gleamed in the moonlight.

His quiet voice calmed her. This wasn't Shark, forcing himself on her. Nothing bad was going to happen. It was just Brett. He was a nice guy.

"I've been sweet on you awhile, Josephine Dupree. You know that?"

"Is that right?" She tried to tame her unsteady voice. Wondered briefly about Shelby and how she fit into all this.

"I had fun tonight," he said.

"Me too." He was a good dancer, and they'd fit well together. He'd flirted and joked with her, and he'd had eyes for no one else. Not even Shelby.

He set his lips on hers again, the motion slow and soft, undemanding.

Josephine returned the kiss. The water rippled over rocks, and crickets chirped. She drank in the familiar night sounds, letting them soothe her as she eased back into his kiss. Tried to like it as much as she should.

When she felt his warm hand on her bare stomach, she startled.

"Shh," he said. "It's just your stomach. Your skin's so soft."

He made lazy circles on her stomach, and she tried to lose

herself in his kiss again. She clasped the front of his T-shirt and breathed in his masculine smell.

*It's just a kiss. It's just a kiss.*

But then his hand closed over her breast.

"Stop." She pushed at him, turning her face away, her heart beating up into her throat. She gulped in a lungful of oxygen, suddenly feeling just plain stupid. Especially when she turned back and saw the stunned look on his face.

"Your friends—" she croaked, then cleared her throat. "They—they'll wonder where we are."

He'd pushed up on his arms, but he still had her pinned to the wooden planks. It was all she could do to keep from pushing him off her. But she didn't want to ruin this. She really did like him. He'd been so fun tonight, and nothing but a gentleman.

*You're so stupid, Josephine! You're ruining everything!*

"They're all drunk. They're not keeping tabs on us." There was a new tension to his voice.

"I'm sorry." Her voice quavered, and she felt every bit the dimwit Eddie said she was. "Can we just, you know, take it slow?"

"If that's what you wanted, maybe you shouldn't have been dancing with me like that." He rolled off her abruptly.

The coolness of the air left her feeling bereft somehow. A blanket of shame crawled over her. She hadn't been dancing any different from the other girls. Had she?

But maybe the other girls weren't pushing their dates off them right now. "I didn't mean—I'm just not—"

He sat up, then pushed to his feet. "Come on then. I'll take you home."

The new strain in his voice propelled her to her feet. He

didn't hold her hand as she trailed after him through the dark woods. She had to walk fast to keep up, and she had a sinking feeling this date was officially over.

"I can't believe you didn't tell me!" Ashlyn said into her ear Monday morning as she caught up to Josephine in the hall.

She'd been dreading school since Saturday night. Brett hadn't called her since prom. Not that she'd expected him to after the way their date had ended. He hadn't even walked her to her door, much less given her a good-night kiss.

"Told you what?" Josephine asked. A junior jock walked by, leering at her. She clutched her algebra book to her chest, looking away.

"You and Brett, silly girl. Why on earth didn't you tell me you did it?"

Josephine stopped in her tracks. "What are you talking about?"

A girl smacked into her from behind. "Watch where you're going."

Josephine recognized her as a cheerleader. "Sorry," she mumbled, but got only a glare in return.

Ashlyn grabbed Josephine's arm and pulled her over to an empty bank of lockers. "It's all over school. Hello, your best friend is the last to know! What in the world?"

"I—no, I didn't—"

"How was it? Tell me everything! You owe me after holding out like that."

"Who'd you hear that from?"

"Who *didn't* I hear it from? What's wrong? Why are you so pale all of a sudden?"

Josephine's gaze darted around the hall. Things were making sense now. Boys had been noticing her today. She'd thought it was because she'd gone to prom with such a popular guy, but now she realized why the looks she'd enjoyed last week were making her uncomfortable today.

She pulled her eyes away from the crowd and fastened them on Ashlyn. "I didn't have sex with Brett," she whispered. "We only kissed."

Ashlyn gave her a suspicious look. "That's not what everyone's saying."

"Well, that's all that happened!"

"All right, all right. Simmer down. I believe you."

She couldn't believe this. Had Brett lied? He must've. And now everyone thought . . .

Shelby Green, of all people, passed at just that second. Her eyes hardened into tiny brown pebbles, her mouth tilting in a sneer as she gave Josephine a look of death. She held Josephine's gaze as she turned into a classroom.

She had to do something. Maybe Brett didn't know what folks were saying. Maybe he could fix this.

She left her next class early and waited for him outside biology so she could catch him alone. When he saw her, his lips thinned into a straight line. He walked right on by.

"Brett. Wait." Josephine jogged to catch up. "Do you know what everyone's saying?"

"I've heard."

"You have to do something!"

He angled a look at her. "It's not like I can keep people from talking."

She grabbed his arm, stopping him. "You can tell them the truth."

His eyes rolled toward the ceiling before returning to hers. "If you want to play with the big boys, Josephine, you gotta roll with the punches."

She gave him a hard look. "You know we didn't do anything, Brett Connors."

He shook her hand off his arm. "You should be thanking me, little girl. You'll be more popular than ever now. And nobody knows what a little tease you were."

Her mouth fell open as he walked away. A stain of shame filled her face. Her eyes stung, and she ducked her head and slipped into the nearest bathroom. She locked herself in an empty stall and stayed there through lunch.

If Josephine thought her day couldn't get any worse, she was wrong. When she finally escaped the bathroom and returned to her locker, something red caught her eye. Turned out *Jo* had an unfortunate rhyme, and someone had written the title all over her locker for the whole world to see.

# Chapter 15

Noah used the last of his laptop power to check in with Mary Beth. She was sick, but her father was there helping her out.

Next he checked the weather. The snow was supposed to stop sometime in the morning. He figured it would take another day or two to get the mountain roads clear. Maybe more. But it looked as if the wind would let up sometime tomorrow afternoon, and he'd be able to take Josephine back to town on the snowmobile. She should be able to make some of her event at least.

He sank deeper into the recliner, releasing a heavy sigh.

"Everything all right?" Josephine looked up from the Tony Dungy book. She was huddled under the blankets Noah had brought from the bedroom.

"Just getting a little stir-crazy, I guess." The laptop screen went black. Well, that was officially gone. He had just a bit of power left on his phone.

The fire was dying down, so he added a few more logs.

"What's the weather saying?" Only the upper half of her face peeked out from the blanket. Her nose and cheeks were rosy. They'd eaten an early supper and settled in for a long evening.

"Snow's supposed to continue through morning, and the wind should die down in the afternoon. I'll be able to take you home then." He set down the poker. "I need to check on the horses."

At her feet, Shadow lifted his head, perking his ears at the magic words.

"I can lend a hand . . ."

"No, you stay warm. I won't be long."

The wind cut right through him as he strode from his truck to the barn. Inside, the horses were quiet, except for Kismet. He was showing signs of agitation again.

"Sorry, buddy. Wish I could put you out to pasture." Noah spent some time talking to the horse, trying to coax him with a flax treat.

Once Kismet had settled, Noah cleaned out the stalls and brushed down a few of the horses. By the time he left the barn his nose was cold, his fingers stiff. He fought the wind and drifts on his way to the truck and headed back to the house.

He called his brother in the cab. "Hey, Seth."

"Hey. How's it going up there on Mount Splitsville?"

"Funny. Our electricity went out last night. I just wanted you to know 'cause my cell battery's going, and I didn't want you to worry."

"*Our*, huh? Sounds like she's already clawing her way back

under your skin. Like a tick. It's not your physical well-being I'm worried about, bro."

"It's not like that. She's in her corner, I'm in mine."

"We'll see how long that lasts. This might be a good time to finish up that attic."

"Yeah." In reality, they'd given up sanding. Cleaning up was too hard with no running water. He pulled up in front of his house and shut off his engine.

"Just keep your walls up, man. And put some barbed wire at the top for good measure. That girl can cast a spell with the best of them."

Noah opened his mouth to defend her, then decided it would be a waste of breath. "Listen, can you call Mom and Dad and let them know what's going on? I don't want them worrying if they can't reach me."

"Sure thing. And don't forget what I said."

Noah turned off his phone, staring at the cottage. It looked like a cozy little refuge from the storm, with its wisp of smoke curling from the chimney.

His brother was right about Josephine. But they'd called a truce. It might've reduced the tension, but it also required him to lower his trusty wall. He wondered how long his heart would survive without it.

Already he struggled to keep his eyes from seeking her out, from just taking in her beauty. His gut clenched when her laughter rang out, her siren's song. He'd always loved the way her eyes arched in half-moons when she smiled. When she'd done it earlier it had been like a sucker punch.

How were they going to pass the time? Lots and lots of time. He looked up at the heavens. *Of all the people in the world to get stuck here, God. My kryptonite. Give me strength.*

On the way up the walk he reminded himself of all the things he didn't like about Josephine. The cynicism that twisted her lips sometimes. The way she tossed her hair and flirted with men. Her manipulative side. The way she wore her sex appeal like a second skin.

Okay, that one had its benefits too.

On the porch he stomped off the snow, thinking of the night ahead. The laptop was dead, the TV useless, and renovations were out of the question. He'd have to find something else to occupy his time. Something without Josephine. He'd pull another book from his shelf. Who cared if he'd already read them all?

He entered the house on a swirl of wind and snow to find Josephine sitting on the rug. She'd pulled the coffee table in front of the fire and set up a Monopoly game. She was snatching at the colorful dollars that had gone flying when he'd opened the door.

When they were together they'd spent many quiet nights playing games. She was a whiz at Monopoly, and he always bested her at Uno.

"I found it in the closet." She looked up at him from a bundle of blankets, her eyes wide.

The childlike hope on her face made a fist tighten in his gut. Because, for all her flaws, she still had that vulnerable part of her that sucked him in like a vortex.

*Idiot.*

He shut the door and shrugged from his coat.

"At least it'll pass the time . . . ," she pleaded.

He pulled off his boots, knowing he was going to give in. He'd lost the battle the second he'd looked at her.

*That girl can cast a spell with the best of them.*

"Noah?" Her smile had fallen from her face. "It's just . . . you know, we've got a long night ahead and all."

He nudged his boots against the wall and attempted a smile. "It just had to be Monopoly, didn't it?"

"I believe that'll be six hundred dollars." Josephine held her hand over the board, palm up, fingers waggling. She'd forgotten how much fun this was. Noah had landed on Boardwalk, and she had two houses on the property.

He gave her a look. "You know I don't have that. I'll give you two hundred and St. Charles Place."

Josephine tilted a saucy smile. "I don't believe bartering is in the rules, Mr. Mitchell. Besides, St. Charles is only worth a hundred and forty."

He leveled a look at her. "It's only eight o'clock. You really want the game to be over?"

"Good point." She scanned his properties. "St. Charles and States Avenue, plus the two hundred."

He gave her a mock frown but handed over the money and properties.

"You're only prolonging the inevitable, you know." A roll of the die landed her on Pennsylvania Avenue.

Noah groaned as she fished through her stacks of money with a flourish and paid the bank for the property.

While she handled business, he turned on his phone to check for calls.

She batted her lashes at him. "Trying to escape reality?"

"As a matter of fact, yes, I am."

A little giggle rose in her throat, surprising her. She'd

forgotten how much fun she had with Noah. It was even more fun when she was winning. And though he was sulking, it was in a playful manner. He was having a good time too, though he'd never admit it.

She settled her Pennsylvania Avenue deed neatly in her long line of deeds, taking care to straighten the others.

He shoved the phone at her. "There's a voicemail for you."

She put it to her ear. The message was already underway—Callie, her tone frantic.

". . . at least two inches of water. I guess the pipes froze or something, and I turned off the water, but—"

Callie went silent.

The phone beeped twice as Josephine looked at the screen. It was black. "What happened?"

"The battery must be dead," Noah said.

"No . . ." Josephine tried to turn it back on, to no avail.

"What's going on?" he said.

"It was Callie. She said something about a pipe freezing. Something about two inches of water."

The look on Noah's face was not encouraging.

"I have to talk to her. Where's your laptop? I can message her on Facebook."

He winced. "Ah . . . it's dead too."

Josephine sank back down. The girls from the Hope House were supposed to start arriving at nine o'clock in the morning. If the shop was flooded, the event would have to be canceled.

"Maybe it's not as bad as it sounded."

"She was beside herself. Did you notice what time the message came in?"

"No. I wish I could call Seth. He has a plumber on staff. But surely Callie would've called someone already."

"I don't know what she would've done. She always runs things by me first. If a pipe did burst, how long would it take to get it fixed? To get it cleaned up?"

He was shaking his head. "It depends how bad it is, what kind of plumbing you have."

Josephine pressed her finger into her temple. "I can't believe this. The girls will be so disappointed if tomorrow falls through."

"Hey, Callie's resourceful, right? I'm sure she'll do her best to get it under control."

"You're right." Josephine's mind spun with all the things she'd be doing if she were at the shop. But she wasn't. She was stuck here without so much as a phone. Completely cut off from the rest of the world. "But I feel so helpless."

Noah gave her a sympathetic smile. "Well . . . I can't fix the pipes or clean up the water, but I'll say a little prayer it all goes off without a hitch. Have a little hope."

"Thanks, Noah."

He was right. There wasn't a solitary thing she could do from here. Maybe God would answer Noah's prayer. Maybe she'd even give it a try herself. Not that it had ever done her any good before.

She shivered and pulled the blanket more tightly around her. The fireplace wasn't big enough to put out much heat, and there was no blower. It was going to be a cold night. A long, cold night, worrying over her shop and tomorrow's event.

Her gaze drifted over the Monopoly board, and she pushed back the worry, searching for the happiness she'd felt only moments before.

*Fretting will get you nowhere, Josephine.*

She pulled her lips into a smile and eyed Noah. "So . . . have I sufficiently humbled you with my Monopoly skills?"

He tucked in the corner of his lips. "If I say yes, does that mean we can officially quit?"

She hiked a brow. "Do you give?"

"Fine. I give." Without hesitation he lifted the board, dumping houses, hotels, and all into the battered box. "I'm sure we can find something better to do."

Immediately ideas surged to mind, complete with images. Noah's lips on hers, his arms around her. Naked limbs tangling in flesh-warmed sheets.

*You are still married, after all.*

*Stop that.*

She forced the images from her mind and grabbed the deck of Uno cards from behind her. She set them on the table with exaggerated flair and withdrew her hand.

He looked up at her, his eyes going from surprised to knowing. "You had those all along, woman?"

She gave an innocent shrug, batting her eyelashes for good measure.

"Oh, you've had it now, lady. You have had it now."

# Chapter 16

*N*oah put down his last set of cards, leaving him empty-handed. He stared across the table at Josephine's handful of cards and tried not to gloat. Okay, not really.

"You're a cruel, cruel man, Noah Mitchell." She pushed out her lower lip.

His eyes fixed on the plumpness for a long moment before dragging his gaze away and gathering the cards. They weren't keeping score, but he was kicking her butt.

"I'm officially humiliated." She surrendered the cards in her hand—at least twenty by the looks of it—and smothered a yawn. "And I think I'm ready to hit the hay."

"It's only ten thirty."

She pulled the blanket around her as she stood. "I know, but I'm tired of being cold. At least if I'm asleep I won't be thinking about the fact that I can't feel my toes."

"Here, let's do this."

She moved out of Noah's way while he dragged the sofa in front of the fireplace, a safe distance away.

It had long since grown dark outside, but the light of the fire kept the shadows at bay. He hoped it would be enough light for her. They needed to conserve the flashlight battery.

She glanced at the recliner back in the corner. "Now I'm blocking your heat."

"You know me. I'm a virtual furnace." He handed her a second blanket, keeping one for himself.

She settled on the couch. She'd put on two pairs of Noah's socks and had thrown a sweatshirt on over her own clothes. Even still, she shivered under the blankets. But then he'd known her to shiver in sixty-five-degree weather, Georgia peach that she was. It was cooler than that now and bound to get colder as the night wore on.

"I'll never take a furnace for granted again. Who knew a house could get so cold?"

"I'm afraid this one's poorly insulated. And the windows are old. I've been meaning to get around to both, but I decided to tackle the attic first. Unfortunately."

Noah put more logs on the fire and set the screen in front of the grate. He turned and spotted Shadow on the floor beside the couch.

He squatted and patted the empty space beside Josephine. "Up, Shadow."

The dog lifted his head, his ears perked.

"It's okay." Noah patted the sofa again. "Come on."

Josephine made room as Shadow leaped onto the sofa, chuckling as he stuck his nose in her face. The dog lay down, stretching along her length.

"Good boy," he said.

"I thought he wasn't allowed on the sofa."

"Special occasion." Shadow would probably test him for the

next month on account of the one allowance, but he couldn't stand to watch Josephine suffer.

Noah adjusted the blanket so it would cover both her and the dog, conserving body heat. He sent a mental apology to Shadow, who was probably going to roast.

"Stay." He ruffled the dog's fur and went to settle on the recliner. The leather was cold, and he still hadn't warmed up completely from his last trip to the barn.

He lay there a long time, the glow of the fire silhouetting the sofa. He shoved his hands into his sweatshirt pockets and pulled up the hood.

Despite his best efforts, his mind went over and over the time he'd spent with Josephine this evening. He could practically feel the ice crystals over his heart thawing. And he knew it was stupid. Dangerous. Seth was right. He'd be a fool to let her in again. Even an inch.

And yet there was something about her. He closed his eyes and had a long talk with God as he lay there. Just putting it all out there. A mass of confusion—and yes, hurt. There was no divine insight, no dreams of angels telling him what to do. Just darkness. The snap of a fire. The continued thawing of his heart.

He woke to a *ting*.

Josephine stood in front of the fireplace, poking at the wood with the metal tool. The fire had died down to glowing ashes, and the room was noticeably colder.

He sat up, pushing in the footrest. "I'll get it."

"Sorry if I woke you."

"It's okay." He grabbed two more logs, setting them on the others.

Josephine held her hands out toward the fire, the quilt draped over her shoulders.

Noah found Shadow lying on his side a few feet away, emitting soft snores.

"I g-guess he got hot," she said, her teeth chattering. "Lucky dog."

He frowned, grabbing one of her hands. "You're freezing."

"I'll be f-fine."

He knew it was stupid. But some primitive need to protect her welled up inside him, compelling him to take care of her.

If Shadow wouldn't keep her warm, that left only Noah. And while the fleshly part of him reached for the idea with greedy hands, the common-sense section of his brain called him all kinds of fool.

He tried to conjure up the anger he'd been nursing just yesterday, but it was nowhere to be found.

"What time is it?" She stepped back, sitting on the sofa.

He held the battery-operated mantel clock in front of the fire. "Two thirty. You should get some sleep." Common sense was kicking in. The fire was stoked. She had her blankets. She wasn't going to freeze.

"I'm t-too cold to s-sleep."

He looked at her. A shivering huddle on the couch.

*Her teeth are chattering, for crying out loud. Suck it up, Mitchell.*

He went to grab his blanket off the recliner and returned to the couch, heaving a sigh. "Move over."

"Whatever for?"

When she didn't move he slid onto the sofa, easing in behind her.

"Noah . . . what are you doing?"

"Come on." He pulled her down, her back to his chest.

She resisted. "No, we shouldn't—"

He pulled her closer, and she gave up the struggle. As she settled against him, he ignored the ridiculous thumping of his heart, adjusting the blanket over them. He tucked it in tight, then draped his arm over her, his hand seeking a safe place to land—the edge of the sofa.

She was as stiff as the two-by-fours framing his attic.

"Relax."

"We—we shouldn't be doing this."

"We're not doing anything. We're just staying warm, that's all."

And man, did she feel good. Not just her warmth either, if he was being honest. His arm rested in the valley of her waist. Her breath stirred the hairs on the back of his hand.

"Go to sleep," he whispered.

The choked sound from her throat wasn't quite a laugh.

He was aware of every inch where their bodies connected. That alone ignited the furnace inside him. All the better to keep them warm. His lip curled wryly at the thought.

His nose was inches from her hair, and the tantalizing smell of her teased his nostrils, reminding him of sweeter days. Of quiet words and petal-soft skin and lingering kisses. From that first kiss, she'd completely ruined him for other women.

He smothered a groan. *Are you happy now?* his common sense asked the greedy, fleshly part of him.

Warm or no, it was going to be a long night. The sweet agony of holding her again nipped at him, making him wish they were back in time. Back when she'd stretched out next to him in their bed, languid and sated, that well-loved look in her eyes.

*Stop it, Mitchell.*

It wasn't two years ago. It was now. And what did he know about her life these days? He hadn't heard anything on the grapevine. But then, he didn't hear much way out here. One of the blessings of living in the mountains.

For all he knew Josephine had a boyfriend tucked away in town, wondering where she was right now. His heart rebelled at the thought, his arm tightening reflexively around her. The possessive feelings had little to do with the recent discovery that he was still her husband.

It was unsettling how quickly she could work her way back into his heart. Or maybe she'd never left at all. That little thought was even more disturbing.

How much time had passed since Noah had lain down behind her? It seemed like a month, but maybe that was just her. Maybe it was just the way her heart was pounding at warp speed.

*Settle down, Josephine.*

She'd told herself as much half a dozen times. But Noah was so close, one of his arms serving as a solid pillow, the other curled protectively around her. Was it any wonder she wasn't thinking straight? How was she supposed to nod off when she was buzzing with tension?

She'd finally managed to relax her body, sinking into the curve of his chest. What choice did she have? Her back had begun aching with the effort to maintain distance. She couldn't deny that his warmth felt like heaven.

She worked hard to steady her breaths, hoping her heart rate would take notice. She let the soothing sounds of the fire, the gentle rise and fall of Noah's chest, relax her.

She stared into the dancing flames, her mind going back to that night when Brett Connors had lured her from the bonfire. She reeled at the role the event had played in her life. Like the first domino, pushed over, the way it had shaped her teenage years.

Once her reputation had been ruined, other boys took interest. She ignored their attention until her sophomore year, when she finally accepted senior Jude Mackey's invitation to the movies. Her heart raced as she thought of that backseat moment at the end of the date. He'd parked on a dirt road and hadn't been as accepting of her no as Brett had been.

She hadn't fought that hard—he was tall and strong, a football player. Her efforts were futile anyway. She forced her mind to go someplace else, her body to go numb. And afterward she wondered if she'd even said no at all. What did it matter? All the boys already thought she was loose. All the girls called her names.

The next Monday she put on a new mask along with her mascara and lipstick. Eddie had been telling her for months that she was only good for one thing. She might as well embrace it. So she flirted. And she dated. And yeah, she did lots of other things. The boys leered, and the girls whispered behind cupped hands. But she was in control now. She would choose *who*. She would choose *when*.

And if somewhere deep down inside a flicker of shame flared now and again, she doused it with smug looks and saucy smiles and the jaunty tilt of her chin. If she was only good for one thing, she was going to be darn good at it.

Josephine closed her eyes, shutting out the fire that licked at the logs. Who was that woman? She'd disappeared when Noah Mitchell came into her life. When he'd slipped out of her grasp. Oh, she kept up with the saucy smiles and the clever quips and the coy looks. But that's where it ended. She could only give her body for so long before her heart would follow.

And she was never letting that happen again.

A cloud of loneliness so big and sudden welled up within her and threatened to overwhelm her. The center of her chest tightened. She sucked in a deep, slow breath and pressed her palm against the ache.

She suddenly needed to know she wasn't alone. If only for tonight.

"Noah?" she whispered.

His breathing was slow and steady. He'd probably fallen asleep ages ago. She should leave him be. He wasn't lonely or needy. He had Mary Beth. He was only taking care of Josephine because he was too good a person to let her suffer.

She shifted back a bit, looking over her shoulder. The stutter of his breath gave him away.

"Noah," she whispered. "Are you awake?"

He stirred, adjusting his arm. "What's wrong?"

"I'm—" *Lonely. Sorry. The biggest idiot in the whole wide world.* "I can't sleep."

"It's easier when you're not talking," he grumbled.

His answer made her smile. "I can't stop thinking." She paused. But when he didn't reply, she went on, not wanting him to fall asleep again. "Does Mary Beth know I'm here?"

He sighed, gravity pulling her body into his as his lungs emptied.

"Yes."

"Does she—does she know the divorce wasn't finalized?"

He groaned. "It's the middle of the night, Josie."

A warmth settled in her middle at the sleepy use of the

nickname. Her lips curled upward. Maybe he was half-asleep, but he hadn't called her that in so long. She didn't know how much she'd missed it till now.

"Are you tired?" she asked.

He shifted, rolling to his back as much as he could in the limited space. "Not anymore."

His breath stirred the hair at the top of her head. The flames had died down, and it was pretty dark. But the darkness had never bothered her as long as Noah was there.

"Want me to stoke the fire?" He sounded more awake now.

"Not yet." She was as toasty as she'd been all day. And now that he was awake she felt infinitely better. She relaxed into his body, the cloud of tension seeping from her muscles.

"What about you?" he asked.

"What about me?"

"Is there some guy who's gonna go ten kinds of crazy because we're still married?"

She breathed a laugh. She hadn't even looked twice at a man since Noah. She was many things, but slow learner was not one of them.

Not that Noah would ever believe that. Men believed whatever they wanted.

"No, there's no one."

"That's good. He probably wouldn't appreciate us being wrapped up tight as a burrito."

"What about Mary Beth?"

A long pause followed. He shifted back to his side, his arm coming around her once again. He felt her hand. "You warm enough?"

"Yeah."

When he let go of her hand, she tucked her fist under her

chin. He was solid and warm. She'd always felt so safe with him. There was something about Noah. She'd known it from the beginning. He had the kind of power to suck a girl right under if she wasn't careful.

"So what ever happened," he asked, a new strain to his voice, "with you and that guy?"

His voice was so calm it took her a moment to realize what he was asking. And when she did, her stomach clenched. A clamp tightened around her throat.

"Never mind," he said. "I don't want to know."

Her pulse sped at the very memory of that night. The overwhelming feelings of shame and fear welled up in her as strong and sudden as a tornado.

"Yes, I do," he said firmly. "I do want to know."

He'd asked her before, the very next day, his voice raised in anger. A mask of fury and hurt she'd never seen on his face before. Never wanted to see again. Her heart twisted at the very remembrance until she felt sick with it.

"Nothing happened," she whispered.

"What do you mean, nothing happened?"

"I-I never saw him again."

She could feel the tension in his arms, in his middle. His breath caught a second, then quickened.

They lay there still and tense for several heartbeats.

"I don't understand." His voice was cold now. As cold as the snow trapping them here.

She suddenly felt tired. So tired. There was nothing she could say to make him understand. It had taken a year of therapy to make any sense of it herself. If she tried to explain it would only come off as excuses. And there was no excusing what she'd done.

"It is what it is, Noah. It was wrong, and I'm sorry."

She closed her eyes against the burning sensation behind her eyes. She wished she'd never awakened him. Because she felt even lonelier now than she ever had before.

# Chapter 17

*Copper Creek, Georgia*

*One and a half years ago*

O uch!" Josephine dropped the hammer and jerked her finger back.

"You okay?" Noah took hold of her hand, examining her throbbing index finger.

"The hammer slipped." Her nerve endings tingled where he held her wrist.

Noah had been in the shop every evening this week, framing the partition between the front door and the lobby. Being as it was a Sunday, and she was closed, she'd insisted on helping him hang drywall.

He gave her a mock scowl that puckered his lower lip. "I thought you said you knew your way around a toolbox."

She gave him a wide-eyed look. "I may have exaggerated my skills just a smidge."

Noah chuckled, giving her wrist a gentle squeeze. "Maybe

you should just observe. You're going to need all those fingers come tomorrow."

"I want to help." She heard the sulkiness in her tone, but it didn't seem to bother him.

Instead, his eyes softened. She was a fool for wanting to spend time with him. Noah had trouble written all over him. Not that he wasn't an upstanding person, but he was a *man*, after all. And when he looked into her eyes like he was now, it was as if he cast a magic spell over her.

He'd already asked her out twice. She'd put him off both times, flirting her way out of it so she didn't hurt his feelings or make things awkward. She had a feeling he wasn't giving up so easily.

She stepped back and picked up her hammer. "Show me." She gave him a look that had never failed her before. She really was a fool.

The look worked.

He pulled a nail from his tool belt and placed it between her index finger and thumb on the drywall, positioning her fingers right under his on the nail. "Hold it right like this."

He was close behind her. So close she could feel his warmth, smell his musky, masculine scent. Feel the rumble of his chest as he spoke.

He moved her other hand on the hammer. "Choke up a bit. It'll give you more control. All right now, go ahead."

She poised the hammer. "Don't you want to move your fingers?"

"I trust you."

She tossed a wry smile over her shoulder. "Well, there's your first mistake, Noah Mitchell."

"You remembered my last name." His voice was low and

smoky. His breath stirred the hairs at her temple. "See, you do like me."

"Your company is Mitchell Home Improvement. It's all over your truck, not to mention the paperwork."

His lips quirked. "You're protesting awful hard there, Josie. Be careful, you're going to give yourself away."

She opened her mouth to deny it, but he'd already moved on.

"Okay, give it little taps like this, until the nail is set." He demonstrated, his hand around hers. He pulled her left hand away as the nail eased into the drywall. "Then you can give it a few good whacks, take it the rest of the way home."

She'd lost track of what he was saying. He smelled so darn good. His work-roughened hands felt like heaven against hers.

"Go out with me this Friday." The low grate of his voice in her ear plucked at her resolve.

"We shouldn't. We're working together."

"Temporarily. That won't change. We have a contract." He gave her a playful look straight out of her own handbook, but somehow more genuine. "Come on, now. I know you like me."

"I'm really busy right now. The shop is my focus, and I really shouldn't be . . ."

He let loose of the hammer and leaned against the drywall beside her, giving her a long look.

"What?" she asked.

"I know you've gone out with other guys since you've been here."

She popped an eyebrow.

"It's a small town. Don't make me name them."

It was true. She'd gone out with three different guys. But

they were only first dates, and those guys posed no threat to her emotional well-being. She hadn't let any of them come upstairs afterward—though two of them had tried.

She'd escaped her reputation in Cartersville and wasn't eager to repeat her mistakes here. Women weren't going to send their men here for a cut and shave if she had a reputation.

"I'm not giving up," he said.

She had a feeling he was telling the truth. And that Noah Mitchell was a man to fight long and hard for what he wanted.

"Why won't you go out with me?"

She gave him a sassy look. "Maybe I just don't want to ruin you for every other woman."

He laughed. "You just might, at that."

"Let me save you a little time, sweetheart. Let's say we went out somewhere, like . . ."

"A picnic by Piney Creek. Followed by a horseback ride through Pleasant Gap."

She blinked. Okay, she hadn't expected that. "All right. So we go out. We eat, we ride, we talk, whatever. I learn a little about you, you learn a little about me. You walk me to the door. We say good night. You ask me on a second date, and I say no." She shrugged.

He gave her a look. "Why would you say no? We had a great time."

She laughed. "Okay. Maybe we did. But . . ." She smiled sweetly to soften the blow and poked her finger into his chest to punctuate her words. "I'm not having sex with you, mister. That's the bottom line."

He gave her a searching look. "I don't recall asking you to have sex, Josie."

"Oh, please. You're a man. That's where this is headed. I'm

just trying to save you the trouble." She delivered the line with just the right amount of sass.

Instead of laughing it off or flushing at being caught, he tilted his head and locked onto her eyes.

Her smile faltered.

"You're pretty cynical, Josie." There was no insult in his tone. Just a statement of fact. "You remind me of my grand-mother."

She gave a lilting laugh. "You need to work on your lines, sugar."

"It wasn't a line. Cynic or not, my grandmother was the finest woman I've ever known."

The compliment filled her with warmth, but it came with a side of guilt. Sometimes she felt a little harsh when she was with Noah. But she couldn't help who she was.

"Thank you for the kind thought. But I prefer to think of myself as a realist."

"Realism leaves room for hope."

He'd hit the target in one shot, and she could swear those eyes were looking down deep into her soul.

She gave a careless shrug and a cheeky smile. "You're right. I'm hopeless. You should definitely give up on me."

"I have enough hope for the both of us." He nudged her shoulder with his. "Come on. One date. What's it going to hurt?"

She gave a hearty sigh. Some guys had to learn the hard way, she supposed.

Her heart thumped so hard at what she was about to do, she wondered if he could see it through her black top. "One date?"

"That's all I'm asking."

"And then you'll give it a rest."

He lifted one muscled shoulder. "If that's what you want."

She studied him closely, meeting his resolute stare with one of her own. "All right, Noah Mitchell. One date."

As it turned out, they didn't end up going on that picnic and horseback ride. The next weekend was the Peach Festival. It started with a parade down Main Street, followed by carnival games and food, and culminated in a dance on the town square.

Josephine worked until five, when Noah was supposed to pick her up. She told herself she should wear some old pair of jeans and a button-up that reached her neck, but in the end she couldn't bring herself to follow through.

And she was tickled with her decision when Noah's jaw slackened at the sight of her in her red wraparound dress.

His Adam's apple bobbed, drawing her attention to his clean-shaven throat. "You're stunning."

His tone, the look on his face, made warmth radiate through her body. She quirked a brow. "Your lines are improving, Mr. Mitchell."

She gave him a bold visual sweep. A black button-down made the most of his broad shoulders, and khakis had never looked so good on a man. "You're not so bad yourself, sugar."

The town square had been transformed into an intimate gathering place. A local band played country music on a stage. White lights twinkled over a makeshift dance floor.

The sweltering summer heat had given way to a mild evening, and the air was heavy with the scent of honeysuckle and freshly cut grass. People crowded the lawn. Neighbors, most of whom she hadn't met, mingled in groups, talking and laughing. Good churchgoing folk. What was she doing here? For a moment she wanted to run back to the safety of her shop.

*This isn't Cartersville. These people don't know a thing about you.*

As they entered the fray Noah took her hand, and she couldn't bring herself to be anything but grateful for the physical connection.

"I'll introduce you around," he said over the noise. "It'll be good for your business."

In the next hour she met so many people her mind was spinning, and her jaws ached from smiling. Noah's presence made it easy to relax. It was obvious he was well liked, his family well respected.

The people she met were friendly and seemed glad to have a new business in town. She began to think she could fit in here. She could make friends and build her business. Nobody was saying bad things about her or whispering behind their hands. Nobody was calling her names or keying her car.

Darkness had fallen by the time Noah tugged her away from a group, giving her a smile she felt clear down to her toes. "That's it," he said. "I'm done sharing you."

He drew her onto the crowded dance floor as the haunting melody of Brad Paisley's "She's Everything" began.

Josephine avoided his eyes as he pulled her into his arms, settling his hand at her waist. She wasn't tall enough to see over his shoulder, so she focused on her hand, resting there. Her red nails were a stark contrast to the black of his shirt.

*Focus on that, Josephine. Not on the way your heart's going wild or the way your mouth is as dry as a cotton ball.*

Then his thigh brushed hers, and she caught the faint masculine smell of him. They moved well together, like they'd been doing this all their lives.

"So, tell me," he said, his eyes laser-focused on her. "How'd you end up in the hair business?"

She shrugged. "I always had a gift for it, I suppose. My girl-friends were always wanting me to fix their hair, so when I graduated, I went to beauty school."

"Did you work at a barbershop in Cartersville?"

"A beauty salon. I'd built up a nice clientele when my dad passed and left me an inheritance. I decided to move here and open the shop. Get to know my nana."

"Why a barbershop and not a salon?"

She laughed. "Men are so much simpler."

He made a face. "I think I'm insulted."

"Don't be. Women are complicated and hard to please."

"Present company included?"

She laughed. "Oh, sugar, you have no idea."

"Tell me about your family."

"What is this, twenty questions?"

"I want to know everything about you. Were you close to your dad?"

"I never even met him. He ditched my mama about the time the pregnancy stick turned pink. He probably left me the money out of guilt. Did you know him? Paul Truvy?"

"I knew who he was, but that's about it. Are you close to your mom?"

A wave of sadness made it difficult to maintain her smile. "She passed when I was twelve. My stepdaddy raised me from there."

"I'm sorry about your mama but glad you had your step-dad."

Josephine brushed an imaginary speck of lint from his shoul-der. "Yeah. I'm real lucky."

By the end of the song they'd somehow drifted closer to-gether. She felt the warmth of his breath at her temple, felt the imprint of his hand on the small of her back, and a pool of longing settled inside her.

The band segued into another slow song, somehow stirring up both relief and dismay. Noah confused her as no man ever had. The pull she felt toward him tangled with her need to push him away. She couldn't make sense of it. Of him.

And right now, in the circle of his arms, she decided she really didn't care to. When he set his cheek against the top of her head, she sank into his chest. Her hand went around his shoulder, her head resting against him.

"You're a good dancer," he said in her ear.

"Right back at you, Romeo."

When the song ended the band kicked it up a couple notches with "I Like It, I Love It." Josephine fought back the disappointment as Noah pulled away. But then he grabbed her hands and began leading her around the dance floor, spinning her until she was dizzy, laughing, and out of breath.

The rest of the night flew by. By the time he escorted her back to his truck, she was flushed with pleasure. She couldn't remember enjoying an evening more. But even as Noah put the truck in gear and drove toward her apartment, she readied herself for the brush-off.

She'd already done the preliminary work. She'd left her apartment messy in case she was tempted to let him up. Her plain-Jane undergarments would put off even the most ardent admirer. But as the night had worn on, he'd somehow managed to slip under her defenses. It was back to reality now. Time to laugh off his advances and wiggle her way out of a second date.

It didn't take long to reach the shop. But by the time he pulled up to the curb, her heart was hammering in her chest, and the back of her neck was damp with perspiration.

*Stop it, silly girl. You've got this. He's just a man, like any other.*

Noah put the truck in park, but he made no move to get out—and he left it running.

*Hmm.* She smiled at him across the darkened cab. "Thank you, Noah. I had a really nice night."

His smile curled even as his eyes searched hers. "Me too."

Josephine reached for the door handle.

He took her other wrist. *Here goes.* She supposed he was going to make his move out here. She looked back at him expectantly.

"I'll get your door," was all he said.

He shut off the engine, and she watched as he walked around the front. He was a gentleman, she'd give him that. He'd treated her with nothing but respect tonight. She liked the way he'd guided her through the throngs of people with his hand at the small of her back. He'd fetched her dinner and drinks and had never left her fending for herself.

Noah opened her door, and she stepped out into the steamy night. The shop entrance was only steps away, but he'd no doubt insist on walking her inside to her apartment door the way the others had. Once there he'd lean in for a kiss. After a few moments he'd deepen it, and his hands would begin to wander, and then he'd ask to come in.

She could handle this. Her stomach fluttered, and her hands shook as she unlocked the shop door. She hoped he didn't notice the way she fumbled with the key.

Once it was unlocked she turned with a polite smile. Her fingers tightened around the keys until they cut into her palm. "Thank you, Noah. I really did have a nice time."

"It was fun." He reached toward her.

She prepared herself for his touch. Her skin tingled with anticipation, and her pulse raced.

But his hand went right past her shoulder, settling on the door handle. He opened the door, and a wave of cool air washed over her, pebbling her skin.

"Good night, Josephine. I'll see you tomorrow night."

She blinked in surprise, then quickly schooled her features. "Good night, Noah."

He gave her one last smile through the glass door as she turned the lock. She wiggled her fingers at him and shut off the entry light.

Her legs shook as she walked through the shop and up the apartment stairs. A strange fluttery sensation filled her stomach. It was only confusion.

Noah hadn't asked to come up. He hadn't asked for a second date. He hadn't even tried to kiss her. And a realization hit as the stale apartment air washed over her: for the first time she could remember, a man had left her wanting more.

# Chapter 18

*Sweetbriar Ranch*

*Present day*

Josephine opened her eyes. The dark of night had given way to the murky light of dawn. She didn't have to look over her shoulder to see if Noah was still lying behind her. Her chilled flesh gave away his absence. The fire had been stoked, fresh logs added. He must've gone to feed the horses.

She mentally reviewed their middle-of-the-night conversation and wanted to sink back into the oblivion of sleep.

Maybe it was for the best. Maybe they'd both needed a harsh reminder of what she'd done. This cozy little cottage, incubated from the rest of the world, wasn't reality. Nothing had changed. Somehow over the past couple days—laughing and sharing, and lying in his arms—hope had gained a foothold. She'd forgotten the truth. That she'd done the unforgiveable. That she was still unworthy of him.

*No man's ever gonna love a girl like you. You're only good for one thing.*

She'd only gotten what she deserved. No penance could wash away her sins. Not really. The familiar wave of shame was still there, staining her with guilt. She'd learned to live with it—or thought she had.

She sat up on the sofa.

Yes, it was for the best. She'd gotten too comfortable with Noah. Had started sliding back into the ease of their rapport. Allowed herself to forget. He'd always had a way of making her do that.

Her eyes drifted across the room, settling on the divorce papers. She'd leave here, take them to the attorney's office, and some judge would finalize their divorce. Then all this would be over.

No more Monopoly or Uno. No more teasing or flirting. And absolutely no more cuddling on the couch.

She was a big fat dope.

Josephine got up and warmed in front of the fire for a few minutes before she got busy on breakfast. She opened the freezer and pulled out a baggie of sliced peaches someone had gifted him. Probably Mary Beth, now that she thought on it. When the woman wasn't giving equestrian lessons for Noah she was running her parents' orchard.

No matter. The peaches would serve as a subtle reminder for both of them. She used the kettle of hot water Noah had hung over the fire to thaw them.

While she waited she put on her coat and boots and took out the garbage, making quick work of it. Drifts had piled up alongside the house. The wind was still raging, though the snow had finally stopped.

Back inside she manually poured hot water through a filter she'd filled with ground coffee. Desperate times and all that. She was warming herself by the fire when Noah returned, Shadow on his heels.

"Morning," he said after shutting the door. His cheeks were flushed with cold, and his breath fogged on an exhale.

"Good morning." She turned back to the fire. Heat filled her cheeks as she thought about the night before.

Noah was quiet as he removed his outer gear.

Shadow nudged her hand with his cold nose, and she scratched him behind his ears. His fur was damp with melted snow. He looked up at her with happy chocolate eyes, his tongue lolling sideways from his mouth.

Noah disappeared into the cold kitchen, probably making himself a cup of coffee. The sound of dog food hitting Shadow's dish had the dog darting through the split in the plastic.

When Noah returned he carried two bowls of steaming peaches.

"Thanks," she said, taking hers.

The recliner creaked as Noah settled into it.

She ate her breakfast standing in front of the fire, her fork clanking in her bowl. In the kitchen Shadow chomped noisily on his food.

"That was good," Noah said after what seemed like an eternity later. "Warmed me right up."

"From Mary Beth's orchard, I presume?"

"Yeah."

"You must be mighty worried about her."

He took her empty bowl, giving her a searching look. "Mary Beth can fend for herself."

Right. Because Mary Beth was a paragon. Mary Beth

wouldn't need a man to split her logs or shovel her snow or keep her warm. Mary Beth wouldn't place a knife in the center of his heart and give it a good, hard twist.

She dragged her eyes away from Noah.

She exhaled in relief when he disappeared into the kitchen, but he returned a moment later, toting a bucket of snow. She moved aside as he hung it on the hook over the fire.

"Once this heats up we can wash up at least. Better than nothing."

"Sure."

Noah joined her by the fire, hands extended. Moments ticked by. The silence was like a tight line, stretched taut between them. Maybe the tension was a might uncomfortable, but it was better than the alternative. Safer.

"What's wrong, Josie?"

She steeled herself against the use of her nickname. "Nothing's wrong." She could feel his gaze on her for a long, painful moment.

"You seem . . . on edge this morning. Are you worried about your event?"

The event. She'd completely forgotten about it. What was wrong with her? Even now Callie was probably up to her eyeballs in work, trying to get the shop ready in time. If they'd even been able to fix the broken pipe. The girls at the Hope House would be waking soon, possibly to some very disappointing news. And all she could think about was herself.

"Josie?"

She gave him a strained smile. "I'm fine. I'm sure Callie's doing everything she can. And I'll be getting back to town just as soon as the wind dies down."

Josephine squirmed as he looked at her long and hard. She was suddenly too warm under Mary Beth's uncomely parka. She moved to the sofa and reached for the book on the floor. Not that she'd be able to pay the story much mind. But maybe it would keep Noah from pestering her.

A moment later the sofa sank beside her as Noah lowered himself. Close, but not touching. Her gaze bounced off him, settling back on the book.

"I'm sorry I brought up the past last night." His low voice rumbled through the quiet room. "We called a truce and I broke it."

Her heart leaped at his words. Leave it to him to bring up the very thing she was working so hard to forget. He'd never been one to beat around the bush.

"Josie?"

She swallowed against the knot in her throat. "It's fine. It doesn't matter."

"What do you mean it doesn't matter?"

She lifted her shoulder in a careless shrug. "It just doesn't."

She ducked her head, focusing on the book. Her hair fell forward, a convenient curtain, blocking out Noah.

*The words, Josephine. Read the words.* She managed a sentence, a paragraph. Not that she understood any of it. She turned the page anyway.

Noah brushed her hair back, tucking it behind her ear. Her skin tingled under his fingers. Her body flushed with warmth. There was no numbness with Noah. No siree.

"What's going on inside that head of yours?"

"I'm just reading, Noah."

"I didn't know you were such a Dungy fan." His tone rang with sarcasm.

Her heart stuttered in her chest. Why couldn't he just leave her alone? He was supposed to be cross with her. He was supposed to sign the papers and tell his friends what a man-eater she was.

The fire snapped and sparks shot up the flue, but Noah couldn't tear his eyes from Josie's face. He could see some kind of battle raging behind those baby blues.

He took the book from her hands and closed it on his lap. "Talk to me."

"You didn't mark my page."

"Talk to me, Josie."

She sighed. "Let's just get through this, all right? It's almost over."

"I thought that's what we were doing."

"There need to be boundaries. We can't be . . . sharing our hearts and—and cuddling up on the couch and playing games like it's old times or something."

"You're the one who started with the—"

"I know, I know. I was stupid. We're divorced, Noah. It will be official in a matter of days, and I just think . . ."

He frowned at Josie. Her cheeks were flushed and not from the cold. Something sparked in the depths of those eyes. Fear? Anger? What he'd give to read her mind right now.

"What, Josie? What do you think?"

She finally turned to him, her eyes snapping with fire. "I think we should just cut this out, that's what. We're not together anymore. We're not married. We're not even friends. We're just—enemies, stuck together by chance."

His gaze roved over her face, his fingers remembering the softness of her skin, his body remembering the feel of her against him.

"You're not my enemy."

She leaped off the sofa. "Well, I should be!"

She moved in front of the fire, arms crossed, chin jutted. Her shoulders rose and fell with shallow breaths.

What was going on here? Everything was fine last night. At least until he'd opened his big mouth.

He'd had plenty of time to ponder his feelings as he'd lain awake for hours. He didn't know what was happening between them. Maybe he just wanted closure. Maybe he wanted to understand what he'd done to fail her so horribly that she'd—

He gave his head a shake. Clearly Josie didn't want to talk about that now any more than she had then. And he'd be a fool to let her back into his heart when he didn't even know what had gone so wrong before.

Right?

Her sharp laugh snagged his attention. "Do you even have any idea how many men I've slept with, Noah?"

He blinked at her. "What the heck, Josie?"

"It's true."

He frowned at her back. At the confidence, almost smugness, in her tone. She'd hinted as much during their courtship, but he'd always shut her down. He didn't care about her past. At least that's what he'd told himself. Mostly he just didn't want to think about it. He still didn't.

"I can't even remember them all. Sometimes I didn't even know their names."

"Stop it."

"I was an early bloomer." She tossed him a look over her

shoulder, her chin jutting out. "I was only twelve that first time."

*Good gosh.* He rocked back in his seat, his breakfast congealing in his stomach.

"Yeah, twelve. He was older though. Much more experienced. I learned a lot."

"That's . . ."

She quirked a brow, gave that little smirk. "Messed up? Yeah, Noah. I'm messed up. And that was just the beginning. I was pretty much the Cartersville High School whore. Did you know that? Need a sure thing for the prom? Ask Josephine Dupree. Feeling lonely? Give Jo a call. Need a little revenge—?"

"Stop it."

"What for? It's all true."

"That's in the past, Josie." Even he heard the hardness in his tone.

Well, what did she expect? He didn't want to hear this. Didn't want to think about all the men she'd given herself to. Not even now. Some part of him argued that Josie wasn't like that anymore. But the part of him she'd hurt, the part of his heart that had been left in tatters, raised a finger of doubt.

He stared at her back, her stiffened posture. Daylight trickled in through the curtains, and he suddenly needed to see the look on her face. The look in her eyes.

She must not have heard his approach, because she jumped when he took her elbow, turning her. Something flickered in her eyes before she blinked it away. Her expression was classic Josephine: proud, carefree, cynical.

"Why are you doing this now?" he asked.

"Just thought you had a right to know."

His eyes pierced hers. "You're afraid."

Her face gave nothing away. Her lip curled in a wry grin. "Whatever do I have to be afraid of, Noah?"

"You tell me."

"I'm not afraid, sugar. I'm just trying to assuage any misplaced guilt you might have over our divorce. It's all on me."

"I don't feel guilty about it." But that wasn't entirely true. How many hours had he spent wondering where he'd been lacking? What he'd done wrong? If he wasn't enough?

"Good. You shouldn't."

He looked closely at her. Past the smirk. Past the jaunty thrust of her chin to the twin pools of her eyes. To the flush that stained her cheeks.

This little show might've worked once upon a time. But he knew better now. Knew her cynicism was just a hard, brittle shell that protected a soft heart.

His gaze sharpened on her. "Did I get a little too close last night, Josie? Is that it? I think you're just feeling a little uncomfortable, and you don't like that. You're trying to scare me away."

She gave a sharp laugh. "Haven't I already done that, Noah? I mean, when your wife rolls around in the sheets with another man—"

"That's enough."

The image flashed uninvited in his mind, repulsing him, making him burn with anger. Heat flushed through him, making his muscles quiver, and his body tensed.

He let loose of her arm and stepped back. If he didn't, he was going to grab her and shake her silly. He took three long breaths and dragged his eyes back to her face.

She'd gone pale, her shoulders were pulled in and upward. The smirk trembled on her lips. Not so brave now.

She curled her arms around her waist. "Let's just go back to our own corners, hmm, Noah?" Her voice was flat, emotionless.

Noah's eyes snapped with fire. "Fine, Josephine. Have it your way."

# Chapter 19

Noah brought the ax down on the log, and it split with a *thwack*. He kicked the halves out of the way and set another log on the stump. His breath fogged in the afternoon air. The snow had finally stopped, and the wind was beginning to taper off.

Good. He was that much closer to getting rid of his houseguest.

He'd put coats on the horses and put them out to pasture. He'd taken extra time with Kismet, trying to settle him. The horse would need a lot more one-on-one time before it really felt at home.

Noah adjusted his gloves, his eyes glancing off the darkened house. This had to be the longest day in history. He and Josephine had hardly spoken all day. Granted, he'd spent much of it in the barn. And it wasn't as if they were out of firewood either. He'd take any excuse to escape the house. Plus, it felt good to work off some steam.

He wished he could call someone. Seth. His mom and dad. Someone who would talk some sense into him.

He stopped a moment to catch his breath. Once he took Josephine home he could start getting back to normal. If all went well it would be safe to take her home by late afternoon. She was missing most of her event—provided it hadn't been canceled—but that was the least of his concerns right now.

His mind reviewed once again the things she'd said this morning. He'd have to be made of stone not to be bothered.

Josephine wasn't the woman he'd made her out to be in his own mind. He'd ignored the things Seth had told him. The warning Jack had tried to give him. He'd told himself her past was in her past. Put her up on a pedestal.

And boy, had she come crashing down.

He needed to remember that. What'd he want with her now, anyway? Hadn't she already caused him enough trouble? What was he thinking, letting her back in?

He brought the ax down with more force than necessary. But he had a feeling there weren't enough logs in the county to work Josephine Dupree Mitchell out of his system.

Josephine shifted on the sofa. She pulled her knees to her chest and covered her nose with the blanket, capturing her warm breath. Her fingers were stiff with cold, and she could hardly feel her toes.

Shadow had deserted her in favor of Noah hours ago. Her husband/ex-husband napped in the recliner behind her, snoring softly. The fire crackled quietly, the flames dancing in the hearth. The wind still howled, though to a lesser degree. It was almost four o'clock now. Her event—if it had even taken place—was practically over. She could only hope that it had gone as planned and that the girls were ready to begin their exciting evening.

Today had been a trial. The hours dragged, even though Noah spent the better half of the day outside. She was up to here in guilt. But she should probably be used to that by now.

She'd second-guessed herself a dozen times. Maybe she shouldn't have pushed him away. He could be behind her right now, holding her tight, keeping her warm. He could be slipping back into her heart, back into her life.

But it was too late to call back the ugly list of things she'd done. The ugly truth of who she was. She was doing the right thing, she told herself. She was saving them both from her, and if that made him angry, it was a small price to pay.

She must've fallen asleep, because when she opened her eyes Noah was donning his coat, urgency in the quick work of his hands.

She sat up. "What's going on?"

He shoved his feet into his boots, not sparing her a glance. "Something's wrong. I heard a crash outside. The horses are agitated."

Now that she stopped and listened she could hear them faintly. High-pitched neighs.

"Do you need any help?"

"No."

She didn't notice the rifle until he grabbed it from its spot against the wall. He rushed out the door, shutting it quietly behind him. A moment later the truck's engine fired up.

She got up and put two logs on the fire, warming her hands. The mantel clock showed ten minutes to five. She listened for the wind and heard nothing for several minutes. It was probably safe to go home now. Once Noah tended to the horses, she'd ask him to take her.

Noah spotted the break in the corral as soon as he pulled up in his truck. He stared at the busted wood and frowned.

*What in the world?*

The snow had been disturbed, but with his horses possibly in danger, he bypassed the broken fence and went to check on them, gripping his rifle tightly.

He was breathing hard by the time he reached the horses. They were huddled in the corner of the corral, ears flicking, eyes wide with fear. He gave a quick scan of the surroundings. He didn't see or hear anything that would have them so worked up.

Whatever the threat, it was gone now.

He shouldered the rifle and advanced slowly, taking care to remain calm. He went to his own horse, Sweetpea, first. She trusted him most and was the leader of the pack. She also had a calm, sensible nature that responded quickly to the unexpected.

"It's all right, girl. Nothing to worry about." The horse stepped toward him, giving one final neigh. But this one sounded less tremulous. "You're all right. Attagirl."

He stroked her withers. Already the other horses had calmed down. They were moving out of the corner, quieting a bit. He kept talking in calm tones as he did a quick head count. *Nine, ten, eleven . . .*

With the horses moving around maybe he'd missed one. He counted again and got the same number. He looked over the herd. Sweetpea, Rango, Bella, Octavia, Gracie, Buffer Zone . . . Where was Kismet?

He scanned the pasture, a sinking feeling in his gut. He trotted back to the break in the fence where his eyes honed in on hoofprints. What had spooked Kismet so much that he'd busted right through the fence?

The prints headed toward the road. Noah walked the opposite direction a short distance, scanning the fresh blanket of snow.

There, up closer to the house. He closed in on the marred snow and frowned. Bear prints. Gun at the ready, he followed them up to the kitchen side of the house. The garbage can was tipped over, the trash scattered. He gave the surroundings a quick scan.

The bear was gone now. He needed to give the fence a quick fix and find Kismet. Hopefully the horse hadn't gone far.

It was around five thirty when Josephine heard the high-pitched buzz of Noah's snowmobile leaving the property. That was two hours ago, and she'd been pacing the living room ever since. The horses had quieted at least. That was good, but it didn't explain why Noah had left.

What was going on? Had he gone to Mary Beth's for some reason? He'd said something about taking the snow machine over there when he'd been on the phone with her.

Josephine was being ridiculous. Whatever was going on with his horses had nothing to do with Mary Beth.

Right?

One thing was certain, he was going to be frozen solid when he came back. Making it back to town was also impossible, since the sun had already set. She hoped the event had gone off as planned and that all the girls were on their way to a magical evening.

She built the fire back up and heated water for coffee. A cup of decaf would warm his insides right up.

Shadow watched her scuttle around the room, his head propped on his paws, his ears perking, probably wondering why she was disturbing his nap.

The water was boiling by the time the door flew open. Noah pushed it shut, and it closed with a slam.

Josephine jumped, her heart kicking into second gear.

He jerked off his knit hat, leaving his hair in disarray. His eyebrows and eyelashes were white with ice, and his nose was pink. None of that distracted from his knotty jaw or the hard line of his lips.

She was almost afraid to ask. "What—what's going on? Are the horses okay?"

His eyes cut to hers. Even in the dim light, they snapped with fire. "Did you take it upon yourself to put out the garbage today, Josephine?"

She blinked at the change in topic. "What—yes. I took it out this morning. Why?"

He gave her a long, steely look that only made her more uncomfortable. "Did you think to put the lid back on the can, by any chance?"

"The lid . . ." She reviewed her actions. It had been so cold, the wind whipping right through her open coat. She was in a hurry. "I-I don't remember."

"You don't remember." He looked away, his jaw ticking, before he found her gaze again.

She crossed her arms over her chest.

"Did it ever occur to you that a bearproof trash can isn't bearproof without the lid?"

"Bears . . ."

"Yes, bears, Josephine. We're in the north Georgia mountains, remember?"

"Bears . . . bears hibernate."

"Bears don't hibernate. Not in the truest sense of the word."

"But—but there's snow on the ground."

"It's early spring and food is scarce." He clamped his jaw shut, started pulling off his boots.

"I'm sorry. I didn't know. Are the horses okay?"

He pulled off his second boot, dropping it beside the first.

She wondered if he was going to answer her. Surely a bear hadn't gotten one of the horses. Her stomach rolled at the thought of one of those beautiful creatures lying dead on the ground. But a bear couldn't get into the corral, could it?

"Kismet got spooked and busted through the gate."

"Oh no. Is he okay?"

"I don't know. I can't find him. But he's bleeding."

*Good job, Josephine.* She was so stupid. Why had she left the lid off the can?

"What are you going to do?"

"Wait till daylight and go back out." He nailed her with a look. "I can't take you back until I find him."

"Of course." Now she knew what was really bothering him. Another night stuck with her.

She grabbed the kettle from the hook over the fire and took it into the kitchen. She made him a cup of coffee and brought it back into the living room.

"It's decaf," she said, extending the mug.

He silently took her peace offering—such as it was. The ice had thawed from his brows and eyelashes. But not from his eyes.

"I'm awful sorry, Noah. I wasn't thinking."

He gave a sharp nod.

But sorry didn't bring Kismet back. It didn't mend a shattered heart or heal a broken marriage. It didn't even begin to soothe the sting of guilt.

Josephine fixed supper, and they ate in silence, then turned in early. She lay on the couch, fretting. She closed her eyes and tried to sleep, but she was too wound up. Somewhere out there a horse was lost and hurt, and it was all her fault.

By the time the gray light of morning filtered into the living room she'd had plenty of time to think and plan. Noah stirred in the corner, the recliner creaking softly. He got up and hung a kettle of water over the fire, moving quietly. The plastic sheet crinkled as he slipped into the kitchen. She heard him filling Shadow's dishes with food and water, then she closed her eyes as he returned, continuing toward the bathroom.

While he was in the bathroom she crept from her makeshift bed and made a large thermos of coffee, adding it to the other things she'd packed in a backpack she'd found in a closet during the night.

By the time Noah came back into the living room, Josephine was suited up in her borrowed winter gear, the backpack hanging from her shoulder.

Noah stopped. "What are you doing?" Sleep hadn't helped his disposition any.

Too bad. "I'm going with you."

"No, you're not."

She notched her chin a few degrees higher. "I sure enough am. This is my fault, my mistake, and I aim to help rectify it."

"It's cold out there, Josephine. And there's nothing you can do."

"I'm not a fragile flower. And two sets of eyes are better than one. I can be looking while you're driving."

"I have no idea how long I'll be out there. It could take the better part of the day." His voice was tight.

She hitched the backpack higher. "That's why I packed some food and supplies. Besides, how are you going to get the snowmobile back if you have a horse to lead?"

Their gazes clashed. She'd made some headway with that bit of reality.

"I'll help feed the horses," she said. "The sooner that's done, the sooner we can get started, and the longer we stand here fussing, the longer Kismet's out there lost."

She refused to wither under his sour look. She was going to do this. Let him try and stop her.

She could tell she was winning when he let out a long breath. "Have it your way, Josephine. Don't say I didn't warn you."

# Chapter 20

*Copper Creek, Georgia*

*Three and a half years ago*

Josephine ran her roller through the paint and smoothed it onto the wall, the paint sucking and slurping. She'd chosen a shade of brown so muted it was almost gray. She stepped back, tilting her head, appraising the color.

"You like it?" Noah asked from his knees where he was taping off the adjacent brick wall. "We can take it back if you don't. Buddy's really good about that."

"No, I think it's just perfect."

"It's a nice contrast with the brick."

"And masculine. I want men to feel welcome and comfortable here. Not like they have to turn in their man card to step foot inside, you know?"

Noah chuckled. "I don't think you have to worry about that, Josie."

She loved the way he shortened her name. She shot him a saucy look. "What do you mean?"

He ripped off the tape and stood, smiling wryly. "I don't think anyone could accuse you of being unwelcoming. You could probably paint the walls pink and butcher the hair of every man in Murray County, and they'd still be lining up at your door."

She tilted a smile at him. "I do believe there's a compliment somewhere in there."

His lips twitched as he wetted his own roller, but he didn't respond.

It had been over a week since their first date. He hadn't called her, much less asked her out again. She knew they'd agreed to just the one date, but she'd honestly expected him to ask anyway.

She'd reviewed the evening so many times. Maybe she hadn't lived up to his expectations. Maybe after spending more time with her he found her vain and shallow. The thought opened a hollow spot in the pit of her stomach.

They'd worked together nearly every evening after the shop closed. It made for a long day on her feet, but it was worth it. He was doing the work for just over half of the bid she'd gotten from the other company. And if she were honest, she didn't mind spending her evenings with him one bit.

They talked about everything from their favorite movies and books to his family and upbringing. She'd skimmed over most of her childhood, somehow making it seem less wretched than it really was. She told him about going to meet her nana at Piney Acres only to find she had advanced Alzheimer's.

Noah was a good listener. Sympathetic and engaged. And he was fun. She loved to hear him laugh.

A knock sounded on the door behind her, making her jump. A middle-aged woman stood on the other side of the glass door. She was short and plump, and her drab brown hair was in desperate need of good color.

Sometimes Josephine fit in a female client if the Clip 'n' Curl was closed. She missed styling women's hair, and it brought in a few extra bucks.

She unlocked the door and pulled it open. "I'm sorry; we're closed. But if you want to stop by tomor—"

"Was my husband in here this morning?"

Josephine blinked. "What—who's your husband?"

The woman's lips pinched together. "Allen Forsythe."

The woman's strained tone and knotted brows made Josephine cautious. "I'm afraid my client schedule is a matter of privacy. I'm sure if you—"

"Now you look here—"

"Mrs. Forsythe . . ." Noah appeared at Josephine's side, roller in hand. "Good to see you, ma'am. How's your daddy faring? I heard he had to cancel his annual fishing trip."

"Don't you go changing the subject, Noah Mitchell. This is no concern of yours."

Josephine tried again. "I'm sorry you're upset, Mrs. Forsythe. Maybe if you simply ask your husband—"

"Do you think I'm some kind of idiot, missy? That cheating scoundrel wouldn't know the truth if it busted him in the jaw. I know he was here. His hair's shorn, and Arlene from the beauty shop said he wasn't in today." She poked a finger in Josephine's face. "I don't want him coming in here again, you understand?"

Josephine's spine lengthened. "I'm afraid that's not up to me."

"Well, I'll have you know I'm a member of the women's auxiliary, and I have a lot of influence around these parts. It'd be a real shame to see your new business go belly-up so quick."

Josephine gave her a thin smile. "I do hope that wasn't a threat, Mrs. Forsythe."

The woman's eyes raked over Josephine's figure, making her mindful of her snug T-shirt and short cut-offs. She resisted the urge to give them a tug as a wave of shame washed over her.

"Well, just look at you . . . dressing like that and tossing your head at every man like some kind of—"

"Hey, now." Noah stepped forward. "That'll be enough of that."

Josephine's heart stuttered before it raced ahead. Heat prickled her face, and her legs quaked under her.

Still, she shouldered right past Noah, her chin thrust out. "Now, you listen here. I run a barbershop, not a bordello. And if a man wants a haircut I aim to give him one. No more, no less. If you have a problem with your husband coming here, I suggest you work that out with him and leave me out of it. You have a good evening now."

Mrs. Forsythe sputtered as Josephine shut the door and locked it in one smooth motion.

Her face tingled with heat and her hand shook as she bent to drag the roller through the tray. She couldn't even look at Noah. She felt exposed and raw. She was right back in high school, those words splashed boldly across her locker. Eyes prying, tongues wagging. She wished she could run upstairs to the safety of her apartment and hide.

*You should be used to this by now, Josephine.*

Outside an engine fired up. Tires squealed as the car pulled away.

She'd just started to feel settled. Like part of the community. Accepted. Included. Would all that be ruined now?

Noah eased the roller from her tight grip, and she realized she'd been laying the paint on the wall in short, sloppy strokes. "Sorry."

He set the roller in the tray, his eyes searching hers. "You okay?"

Josephine drew a long, slow breath and gave a smile that felt strained. "I'm just fine."

"Is that right? 'Cause your hands are shaking and you look like you've just seen a ghost."

Josephine gave a sharp laugh.

"You didn't do anything wrong, Josie."

How was it he knew exactly what she was feeling? She swallowed against the lump in her throat. "She's going to bad-mouth my business."

"She doesn't have the kind of influence she thinks she does. Everyone knows Allen's a cheat. She's just jealous and hurt, and looking to control everyone else 'cause she can't control her husband."

Josephine winced. "I almost feel sorry for her."

"Everyone does. I don't imagine she likes that much either. Try not to take it personally. Last spring she went on a rampage in the Rusty Nail over some waitress her husband was making eyes at."

"Why on earth doesn't she just leave him?"

"Beats me. You'd think she'd be happier alone."

"I hope she doesn't come back when I have customers." Bad enough Noah had been here. Worse, actually, now that she thought on it. She cared more about his opinion than that of a whole shop full of clients.

"Did Allen really come in this morning?" he asked.

She nodded. He had flirted with her, but she hadn't thought much of it. "I think I'll be a mite less friendly if he comes back. Hopefully he'll stop coming in altogether."

"You didn't do anything wrong."

She quirked a brow. "And how do you know that?"

He gave her a little smile, and his gaze seemed to dig right down to the secret corners inside. "I know you better than you think, Josie. You may be friendly, but you don't cross the line."

The vote of confidence soothed a place deep inside her. Made her want to live up to his expectations. She got lost in his honey-colored eyes. Couldn't have dragged hers away if she'd wanted.

His gaze traveled over her face, and her breath hitched. Have mercy, he was a beautiful man. That thick black hair. Those long eyelashes. He currently sported a five o'clock shadow, and it was making her want to whisk him right over to her bowl. Not that he wasn't as handsome as sin with that dark stubble.

Her fingers tingled with the need to touch his face. She curled them into her palms until her nails bit the flesh. She didn't need to touch him. She needed to gather her wits, that's what she needed.

Falling back on the persona that was like a second skin, she gave him a cheeky grin. "If you think so highly of me, Noah Mitchell, why is it you haven't even asked me for a second date? Hmm?"

His lips twitched as he stared steadily at her, and his eyes danced with humor. "Because, Josephine . . . you'd only tell me no."

She reared back slightly, feeling her smile waver. His ability to read her mind was a bit unsettling. "Oh, you know that, now, do you?"

"I believe I do."

She tossed her hair, forgetting for the moment it was tied back in a stumpy ponytail. "And so you're gonna just give up so easily? I didn't take you for a quitter, honey."

His eyes traveled over her face with the weight of a touch. Her heart skittered across her chest, and a flush of heat flooded through her, making her skin tingle.

"Who said I'm giving up?" His low voice scraped across the corners of her heart, nicking it good.

He reached out and brushed her cheek with the back of his knuckles. Every neuron fired up, leaving a trail of heat in its wake. She couldn't have drawn a breath if she'd tried.

He lowered his head and gave her lips a slow, gentle brush. It was warm. Delicious. Heaven. Her heart didn't dare to beat.

But it was over almost as soon as it had begun. He backed away, and her eyes fluttered open. Her body hummed like a live wire. She was the very opposite of numb.

His eyes locked on hers, steady and intense. "That was your last first kiss, Josephine Dupree," he said softly.

The words made her chest tighten. She choked off a strangled sound that threatened to escape and gave a saucy smile instead. "You're a funny guy, Noah Mitchell."

She retrieved her roller and worked hard to affect a casual manner. To steady the tremor in her hand. To quell the fear that had struck hard.

A moment later Noah picked up his roller and began working the wall beside her in long, steady strokes. He brought the conversation back to safer topics: the town's new council, their favorite pastries at the bakery, the pros and cons of social media.

It was all she could do to make casual conversation when all she wanted to do was escape Noah's magnetizing presence. Either that or kiss him senseless.

She gave her thoughts a mental shake. She'd known he was trouble. Had known it from the first time she'd laid eyes on him. Because as much as she feared letting him into her heart, he somehow made her want it too.

She made it through the rest of the evening, claiming fatigue and calling it quits a little early. They wrapped the rollers and put away the supplies, and Noah confirmed he'd be back the next evening. She could hardly wait.

"Night, Josie," he said at the door.

"Good night."

"Lock up behind me." He gave her a toe-curling smile as he slipped through the door.

"I will."

The kiss was nothing, she told herself as she walked up to her apartment, her legs trembling beneath her. Hardly more than a peck. Downright chaste, really. But she couldn't deny that it had left her wanting more. Or that it had stirred her up more than all the kisses she'd had before combined.

# Chapter 21

*Present day*

Noah gave the snowmobile some gas as he took the incline in the road. The droning buzz of the machine shattered the silence. They'd been trailing Kismet's prints farther into the mountains for the past half hour. So far the horse had stayed on the main road, and there had been no more traces of blood.

As they took a corner Josie leaned into his back, and he steeled himself against the feelings her nearness provoked.

He wasn't one bit happy about having her along. He'd more or less agreed only to make her suffer. If she thought the house was cold, she was in for a rude awakening. A few hours with the wind blasting her face would teach her to heed his advice.

He felt a prick of guilt. She needed a helmet and something warmer than his work gloves, and he knew just where to get them. He took the next fork in the road, though Kismet's prints went on straight.

"Where are we going?"

"To Mary Beth's." It would take them ten minutes out of their way, but he wanted to check on his friend anyway. He'd also brought his phone and charger in case she still had power. It was a long shot, but if she did, he could pick up his charged phone on the way back home.

Josie had gone silent behind him, but he couldn't bring himself to care.

Several minutes later he pulled into the drive. He drove through the orchard of dormant peach trees and stopped beside the small red-roofed cottage. A wisp of smoke escaped the chimney.

He got off the machine, pulling off his helmet, but Josie didn't budge. "Aren't you coming?" He'd figured she'd want to warm up, if nothing else.

She leaned against the spare gas container he'd clipped onto the back. "I'll wait here."

He noted the stubborn tilt of her chin. "Suit yourself."

Josephine knew she was being plain silly, but no amount of cold was making her go inside that house. She didn't want to watch Noah embrace Mary Beth or worse yet, give her a big old smooch on the lips.

She shook the image from her head. She refused to think about what Noah and Mary Beth might be doing inside. As Callie was fond of saying, "You can't keep birds from flying over your head, but you can sure keep them from building a nest in your hair."

Josephine got off the machine and stretched, stuffing her

hands into the deep coat pockets. It had been slow going, tracking Kismet. Some of the roads were windswept, covering the tracks, and in other places deer and other animals had left prints, forcing Noah off the snowmobile for a closer look.

She got into the backpack and took a sip from the thermos. The warm coffee felt good going down. She capped the thermos and secured the pack to the back, forcing it into place.

A few minutes later Noah came out, striding toward the snow machine. He held out a helmet and a pair of women's gloves.

It galled her to borrow from Noah's girlfriend, but her hands were freezing, and he'd probably insist on the helmet.

She took the items with a smile, blinking innocently. "And how's little Mary Beth?"

"She's still sick, for your information."

If he'd meant to make her feel bad, it worked. But he didn't have to know that. "Maybe you should stay and take care of her."

"She's got her dad here, and I have a horse to find, remember?" He shoved his helmet on his head. "Are you coming or what?"

Josephine slid the helmet on, adjusting its weight. It felt heavy and awkward on her head, but she was glad for the visor, which would block the wind.

The snowmobile surged forward, and she grabbed onto Noah's coat, trying to keep some space between them. But it was hard with their gear crowding her from behind. When he got out to the road he gave the machine more gas, pressing her farther into the gear. Something hard poked into her back. She must've displaced things when she'd replaced the backpack.

Holding tight with one hand she elbowed the gear behind

her. The pressure against her back finally gave. She adjusted her helmet and grabbed onto Noah's coat again.

When they reached the main road, he slowed a bit to follow Kismet's trail. As they rode farther into the mountains, the road curved and wound. The hilly pastures had given way to rugged mountain terrain, steep on one side of the road and dropping off on the other. Up and down and around. Her stomach was starting to feel unsettled. Not that she was going to complain.

After what seemed like an hour later he slowed the machine. The hoofprints left the road, heading into the woods. Pine trees swayed high overhead, but there was little low-lying brush to impede a horse or a snowmobile. There was, however, a creek off in the distance.

Noah turned off the machine. "I'll be right back."

He followed the trail toward the bubbling creek, about twenty yards from the road, and stopped, hands on hips. Josephine stood, stretching, and scanned the distance, hoping to sight the horse. Even with the face shield and gloves, it was cold. The wind seemed to blow right through her coat.

A few minutes later he returned. "Have you ever driven one of these?"

"No."

"Kismet crossed the stream. I can't see where the trail leads, but there's a forest service road across the creek. It'll save time if I track while you drive to the other side. It's pretty straight-forward."

She nodded, easing forward on the seat, and Noah gave her a quick tutorial.

"Got it?" he asked when he was finished.

"I think so."

"You'll see the road on the right. It's one lane. Take it a couple miles." He pointed into the distance. "See that outcropping of rock?"

"Yeah."

"I'll meet you there."

"Okay." She turned the key and the machine fired up, rumbling beneath her. Following his instruction, she eased away. Ten slow minutes later she was wondering if she'd missed the turn. But then, just up ahead, she spotted a turnoff. It was narrow and uphill and had a little sign sticking out of the snow that read *SR 259*. This had to be it.

Josephine gunned the engine and took the hill easily enough. It was even kind of fun. She could see why people did this for sport. Gaining confidence, she took the next stretch a little less cautiously. The road turned and curved and went up and down over the mountain. She was starting to wonder if she was ever going to end up by that outcropping when she spotted Noah by the road ahead.

She eased to a stop beside him. "Did you find Kismet's trail?"

"Fortunately for us, he likes the roads. It picks up just down the way."

She scooted back on the seat as he put on his helmet.

"I can't believe he's still going," she said. "I didn't think he'd get this far."

"He's pretty high-strung. That bear scared him good."

She felt a prick of guilt at the thought of the bear, but Noah didn't seem angry anymore. Not that he was warm exactly either.

He hopped on, and they pressed forward. Josephine kept her eyes peeled over Noah's shoulder. Her back began to ache from the distance she kept, and her fingers grew stiff from gripping his coat. She found herself sinking into him, inch by inch.

One of her arms slid around him, clutching tighter as he took a turn.

How long had they been out here? It had to be going on noon. Her bladder was crying out, especially when they hit bumpy spots. They'd followed Kismet's tracks onto numerous unmarked branches of the service roads. The current one seemed more like an ATV trail than a road, and she had a feeling there was nothing but dirt beneath the layers of snow.

A short while later Noah slowed to a stop.

"What's wrong? You see something?"

He shut off the engine. "Time for a break. I need to gas up."

She saw the thick groves of pine and underbrush on both sides of the road, and her bladder cheered.

She got off the machine and pulled off her helmet. "Where does this road even go?"

Noah stretched. "Who knows? Service roads go on for miles and miles. It's a virtual maze spread over a thousand square miles. Don't you worry though. We can follow our tracks out."

"I think I'm gonna . . ." She pointed toward the woods, heading that direction.

She waded through the snow—at least seven or eight inches. The smell of pine was so heavy in the air it suffused each breath. And the snow-covered mountains were a sight, even if she was shivering from the cold.

Once she emptied her bladder she was going to have a nice warm cup of coffee. And one of the granola bars she'd found in the bottom of the pantry.

*"Josie . . ."*

She turned at Noah's strained voice.

He was frowning at the machine. Then at her. "Where's the gas?" His words were clipped.

"What—what do you mean?"

"The red gas container I strapped on the back." His tone was sharp as a knife.

She waded slowly back to the machine as if she might find the container if only she had a better view. Or maybe find it lying on the other side, out of sight.

But inside she was remembering. She was visualizing the plastic container strapped between her and the backpack. The pack was still there.

Oh no. She bit her lip.

"What. Did. You. Do?"

Her gaze bounced off him. Her chest felt weighted with the words she had to say. "The—the belt thing was digging into my back. I gave it a little shove to make room, that's all."

His face was like rock. "You gave it a little shove."

This wasn't good. Not at all. Even she could see that.

He ran his hands over his face, then shelved them on his hips. "Josie, that buckle was a push-button release. You released the belt, and the gas container went flying off the back." His chest expanded with a breath, and he sighed hard. "Where? When did this happen? We'll just have to circle back and get it."

She didn't want to say the words out loud. Not the way he was looking at her. She was such an idiot. Why couldn't she do anything right?

*"Josie?"*

She swallowed hard. "It was a long time ago."

"How long?"

"Right—right after we left Mary Beth's."

He turned away, looking skyward, laughing. Not the good kind either. She'd never seen a madman, but he was giving a good impression.

She closed her mouth, giving him a moment. It looked like he needed a really long one. And she could hardly blame him.

By the time he turned around his eyes had lost that wild look. His jaw still twitched though. He gave a hard exhale, his breath fogging in front of him.

"We—we don't have enough gas to get back?"

"No, we don't have enough to get back, Josie. We're running on fumes right now."

"Oh." Her word was barely audible.

The urgency to urinate pressed on her, and she fought the urge to squirm like a little girl.

"Go . . ." He flung out his hand. "Use the facilities. I have to think."

The "facilities" were a snowy spot about fifteen yards off the road in the middle of a thick copse of small evergreens.

When she was finished she made her way slowly back to the road, dread weighting each step.

Noah was perched sideways on the seat, hands on his knees, when she returned. He looked up at her approach. The expression on his face made her think she might fare better back in the woods with the wild animals. She stopped a safe distance away, squirming under his stony look.

She crossed her arms over her chest and forced herself to ask the question. "What are we going to do?"

"We're going to backtrack. Take the machine until it stops and walk from there."

"Walk? But we've come miles and miles."

His eyes snapped with fire. "I'm aware of that."

"Shouldn't—shouldn't we just keep heading the way we're going? Maybe we'll come across Kismet soon."

"Even if we do, he's not going to be in any condition to carry us. Even if I trusted him—and I don't."

"Well, surely we'd find civilization sooner if we just continue on. We've been on this road for an hour. It must lead somewhere."

"Weren't you listening before? This road could go for miles and miles without so much as a mailbox. We could take branch after branch and freeze to death before we ever found our way out of here."

The blood blanched from her face. "But it's such a long way back."

He cupped the back of his neck. "We have some supplies. And we can take some shortcuts through the woods. We don't have any other choice."

# Chapter 22

Ten minutes later the snowmobile began sputtering. Noah had used every bit of those minutes to deep-breathe away his frustration. Too bad it didn't seem to be working. He'd also done some math. They had to make it back to the main road for any chance of help. They'd been on the service roads two hours, going about twenty miles per hour. They were forty miles from help, minus a couple shortcuts.

They had roughly six hours till sunset. Even if they could walk four miles per hour—almost impossible in the deep snow— they'd only cover twenty-four miles. Unless they came across someone—also unlikely—they were going to be stuck out here tonight.

The machine finally sputtered to a stop, the engine dying. The sudden silence was ominous.

"End of the road." He heard the tightness in his voice, but who could blame him?

He took off his helmet and waited for Josephine to dismount, his mind in gear. While she replaced her helmet with the coat hood, he unbuckled the backpack from the machine and shouldered his rifle. Then he reached into the closed compartment for the unopened emergency kit his mom had gotten him for Christmas a couple years ago. Thank God for moms.

A glance at the label gave him a measure of comfort: lighter, utility knife, mini-saw, mini-flashlight, and a few first-aid items.

He stuffed the kit into the backpack and considered taking the helmets for warmth tonight. In the end he decided against the extra weight. They should be warm enough with a fire and whatever kind of shelter he could find or make. Instead, he opened the visor on his helmet, worked it off, and stuffed it into the backpack. It would work as a handy little shovel later.

Josie's stomach gave a rumble that sounded like an approaching avalanche. They both needed sustenance for the long walk. He rooted through the bag to see what she'd packed. It was going to have to last them awhile. He pulled out two plastic bags, one full of snacks, the other water bottles. He grabbed the granola bars and handed one to her.

Her face peeked out of the fur-lined hood. "Thanks."

"We should walk as we eat. We have a lot of ground to cover." He shouldered the bag and started off.

She trotted after him. "I can carry something."

"I got it."

He set off at a challenging pace, plowing through the snow. "It'll be easier if you follow in my footsteps," he said over his shoulder.

And easier for both of them if he didn't have to see her for a while.

Josephine's face tingled with cold, and her lungs burned in her chest. She almost had to trot to keep Noah's pace, but she was determined not to slow him down. She'd caused enough trouble.

They'd been walking in silence a couple hours when he finally slowed, looking out through the woods.

Josephine stopped, grateful for a chance to catch her breath. It was official. She was woefully out of shape. When she got home she was starting an exercise regimen. Her shallow puffs of air were all that broke the silence. Irritatingly enough, Noah wasn't even breathing hard.

"We're going to take a shortcut," he said a moment later. "The road switches back, around the corner ahead." He pointed across the woods. "See the road through there? The terrain's a little more challenging, but we can cut half a mile or so."

Josephine nodded. "Lead on."

She followed him down the slippery slope beside the road, then through the evergreen forest. The ground was uneven, and the undergrowth thick in places, but when they made it back onto the road, she had to admit it had been a good trade-off.

She remembered this next stretch of road and realized how far they had yet to go. The weight of that was like a boulder in her stomach.

"We're not going to make it back tonight, are we?"

"No."

Her feet were already half-frozen from plowing through the snow, and her toes were numb. She thought of a full night out here, where the temperatures would surely drop . . . to say nothing of the other dangers. Bears and heaven knew what other creatures might be prowling around out here.

*And the dark. Let's not forget about that.*

A shiver of fear clawed up her spine. "Noah . . . are we going to be all right?"

He glanced over his shoulder, probably hearing the tremor in her voice. "We'll be fine. It won't be a picnic, but we'll survive."

His reassurance gave her a measure of relief. She trusted him, she realized. If he said they'd be fine, they would. He'd been a Boy Scout and a US Marine, for pity's sake.

"You doing okay?" he asked.

"Yeah."

It was the kindest thing he'd said since they'd started off. The sharpness was gone from his tone, and she was grateful for that at least.

"What about Shadow? And your horses? Will they be all right overnight?"

"Shadow will make do. He's never been shy about drinking from the toilet. As for the horses, the hay hut's full, and they have water. No need to worry."

His kindness was enough to carry her through the next few long hours. Through the deep ache of her leg muscles. Through the bone-deep chill of her fingers and toes, and the blisters burning on her feet.

She was ready to drop when Noah finally stopped, hours later, and scanned the surrounding area. To the right of the road a hill rose at a sharp incline. To the left there was a short drop-off. Evergreens abounded, shielding them from the wind.

"This is a good place to set up camp. Sheltered from the wind, plenty of pine boughs for a makeshift bed. And I can hear a creek somewhere close by."

She thought they had at least an hour before they lost light, but she wasn't going to complain.

She followed him through the woods, and he helped her down the steep incline. Her legs trembling with exhaustion, she made a beeline for a fat, snow-covered log.

"Wait," Noah said before she could brush the snow away. He dug in the backpack and came up with the windshield he'd pried from the helmet. "Use this. Try not to get your gloves wet. Are your feet dry?"

She gave a wry laugh. "I don't know. I can't feel them anymore."

"Well . . . check and see. If they're wet we need to dry out your socks and boots over the fire."

Her eyes shot to his. "We're going to have a fire?"

"I hope so." He pulled a kit from the pack, removing a lighter. One click later a flame danced at the end.

She smiled at the sight. They were going to have a fire. That was the best news she'd heard all day.

"Rest awhile. I'm going to gather some kindling."

While Noah was gone, Josephine looked around. She'd hardly even caught her breath, but she wasn't going to sit around while Noah gathered wood.

He'd said something about pine boughs. She opened the kit, rooted through it, and found a sturdy-looking folding knife. When she pulled out the blade, she was happy to see it had a saw-toothed edge.

She wandered over to the nearest low branch and set to work. Her fingers were stiff and uncoordinated, and the blade was only five inches or so, making for slow going. She'd only managed a few boughs by the time Noah returned.

The kindling clattered to the ground as he dropped it at the base of the incline. "I'll do that after I get the fire going," he called.

"I'm fine."

She kept sawing on the bough until it broke off, then she brought it over with the others. It was a meager start. She was beginning to see why he'd stopped an hour before dark. There was a lot to do. Her stomach twisted with hunger, but they'd have to ration the snacks: a baggie of Life cereal, a few sticks of cheese, and half a can of peanuts.

Noah had cleared a spot for the fire and was arranging the wood into a tepee with the smaller kindling in the middle. She was mesmerized by his meticulous efforts.

When he finished arranging them, he dug in his coat pocket and came up with one of the paper granola wrappers he'd shoved in there earlier. He twisted it tightly like a candle-wick and lit the end.

Josephine held her breath, waiting for the kindling to catch fire. When it did, Noah blew gently on the flame to encourage it. A few minutes later it caught. The flame flickered steadily and began spreading to nearby twigs.

"That is the prettiest sight I've seen all day," she said.

He spared her a smile as he held his hand out for the saw. "I'll get more boughs. Why don't you use the shield to clear out a spot for us to bed down? Right here between the hill and the fire."

"Okay."

She looked at the appointed spot as he disappeared into the evergreens. There was barely room for the two of them to stretch out along the hill.

She wasn't saying no to body heat tonight, that was for sure. Her heart gave a couple of heavy thumps at the thought of sleeping in Noah's arms again.

By the time she finished carving out a bed, the fire was

going strong, and the sky was getting dark. She sat back on her heels, breathing hard from her efforts, her back damp with perspiration.

Where was Noah? The wind whistled through the treetops, and the creek gurgled in the distance. In ten minutes the last of daylight would seep from the horizon, leaving total darkness. There would be no starlight or moonlight tonight. Only a bit of firelight. That would leave an awful lot of darkness beyond the glowing circle.

What if something had happened to him out there? What if she were left out here all alone? Adrenaline flooded into her blood, making her heart pound and her breaths go shallow.

*Stop it, Josephine. Everything's going to be just fine.*

A twig snapped somewhere in the distance, and she sagged against her heels as Noah emerged from the darkening woods.

"Getting dark quick." He dumped the load of boughs into the area she'd carved out.

She didn't know how he'd cut all those so quickly.

"Why don't you spread these out? I need to lay in enough wood to carry us through the night."

"I'll go with you." She couldn't keep the bit of panic from her voice.

He gave a little nod. "All right."

They swept through the area, gathering fallen, half-buried branches. By the time they'd laid in enough for the night, Josephine was ravenous and thirsty. They settled on the fallen log and broke out the cheese sticks and bottled water. It wasn't nearly enough.

"I think we can afford a bit of cereal too," he said. "But let's save most of it for morning. We can have some of the nuts for lunch and what's left in the afternoon."

"Is the coffee still warm?"

"I don't know, but we should probably save it for morning. We can heat it over the fire. That'll help warm us up and give us some energy."

She looked over at him, his face glowing in the firelight. His elbows were perched on his knees as he stared into the wavering flames. If he was worried, he surely hid it well.

"Noah . . . we'll make it back tomorrow, right?"

He gave her a sideways glance. "It should take about eight hours to get back to the main road if we keep a good pace. And who knows? Maybe we'll get lucky and come across some hunters or something."

Her teeth chattered in the waning light. "Speaking of hunters . . . What kind of wildlife should I be worried about besides bears, which I now know are *not* hibernating?"

The corner of his lips turned up. "I got my rifle. You don't have to worry about the wildlife."

She surveyed him for a long moment, the full weight of their predicament hitting her. It was her fault they'd come out here to begin with. Her fault they were stuck without the snowmobile. If she was shivering and numb and miserable, it was her own fault. He surely didn't deserve any of this.

"I'm sorry I lost our gas can." She waited a long time for his reply.

"We'll get through it."

It wasn't the response she longed for, but it would have to do.

"Your feet are dry?" he asked.

"Yes."

"You warming up?"

Her toes were numb, and her fingers were stiff with cold. "I am. The fire feels divine."

Thank God for the rugged boots and coat. She supposed she had sensible Mary Beth to thank for that. She'd bet Noah wished he were with his girlfriend right now. It was probably driving the woman batty to know he'd gone off into the woods with his wife/ex-wife.

"I'm surprised Mary Beth didn't object to our little excursion today. She must be awfully understanding."

He poked at the fire with a stick. Sparks shot up into the sky, flickering out a ways up. The smell of burning wood consumed her senses.

"She's not my girlfriend." His low voice scraped the night air. He stared into the fire, quiet, his mouth pinched. Seemingly nothing more to add.

"But you said—"

"I never said anything." He lifted a shoulder. "You just assumed."

And he hadn't corrected her. Not once. She tried to be angry over the omission, but relief bubbled up instead.

*You stop that right now, Josephine. There's no reason to be relieved. Not a single one.*

"Well . . . rumors abound," she said.

"You can't believe everything you hear." He got up and started adding more wood to the fire. "We should probably turn in early. We have a long day ahead and need to get an early start."

Josephine made herself busy arranging the pine boughs over the frozen ground at the base of the incline. They would lie lengthwise, the hill on one side, the fire on the other. The snowbanks would provide extra wind blockage.

The body heat extra warmth.

Her heart gave an extra thump as she lowered herself onto the boughs, crossing her legs pretzel-style.

Noah finished up with the fire. Approaching, he held the backpack aloft. "Pillow, meet Josephine. Josephine, pillow."

"Sure beats nothing." Her heart flopped at the thought of curling up with Noah again. She told herself it was his warmth she sought. "How—how do you want to do this exactly?"

"Lie down. I'll climb in behind you."

She did as he said, facing the fire, which was burning a safe distance away. Her breath caught in her throat. She could hardly wait for his . . . warmth.

He climbed over her and lay down, stretching along her length, his knees tucked up behind hers. He settled the backpack under their heads and slipped one arm under her neck and the other over her waist.

"This okay?" His breath fanned her cheek.

"Y-yeah."

His warmth felt so delicious. Instinct relaxed her tense muscles. The crackling fire warming her front, Noah warming her back . . . It wasn't the worst position she'd ever been in.

"I'm blocking your heat," she said.

"I'm warm enough. Try to get some sleep."

Even when she was a big fat idiot he still put her needs first. He always had. How could a woman not fall for a man like that? And if she were honest she had to admit she *was* falling, bit by bit, all over again. As quickly and helplessly as she had the first time.

# Chapter 23

*Copper Creek*

*Three and a half years ago*

Noah never did ask her out on that second date. Instead, he took her to the hardware store to pick out trim . . . and it was late, so they ended up stopping by the diner on the way home. Then he insisted she check out the stain color of the wood floor in Ellijay's barbershop. And hey, there was a great coffee shop just down the street—had she ever been to the Martyn House?

By the time the renovations on her shop were completed, they'd been on no fewer than seven field trips and had spent hours working and talking and laughing.

But no more kissing. Which had Josephine a tad disappointed. No, not disappointed—befuddled. Yes, that's all it was.

As she wrote him the final check for his work, she couldn't deny the pinch in her throat or the worry twisting her insides. She'd only met him two months ago, but he'd grown on her.

She couldn't even imagine the next week without him at her side.

He had a way of looking at her. Not like other men did, exactly. Oh, she definitely sensed his attraction. It was assuredly mutual. But when she did silly things like get paint on her nose or trip over thin air or laugh like a hyena . . . The way he looked at her—like he just might adore her—stole her breath away.

Her last customer had long since gone for the night, and Noah stood beside her at the new counter. The smell of fresh paint and stain lingered in the air, mingling with the scents of her styling and shaving products.

She'd swept up as Noah had put on the finishing touches—filling nail holes on the new trim and replacing the electric plates. He was officially finished now. Not a single thing left to keep him around another minute.

She ripped the check from the ledger and handed it to him with a big smile. "Thank you, Noah. I'm very pleased with how everything came out."

He took the check and tucked it into his shirt pocket, his eyes never wavering from hers.

Her heart gave a little wobble at the intensity she saw there. "Everything?" he asked.

She held her smile steady. "Of—of course."

She was helpless against the pull of him. No man had ever had this effect on her. They hadn't even had a second date, and she was already half in love with him. The realization made her want to run upstairs and hide under her covers.

His gaze dropped to her lips, and she suddenly changed her mind. She didn't want to run. She wanted his kiss, and she wanted it more than her next breath.

He ran his knuckles along her cheek. Did he notice the shiver that ran through her? Her heart threatened to jump right out of her chest, and she pressed her fingers against it.

He lowered his head and brushed her lips in a kiss as soft and tender as the first one. Heaven knew she'd relived it in her mind often enough. She'd wondered if she'd built it up in her mind to such monumental proportions that another kiss couldn't possibly compare.

But nope. She surely hadn't. And she didn't think she could bear it if he ended it so quickly again.

She didn't have to fret, however. He cupped her jaw, slid his other hand around her waist, and brushed her lips again.

Every nerve ending came to life, buzzing, tingling, until she was lightheaded with the sensation. She slid her hands up the solid curves of his biceps and around his neck. He wasn't going anywhere. She was going to make sure of it.

He deepened the kiss and Josephine melted into him helplessly. She'd never waited so long for a man to kiss her—really kiss her. And the wait had only sharpened her need. Her fingers forked into his hair, finding it as thick and soft as she remembered.

He pulled her closer, his hand sliding to the back of her head. Heat flushed through her, making her burn. Making her legs go weak and her pulse skitter wildly in her chest.

A long, heady moment later he broke the kiss, setting his forehead against hers. Their raspy breaths mingled in the quietness of the shop.

"You make me lose my mind," he whispered into the gap between them.

She kept her eyes closed, trying to find some semblance of control. Impossible. She was as weak as a newborn kitten and twice as needy.

"Go out with me Friday," he said.

She breathed a laugh. Oh, the man knew what he was doing. How could she say no now? He'd just given her a tiny dose of his drug, and she was already addicted. Hopelessly addicted.

He eased away, tipping her chin, and she opened her eyes.

He held them for a long, steady moment. "Go out with me, Josie," he said, his voice as thick as honey.

His thumb slid along her jaw, stealing her breath, her common sense. She tried to dredge up the voice that told her she was just asking for trouble. But one look in his eyes, and the words scattered like pollen on a summer breeze.

And in its place something unfamiliar. Something beautiful and unexpected and dangerous.

Hope.

She swallowed hard against the knot in her throat. "All right."

That weekend Noah finally took her for that picnic. Afterward he saddled up two of the horses from Sweetbriar Ranch, and they rode through Pleasant Gap. It was beautiful land: tall grass, towering evergreens, and a rippling creek winding through it all.

He told her about working one summer on the ranch as a stable hand when the construction business was slow. She could tell he'd loved every minute of it.

They talked about his faith, and she told him about the white bus that picked her up for Sunday school when she was little, about asking Jesus into her heart. He listened carefully, and she had an inkling he heard more than she actually said.

It was her first time on a horse, and he was patient with her, going slowly, giving direction. They rode so long that she was saddle sore by the time they returned to the stables, and he chuckled as she limped to his truck.

She gave him a mock scowl and smacked his arm, but he only caught her hand and pressed a kiss to the palm. Her heart turned over in her chest at the look in his eyes. And she wondered how he stirred so much with just a look when other men only left her numb.

At her door he kissed her good night, and she was loath to let him go. Her heart pounding in her chest, she searched his eyes.

"Come upstairs for a drink." She pressed closer, already imagining the hard planes of his muscles under her fingertips.

He looked down at her with hungry eyes, a wry smile forming slowly on his lips. "You make it hard for a man to say no, Josie."

She gave him a lazy smile, her lashes fluttering. "Then don't."

Indecision flared in his eyes. A muscle in his jaw twitched, making shadows dance under the exterior light. His lips turned up in a gentle smile a moment before he eased away.

Josephine's chest tightened. She felt the sting of rejection.

"Come to church with me tomorrow."

She blinked. He was nothing if not unpredictable. "Church?"

"You'll like it. I promise."

He'd told her a bit about Faith Community today. He talked about his faith with such ease. It was an important part of his life, that much was obvious. It used to be important to her too. But that seemed so long ago. Almost like it had happened to somebody else.

He slipped his hands into his pants pockets. "What do you say? I'll pick you up at nine fifteen."

She was closed tomorrow. And she did want to spend more time with him. And maybe, some tiny voice inside whispered, going back to church would help.

"All right," she whispered, mainly because she seemed incapable of saying anything else when he looked at her that way.

He'd been right, she found the next morning, sitting with his family on a pew near the front. She did like his church. The people were friendly, the pastor down-to-earth, and the walls hadn't come crumbling down when she walked through the oversize wooden doors.

Noah began calling her every night, and she found herself looking forward to the calls. He made her laugh, made her feel wanted—more than just physically. He took her to the Rusty Nail on a regular basis, and they danced, moving together as if they were two halves of the same whole.

It was at the Rusty Nail that they ran into Pastor Jack.

Noah slipped his arm around her shoulders as Jack approached their booth. The men shook hands.

"Jack, meet Josephine Dupree. Josie, this is my good buddy, Jack. He pastors the Lutheran church down the street, but we Baptists try not to give him too much grief."

Josephine's face burned as she shook his hand. "Hello."

He gave her a nod and a smile that seemed strained. "Josephine."

She couldn't quite meet his eyes. She was certain her face turned a dozen shades of red at the memory of all her secrets. Her confessions, laid bare in the privacy of his office.

Discreet confessions, she reminded herself, smiling through her discomfort. Pastors were surely bound by confidentiality.

Weren't they?

Jack knew everything there was to know about her. Every dark, ugly sin she'd committed. The temporary relief she'd found through her confessions now seemed worthless in the face of what she stood to lose.

What if he told Noah what he knew? Noah would know what she was. That she was unworthy of him.

Worry welled up in her soul as the men caught up. She kept a smile plastered on her face as her mind spun. Perspiration broke out on the back of her neck, and she cupped it in the coolness of her palm.

Time dragged as they made small talk, and finally Jack wandered off to another table. Josephine tried to act normal, and if Noah noticed anything amiss he didn't say so. Later he gave her a long, heart-stopping kiss on her stoop and sent her inside with a sweet kiss to her forehead.

The next few days she waited for the other shoe to drop. She envisioned Pastor Jack calling Noah to warn him about her. She envisioned Noah showing up one night after closing, saying he needed to talk to her.

Each time he called, her stomach rolled, her fingers grew cold, and her knees weakened.

But nothing changed. Noah continued to call, and he took her out, and they talked and laughed until, little by little, he'd stolen every last bit of her heart.

The realization was altogether unpleasant, made her feel raw and vulnerable. Especially since he had yet to say the words she longed to hear.

A couple weeks after their run-in with Pastor Jack, they made their relationship exclusive. It gave her a measure of peace to know that the women whose heads turned when Noah walked by had no claim on him.

She shifted in the passenger seat on the way home from a restaurant in Ellijay late one Saturday evening. She reminded herself she had no reason to expect anything from him. He was just a man, like any other.

But, came a whisper from some corner of her mind, he had yet to take her up on her offer. He'd come up to her apartment on occasion . . . to watch a movie or eat a meal she'd fixed. But he never took things further than a passionate kiss. And after that first rejection, she hadn't put herself out there again.

He was a man of faith, a man of conviction. She admired that, even while the rejection left her feeling insecure and uncertain.

When he pulled into the diagonal slot in front of her shop, they unbuckled their belts. The truck idled quietly, and a country tune played softly on the radio. He didn't turn off the truck and get out as he usually did. Instead, he shifted toward her.

He lifted their hands, their fingers laced together, and placed a kiss on her knuckles. "I had a nice time, Josie. I always have a great time with you."

Her lips curved upward. "Likewise, Noah Mitchell."

The golden glow of the exterior light filtered through the cab, allowing her to see the look in his eyes as he leaned toward her. He nudged her chin up and swept her lips in a soft, sweet kiss, his eyes still open as if he couldn't bear to tear them away from hers for even a moment.

He pulled back, a whisper away, and drew his thumb along her cheek.

Her pulse fluttered at his reverent touch, making words scatter from her mind. Feelings, sensations were all that remained.

That and the musky, manly smell that wove around her like a net.

"I love you, Josie."

The rough texture of his voice rippled over her, the words causing a quake deep inside.

"I love you too," she said on a soft breath, the words flowing out of their own accord.

His lips tipped up an instant before they were on hers again. He kissed her longer this time, deeper, as if backing up the declaration. Sealing the deal. By the time he pulled away, she was gasping for air. But the feelings inside . . .

She was floating. She was melting. She suddenly understood every cliché she'd ever heard about love. The cynicism encasing her heart gave a loud, hard crack.

It didn't always have to end badly, did it? Love worked out for some people. Noah was different from the others. Maybe her past didn't matter. Maybe she could deserve him if she tried hard enough.

Noah dragged his thumb over her lips, his gaze finding hers again. The look in his eyes, on his face, stole her breath. It said *forever*, and the thought made hope bloom inside like the brightest, freshest spring flowers.

*He really loves me*, her heart whispered.

*You're just asking for it with that thought, Josephine Dupree.*

She took a breath, then another, trying to temper her expectations.

But another sweep of his thumb made her fears vanish like a dissipating vapor.

Later, when she lay in bed reviewing those moments over and over, she decided to banish the voice from her mind. Instead, she memorized the feel of his lips on hers, the sensation of his touch on her skin, the smoky sound of his voice as he professed his love.

And, if only because she needed it so desperately, she allowed herself to believe she was worthy of that love.

# Chapter 24

*North Georgia Mountains*

*Present day*

The first thing Noah noticed as he awakened was Josie's body curled into his. Her leg was tucked between his own, her face buried in his chest.

One of his arms was wrapped around her as if she were a life preserver, and his other lay beneath her, tingling. He became aware of other things then. His toes, numb, his fingers, stiff. Beyond Josie, orange ashes glowed, the remains of their fire.

As if sensing his wakefulness, Josie stirred. Her head tilted up until their eyes connected. He knew the moment she realized their position.

Her eyelashes fluttered down, and she stiffened. "Sorry," she muttered.

She pushed away, taking her warmth with her, then sat up, huddling against the cold. "What time is it?"

"About six thirty, I'd guess. Sleep okay?"

"Surprisingly, yes. You?"

He'd gotten up to replenish the fire three times and had trouble settling each time. "Yeah."

He got up and nursed the fire back to flame as Josie went into the woods. His stomach rumbled with emptiness. He filled the thermos's metal lid with the last of the coffee and set it in the glowing ashes. By the time they'd eaten the rest of the cereal, the coffee was warm.

The sun was peeking over the horizon as they set off on the service road. If they made good time they'd reach the main road around three or four this afternoon. He wasn't sure if Josie could keep that pace through the deep snow, however. The cold made his own muscles less than cooperative.

The road curved and wound, and a long uphill stretch a half hour into their walk left them both winded. He stopped halfway up so they could catch their breath.

He handed her a water bottle and sipped from his own. "Doing all right?"

"Yeah," she said, panting between gulps.

Her nose and cheeks were pink, the rest of her skin pale against the fur trim of the hood. Her teeth were chattering, and he was sure her hands and feet were colder than his—and his were plenty cold.

Their breaths fogged in the stillness of the morning. A squirrel nattered from a nearby branch, and high branches clacked together in the breeze. The fragrant smell of pine scented the air.

Noah assessed their position. The road turned sharply ahead. Across the wooded valley he could see where it doubled back, going downhill. They could save a lot of time, not to mention the uphill climb, if they cut across.

There was a fairly steep and long drop-off to the valley floor, but once there it would be an easy walk to the road.

"Feel like taking a shortcut down that hill?"

She followed his gaze across the valley. "You had me at 'downhill.' Can we get down in one piece?"

"We'll take it slow."

Noah took her arm as they started down the slope. He caught her each time she slipped. He lost his own footing a couple times.

"Too bad we don't have a sled," she said.

"That'd be a lot of fun until we ran headlong into one of these trees."

"There you go, throwing cold water on my bright ideas."

"Can we not talk about cold water right now?"

"Good point." She stepped over a log, Noah grasping her arm tightly. "Let's talk about hot things. Like campfires and hot cocoa."

"If we're talking beverages, I'll take a latte. Vanilla with an extra shot of espresso."

"A latte, huh?"

It was a recent addiction. "I'm secure in my masculinity."

"Well, since we're dreaming of hot and yummy, I'll add beef stew and toasted marshmallows and—"

"Stop, you're making me hungry. Let's stick to nonfood items."

"All right then. Electric blankets, hot baths, curling irons."

Noah held a branch out of her way. "Running engines."

"The sun."

"Hot tubs."

"Passionate kisses."

His eyes cut to hers as he lifted a brow.

"Well . . ." She hitched a shoulder. "You can't deny it."

Heaven knew they'd shared enough of those. They were like fire and gasoline when they came together—always had been. He hadn't experienced anything like it before Josie and surely not afterward. Just thinking about it had raised his temperature a few degrees already. At least something good came from it.

He reminded himself that Josie had probably had plenty of passionate kisses since they'd separated. All while they were still married, technically.

They grew quiet as they reached the valley floor, and Noah was fine with that. This thread of conversation was dangerous. After spending the night holding Josie in his arms, he was all too aware of what he was missing.

They followed the valley floor, trudging through the deep snow, skirting trees and fallen branches. A few minutes later they came to a creek he hadn't seen from the road. It was about twelve feet across, covered in snow, and lumpy with buried rocks.

He paused on the bank, but Josie kept going.

He grabbed her elbow just before she reached the edge. "Wait."

She searched his face. "It's got to be iced over, right?"

"Listen."

The brook bubbled quietly beneath the layer of snow and ice. "Too much movement. The ice'll be thin."

"Well, there are plenty of rocks. We can make it."

He looked both directions searching for a better place to cross, but they seemed to be at the narrowest point. The rocks would be slippery, and getting wet would be a disaster.

He turned around, looking behind him. The steep incline

they'd just descended seemed formidable from down here. They'd never make it back up. And even if they did, they'd face another uphill climb.

They'd be better off taking their chances with the creek.

"All right, let's go." He hitched his gun strap higher on one shoulder, the backpack on the other, and took her elbow.

They started off, wobbling here and there, using each other to catch their balance. The rocks were flat and close together near the shore. In the middle they were smaller, farther apart, and slippery.

When Josie stepped onto the next rock, her foot slipped. He tightened his grip on her elbow as his own foot slid on a rounded rock. Fearing he'd drag her down, he let go, trying to catch his balance.

Josie's arms flailed and she shrieked.

Tottering himself, he watched helplessly as her foot plunged through the snow. The brittle ice gave a loud *crack*, and her other foot followed with a splash.

"Josie!" Having caught his balance, he reached out and plucked her from the knee-deep water. He half carried, half dragged her across the rocks to the bank.

After brushing off a rock ledge he guided her down onto it. "Sit down."

"Oh my gosh. Oh my gosh. S-s-so cold!"

Kneeling in front of her, he pulled off her boots, peeled off her sopping-wet socks, his cold fingers fumbling.

He took off his gloves and tried warming her bare feet with his hands. But after a moment he realized they were too cold to do any good.

Sitting beside her, he pulled off his boots, removed his

socks, and put them on her, pulling them up over her calves. Her pant legs were wet up past her knees and already growing stiff with ice, but there was nothing he could do about that.

He had to get her feet warm. The icy water would cause a drop in her body temperature, and she'd already been awful cold. She was shaking uncontrollably, and the danger of hypothermia, not to mention frostbite, had just become very real.

"W-w-what are w-we going to do?"

He hated the fear in her voice, in her wide blue eyes.

He put his boots back on, then wrapped his hands around her stockinged toes. They had a long walk, but her boots were wet now. He could build another fire to dry everything out and warm her up a bit, but that would take hours and mean another night out here.

They had to keep moving, keep her blood circulating.

Mulling over their dilemma, he mentally reviewed their supplies. Then he opened the book bag and pulled out the two grocery bags she'd kept the snacks in.

"These should keep you dry." He slipped the bags on over her feet.

"W-what about you? I can't take your s-socks."

"My boots are good and warm—don't worry about me."

He wished he could soak up the excess water from the inside of her boots, but there was nothing to soak it up with. He slipped her boots back on her feet and prayed the plastic would keep her dry.

Josephine's feet no longer ached. In fact, she couldn't feel them at all. The cold air seemed to cut right through her clothing, making her shivering muscles tighten. Her frozen pant legs scraped together with each step.

The numbness in her toes made her uncoordinated, and she tripped over another rock, buried beneath the snow.

"Doing all right back there?" Noah called over his shoulder.

"Yeah."

It had surely been less than an hour since she'd plunged into the ice-cold water, but everything had changed. She could no longer control the shivering, and her balance was off.

She could tell Noah was trying to plow through the snow to make a path for her, but it didn't seem to matter. They'd been walking uphill for the past twenty minutes. Her lungs struggled to keep pace. A fine sheen of perspiration coated her skin, chilling her further.

Her foot hit something buried beneath the snow, and she tripped. She flung out her arms, but she was too late. Her knees stung with the impact, and a grunt escaped.

Noah was at her side in a heartbeat. He helped her to her feet, brushed away the snow, searching her eyes. A frown crouched between his brows. "You okay?"

Out of breath, she nodded.

"Need to stop and rest a bit?"

If she sat down she wouldn't be able to get back up. "No."

A moment later he resumed his position in front, and they carried on.

But she wasn't okay. The bags were leaking—the wetness from her boots seeping into the socks. Her limbs quaked, her muscles ached, and she couldn't seem to catch her breath. Would this hill never end?

She stopped. Just for moment. But Noah didn't notice, and she hadn't the breath to tell him. After a brief rest she trudged ahead, trying to catch up, but it was impossible. She stumbled over something in the road. Or maybe it was her own feet. But somehow she caught her balance and continued on.

They had hours to go. She was never going to make it. She didn't know how she was remaining on her feet as it was. The snow she plowed through seemed to weigh a thousand pounds, and her body begged for reprieve.

Noah looked over his shoulder. Josie had fallen behind. He slowed his pace. He hadn't liked what he'd seen when she'd stumbled. Her face was pale, her lips drained of color. It wasn't fear flickering in her eyes any longer, but resignation.

At a scuffling sound, he whipped around just as Josie hit the ground. He rushed back to where she lay on her stomach. Her elbows were the only thing keeping her face out of the snow.

He tried to help her up.

"No." She pushed his hands away.

"You're getting wet."

"This is too hard. I can't do this anymore." Her head sagged between her shoulders, her torso rising and falling with her shallow breaths. She looked as if she were ready to lie there and give up.

Not on his watch. He reached down and lifted her out of the snow, setting her on her feet. When she wavered he tightened his grip around her waist.

"Go on, Noah . . . Just go on without me."

"I'm not leaving you. Come on, I'll help you."

Before he could take a step, she shrugged him off.

"I can't!" Her eyes filled with tears. "I just can't."

He hated the surrender in her eyes. Hated the way her body quaked with cold. And hated most of all how helpless it made him feel.

"You go on." She looked ready to drop on the spot. "Go for help. I'll w-wait here. I'll be fine."

He was shaking his head before she even finished. Having grown up in the mountains, he knew the rules. Splitting up was a bad idea. Something could happen to the person who went for help, leaving the other person stranded. And the one left behind often suffered from despair and mental fatigue from being alone and bereft. They gave up hope.

Josie wasn't a quitter, and she wasn't a complainer. If she said she couldn't go on, she really couldn't.

So he couldn't either. "All right. We'll stop and rest awhile. I'll build a fire, and we'll get you warmed up and dried off." They could still make it back today. Maybe not before dark, but they had a flashlight. Maybe someone would even see the smoke from their fire and come to investigate.

But when they'd settled at the base of some nearby boulders, and he removed her boots, fear clawed at his throat. The plastic bags had leaked, leaving her feet wet and frigid.

# Chapter 25

*Copper Creek*

*About three years ago*

Noah had never believed in love at first sight, but his experience with Josie made him a believer. It had been all he could do to wait three months before professing his love to her.

In the two months since, he'd been on cloud nine. Having Josie in his life . . . There weren't words to describe how it had changed him. He thought of her every hour of every day. He couldn't wait to see her again. Couldn't wait to touch her, to kiss her, to hold her in his arms. But even that wasn't enough.

He was caulking one of the new windows he'd installed at the Willoughbys' house when the realization struck with the force of a lightning bolt. The caulk gun slipped from his hands, hitting the windowsill before thunking onto the carpet.

He wanted to marry her. It wasn't as if the idea hadn't occurred to him before—it occurred every time he went home alone after one of their dates.

But this was a *knowing*. A knowing deep in his soul that this was right. And an urgency. What was he waiting for? He loved her. She loved him. He wanted nothing more than to start their life together.

He hummed with energy. His hands shook with adrenaline. He couldn't finish this job right now. It was Saturday anyway, and the Willoughbys would be out of town for another week. He wiped his fingers on his rag and picked up the caulk gun.

He had to tell someone. His family seemed lukewarm toward Josie, at best. Besides, his parents were helping friends move into their new house today, and his brother was on a roof.

But he knew just where to find his buddy Jack.

Noah stopped in front of Jack's closed office door. He tried to calm his racing heart. He'd always thought the heavy wooden door looked like it belonged on some ancient antechamber. It had cast iron straps and an open rectangular window filled with black filigreed scrolling. The builder in him appreciated the quality hardwood and detailing absent from today's construction.

Feeling giddy with his new decision, he sidled up to the door, out of Jack's sight. "Bless me, Father, for I have sinned."

He heard a heavy sigh from beyond the metal scrollwork. "Come in, Noah."

"Isn't this supposed to be anonymous?"

"As you know, Lutherans don't practice confession. Are you going to come in or are we going to talk through the door?"

Noah opened the door, appreciating the weight and solidness of it even as his eyes fell on Jack, sitting behind his tidy desk.

Jack folded his arms on his paperwork, frowning. "I realize

you're somewhat ignorant of the practices of various denominations, and though we don't practice it in our own, private confession is a serious matter in the Catholic church, and as such—"

Noah threw up his hands. "Oh, for pity's sake, don't start. I didn't mean to make light. I'm just feeling a little crazy right now, and that door has always reminded me of a confessional. Even though I've never actually been to one. Anyway . . . I had to talk to someone, and you're it. Am I interrupting anything?"

Jack sighed. "Just my sermon preparation, but go on. I can see you're about to bust."

"I'm going to ask Josie to marry me." The words gushed out like water over a fall. Saying them out loud felt even better than thinking them. He knew he had a big, goofy smile on his face, and he didn't care.

He had plans to make. A ring to buy. He didn't even know her size. Or how he'd ask her. It had to be perfect. He cleared his thoughts long enough to realize his friend had yet to respond.

Jack's face was inscrutable.

"Well?" Noah said. "Aren't you going to say something?"

Jack gave him a tight smile. "Why don't you sit down?"

"Okay . . ." He settled in one of the padded chairs opposite the ornate desk and planted his elbows on his knees.

Jack clasped his hands. "This is awfully fast, isn't it? How long have the two of you been dating? A few months?"

"Five, to be exact. But sometimes you just know. I don't expect you to understand."

Jack bristled. "Why's that? Because ministers are somehow incapable of romantic feelings?"

"Nooo . . . because you've never been in love."

"What's the hurry? If God ordains, you'll still love her six months or even a year from now."

"But that's just it. If we know now, why wait? I'm ready to get started on the next phase of my life. Besides, I'm trying to be a gentleman here, and I'm running out of willpower, if you know what I mean. Better to marry than to burn with passion and all that."

Jack tugged at his collar. "What do you know of her spiritual life, Noah?"

"I know she made a profession of faith as a child, and I know she attends church with me every Sunday."

"There are a lot of years in between. What of her fruit? Tell me what fruit you see in her life."

Noah's neck muscles tightened. "I've never known you to be judgmental, Jack."

"It's a legitimate question. The Scriptures say, 'You will know them by their fruits.'"

Noah thought of Josie's heart for people. The way she'd responded when she found out about the Hope House. She'd already offered free haircuts to the girls there, and he knew she could scarcely afford to give her services away.

But he wasn't going to sit here and defend Josie to Jack. "What have you got against her? She's been nothing but kind to everyone in town."

Jack's eyes flittered away, and he tugged at his collar again. Noah remembered the early rumors about Josie when she'd come to town.

"Don't tell me you're buying into rumors these days."

"Don't be insulting."

He looked Jack over, noting his dark good looks, his short, neat haircut. Half the single ladies in his congregation had a crush on him. An unwelcome thought surfaced. One that made jealousy spring up like a thorny weed in a flower garden.

"Did she come on to you, is that it? I admit she can be a little flirtatious, but she doesn't mean—"

Jack waved a hand. "No, no, it's not that."

A quiet breath tumbled from his lips. Noah didn't want to admit, even to himself, how quickly he'd jumped onto that thought.

But Jack still wouldn't meet his eyes. The struggle was there on his face in his tightened eyes, his furrowed brow.

"What then?"

"I can't say."

"But you know something." Noah continued to search his friend's face.

Jack's eyes finally met his, something surfacing there even as his lips pressed together.

Noah tipped his head back as light dawned. "She's counseled with you."

He saw the admission in Jack's eyes. "You know I can't talk about that."

"But it's true, isn't it?"

Jack stared back, resolutely silent.

"Well, that only proves she's trying to do better, for crying out loud. Whatever she's done that's got you all heated up, she obviously regrets it." Noah gave him a pointed look. "And she's trying to work it out—isn't that the whole point of counseling, Jack?"

The longer his friend stared silently back, the more agitated Noah became. Sometimes Jack thought his bachelor's in psychology made him the premier font of wisdom.

"You know what? I don't care. I don't care about any of that. It's in the past. You may know what she's done, but I know *her*. You don't. She may come across as cynical and a little . . . provocative, but she's got a soft heart, a good heart."

Noah's skin tingled as sweat broke out on the back of his neck. He didn't know what Jack's problem was, but he rejected it. Whatever it was.

"How long have you known me, Noah?"

"I know you mean well. But you're wrong about her."

"I just want the best for you. What would it hurt to slow down a little?"

"Slow down a little, or put an end to my relationship with her?"

The truth flickered in Jack's eyes before he lowered them.

"Yeah, that's what I thought." Noah slapped the chair's arms with his palms and stood. "Thanks for the support, man."

"Noah, come on."

He strode out of Jack's office, wanting out of there more than he could say. A moment later he gave the exterior door a hard shove and walked into the sun's bright light.

He loved Josie, and she loved him. Anything else they could work out together.

Noah had been acting strangely all night. He'd been unusually quiet through supper. The Blue Moon Grill was on the outskirts of town, adjacent to Copper Creek. It had become one of their favorite spots, not only for the delicious food, but for the moonlit strolls on the walkway afterward.

Josephine had kept the conversation rolling through supper,

mostly talking about her week at the barbershop, filling the gap with little anecdotes meant to make him smile.

But he hardly seemed to be listening. He fidgeted with his collar, his eyes never focused too long on one spot. By the time they finished eating, a terrible dread had seeped into her blood.

He'd gone to supper with Pastor Jack this week. Whenever they spent time alone together Josephine worried. What if Jack had told Noah about her past?

Judging by the tense silence that hovered over their table, she was afraid that her worst fears had finally come true.

Noah took the bill folder from the server and pocketed his credit card. He gave her a strained smile. "Take a walk?"

Her smile trembled on her lips. "Sure."

This was it. This was where he was going to break up with her. Out on the walkway or on the bench in front of the covered bridge where they'd spent so many happy hours talking.

Her legs wobbled as they stepped into the chilly night. He shrugged out of his jacket and slipped it over her shoulders. Always the gentleman.

The still November air was laden with the smells of pine and burning wood. The moon had risen, and it hung over the water like a big white balloon. But she couldn't appreciate its beauty. All she could do was try to breathe past the hard stone lodged in her throat.

She had to get ready. Buck up. She was a survivor. She'd suffered through much worse than this.

But suddenly losing Noah seemed like the worse thing that could ever happen. She'd come to love him more than she'd ever loved anyone. Had come to depend on him.

*You're so stupid, Josephine! You knew better than this.*

She already felt the impact of his rejection like a sucker

punch to the stomach. Her chest constricted, making her heart ache. Making her ache all over.

He took her hand when they reached the walkway that led beside the rippling creek. He was going to break it to her easy. Of course he would. She'd nod and tell him it was all right. Easy come, easy go. He didn't have to know about the vise tightening around her heart or the white dots speckling her vision.

His hand was clammy. He was nervous. Of course he was. He was a nice guy, and he'd take no joy in hurting her.

Could he tell her own hands were cold, despite the rather mild evening temperature? Or that she trembled like the last withering leaf on a dead oak tree? Suddenly she just wanted to get it over with. So she could go home, shut her door, and curl up in a quiet corner.

"You're awful quiet tonight," she said.

She felt his perusal. "I'm sorry. I guess I'm just preoccupied. And a little nervous."

*Here it is, Josephine. Get ready.*

She made a futile attempt to slow her breathing, settle her heart rate as they neared the covered bridge.

Noah suddenly stopped and turned to her. There was a look on his face she hadn't seen before. So serious, his eyes blinking rapidly. He jabbed his free hand into his pants pocket.

Josephine fought the urge to pull her hand from his. To wrap her arms around herself.

"You know how I feel about you, Josie . . ."

She pasted a smile on her lips, her spine rigid straight. *Easy come, easy go.* "Of course."

He dropped to the ground. And for a moment she thought he'd dropped something. But then he looked up at her. The moonlight caught the amber flecks in his eyes, and they flashed like fire.

He dropped her hand, pulled something from his pocket. And then she was staring at a diamond that winked in the moonlight.

She sucked in a breath, her fingertips covering her mouth. Her heart beat erratically in her chest.

"I love you, baby girl." Noah's voice was warm and liquid. "I've loved you since the first moment I saw you, and my feelings have only grown with every moment we've spent together. I want nothing more than to spend the rest of my life with you. Make me the happiest man alive and tell me yes, Josie."

Her eyes burned with tears, and the knot in her throat grew even as it softened. "Oh, Noah."

"I know it's quick. If you want to wait awhile or have a long engagement, I'll understand. Whatever you want."

Wait? After the dread building inside her the past hour, she wanted a wedding band on her finger yesterday. "I don't want to wait. I want to marry you and soon."

A smile curled on his lips, making his eyes crinkle at the corners.

"Are you going to put that ring on my finger or what, Noah Mitchell?"

He fumbled with the box, both of them laughing at his clumsiness, then he slid the ring into place and stood, drawing her into his arms.

She swallowed against the lump in her throat, dizzy and shaking from the emotional U-turn she'd taken in the last minute.

She slipped her hands up his chest, admiring the ring there on her finger. "I love it. It's so beautiful."

He tipped her chin up. "*You're* beautiful, Josie. Inside and out."

It was the inside that worried her. She wondered suddenly what his family was going to say about this. What Jack was going to say. But she managed to smother the glimmer of fear as Noah lowered his head and placed a soft kiss on her lips.

As it turned out, his family took the news pretty well. His mother was nothing but kind, offering to take her shopping for a dress and lending a hand with the wedding preparations. His father was supportive and said all the right things. They threw a small engagement party and tried to make Josephine feel like part of the family. Jack, too, wore a smile as he served as best man during their simple Christmas ceremony.

A feeling of relief swamped Josephine once that wedding band was on her finger. Following a short honeymoon in Savannah, they began house hunting and settled into a darling little cottage on Katydid Lane. Josephine loved the kitchen with its white beadboard walls and old farm sink.

They cuddled in front of the fire on cold winter evenings, and when spring arrived, Noah tried to teach Josephine how to garden. It soon became obvious she had no talent for growing things, but instead of getting cross with her, he swatted her rear end and told her to just keep the iced tea coming.

She was happy in those early days. All except for that little voice in the back of her mind. The one that warned that the other shoe was about to drop. No matter how much she tried, she couldn't quite drown it out.

# Chapter 26

*North Georgia Mountains*

*Present day*

Josephine hugged her knees on the bed of pine boughs while Noah gathered wood for a fire. He returned from the nearby copse of trees, his arms loaded with more logs.

"Doing all right?" he asked.

"Sure." But the truth was, she still couldn't feel her toes, and she was cold to the bone. The perspiration from their hike had left her skin chilled. She couldn't wait to feel the warmth of the fire.

"You're going to have to move back when I light this. If you're not careful you'll burn your skin and not even feel it."

He dumped the branches on a nearby ridge.

That was a lot of wood. Was he expecting to spend the entire day out here? Surely not another night. She didn't know how she'd make it another night.

"That's a lot of w-wood."

His eyes glanced off hers as he began stacking the logs. "I'm making a signal fire. Once it's going, I'll put some green wood on so it'll burn black. Then I'm going to fire off a few rounds. Hopefully that'll draw someone's attention."

She should've known he'd have a plan. Hope flooded through her veins. Maybe they'd be back to Noah's place in a matter of hours.

"Do you suppose it'll work?"

"I'm saying my prayers."

While Noah broke up the branches, Josephine loosened the ties on her boots and set them near the logs to dry with both pairs of socks. Surely it would take hours to dry them out. She whispered a prayer for rescue even though she was sure her plea didn't make it past the treetops.

Once the wood was arranged into a tepee shape, Noah dug in the book bag for the lighter. He peeled the paper from the peanut can, made a wick of it, then pushed the lighter button.

It clicked but produced no flame.

He tried again. After it failed to light a third and fourth time, the corners of his mouth tightened.

"What's wrong with it?" she asked.

He said nothing as he blew on the lighter tip and gave it a few more unproductive tries.

Josephine's sluggish heart pumped faster. If he couldn't get that thing working there'd be no signal fire. No one would know they were here. There'd be no way to warm themselves or dry anything. A niggle of fear wormed through her.

He blew on the top of the lighter and tried again. Nothing. After a few more tries, Noah sat back on his heels, staring silently into the cold fire pit.

"Noah?"

"The bottom of the bag got wet back at the creek."

"Maybe it'll dry out."

"Maybe." He blew on the tip one more time and gave it another try, to no avail. "In the meantime, I think I'll go ahead and fire off those shots."

"But they'll only echo off the hills, won't they? No one will be able to tell where they came from."

"I have six rounds. If we get a fire going later, I'll shoot the last three then."

"Maybe Mary Beth will hear it. D-didn't you leave your phone charging at her place? She must be wondering where you are."

"She didn't have power either, so I didn't leave my phone."

"Oh."

Would anyone notice the gunshots when nobody even knew they were missing?

Was this really their best chance? She'd never make it the rest of the way back. But Noah could. It would be miserable being out here all by her lonesome, freezing, and it would be infinitely worse if he didn't make it back by dark.

Still, she made herself say the words. "Noah . . . maybe you should just g-go for help."

He chucked the lighter and grabbed his gun where it leaned against a tree. "I told you I'm not leaving you out here."

"But—"

"Let's just sit tight and hope someone takes note of the shots. It's our best bet."

Noah had never been so afraid. He'd had moments in his life. What man didn't? A thumb almost caught in a jigsaw. An o'dark hundred phone call from his distraught mom. A ladder tipping precariously while his dad clung to the eaves.

But this.

He was sitting behind Josie, both arms wrapped around her. Her weight sank into his chest, and her whole body shook with tremors even though she'd fallen asleep a long time ago.

The sight of her feet had sent a shiver of apprehension down his spine. They were red and swollen, and she'd lost all feeling. There was no way she could walk for miles. He'd put his dry boots on her and covered his own with the dry neck of his socks. They stung from the cold air, but he was faring better than Josie.

His palms stung too. He'd spent hours trying to spark a flame using the only tools at his disposal. He'd "drilled" a hole in a dead tree stump with his blade and found a dry stick. After making a nest of dry wood slivers and lint he'd scraped from his jeans pockets, he'd set to work. After placing the stick's end into the hole, he rolled the stick rapidly back and forth, producing friction. He'd come close a couple times, had made plenty of smoke, but he couldn't quite get the nest to catch flame.

A few hours had passed since then, and as evening drew closer his hopes were fading. Josie had been right about the gunshots. They'd echoed off the hills. Even if the sound had attracted attention, no one would know where to look. They might even assume someone was just hunting.

He'd tried the lighter periodically, but it still wasn't working. He picked it up again, palming it, and looked heavenward for a long, heartfelt moment.

*God, we need Your help. I can't do this alone. We need a fire, and we need it bad.*

He looked down at Josie, where she rested on his shoulder. Her delicate eyelashes swept the pale skin of her face. Her lips, bleached of color before, now had a bluish tint.

The trickle of fear seeped into his blood, spreading rapidly. He didn't know how long she'd last out here without a fire. She'd gone downhill so fast after getting wet.

*Please, God. For Josie's sake.* He blew on the lighter's top and gave the switch a flick.

Nothing.

Frustration poured through his veins. He had to do something. He couldn't just sit here, waiting around for help that may never come. Even though he knew better, he considered starting off on his own. Without a fire, did they even stand a chance of being found?

There were still the snowmobile tracks. They'd be gone once the plows came through, but at that point Mary Beth would go to his ranch to check on her horse. She'd see they hadn't been fed or tended to. That he wasn't there, though his truck was. She might notice the missing snowmobile and come looking.

His brother would worry too, when he couldn't reach Noah. Once the roads were plowed, Seth would come check on him. The question was, how long would all that take?

Josie stirred in his arms, and she tipped her head back, looking at him. "Is the c-cavalry here yet?"

"Not yet, but my fingers are crossed." Or they would be if he could feel them.

She sat up a bit, stretching, her teeth clacking together. She caught sight of the lighter, still clenched in his hand. "Still not working?"

"Afraid not."

He handed her the last water bottle. "We need to stay hydrated."

She looked around the white landscape. "Water's one thing we have aplenty."

That might be true, but eating snow would cause their body temperatures to drop further. He hoped there was a stream nearby. It would be cold, but it was better than snow.

She took a long drink, then handed the bottle back to him. "I'd trade all my worldly possessions for a warm b-bath right now."

"I know what you mean. How are you feeling?"

Her coat swished as she crossed her arms. "Seems colder today, doesn't it?"

Were her words a little slurred? She'd already exhibited signs of imbalance, and her skin had taken on a gray tint. He feared she was already mildly hypothermic.

"I think it just feels that way." He unzipped his coat. "Lean back. Let's try and get you warmed up a bit."

She sagged against him, and he wrapped his coat around her, followed by his arms.

"That feels good," she said softly.

He tucked her under his chin. He couldn't deny it. Having Josie close felt good for all kinds of reasons.

"Think anyone'll come?"

Definitely slurring. He hunched his body over hers, hugged her legs tightly with his own. "There's a good chance. Seth will worry when he doesn't hear from me. Mary Beth'll come to check on the horses."

"Didja say your prayers?"

"Of course. Did you?"

"Mmmm. He's more likely to answer yours though."

It wasn't the first time she'd said such a thing. "Why do you say things like that? God loves you as much as He loves me."

"He's never really answered mine."

"Sure He has. He doesn't always say yes, that's all."

He waited for a reply, but she only let out a long, slow breath.

Overhead the barren branches knocked together in the breeze, and a couple of squirrels nattered somewhere nearby. The air smelled of cold and pine, and he detected a hint of his shampoo on Josie's hair.

A distant honking sound echoed through the air, growing louder. Noah looked overhead as a flock of geese passed in their V-shape formation. He sure wished he and Josie could fly out of here.

"Lucky ducks," Josie said.

He set his chin on her head, seeking her warmth, as he closed his eyes and whispered another prayer. This one was longer and more specific. He prayed for his brother to grow alarmed at his absence and for Mary Beth to check on her horse sooner than later. He prayed for supernatural warmth for Josie, who was too apathetic for his liking. And fire. He prayed for fire.

"Remember what I told you before?" Josie said softly.

His eyes opened, and his stubble scraped against her nylon hood as he set his cheek against her head. "About what?"

"About, you know . . . losing my virginity at twelve?"

His stomach tightened. A man wasn't likely to forget such a thing. But he wasn't sure he wanted to hear this. "We don't have to talk about that right now." Or ever again. Some images were best forgotten.

"Thing is, Noah . . . I wasn't exactly forthcoming before. When it happened, I-I wasn't exactly a willing participant."

A heavy feeling settled in his stomach even as his muscles tightened. "You were raped?" He stilled, waiting for an answer that was slow in coming.

"My s-stepdad . . . Eddie? He lost me in a poker game."

The words hit him in waves, each one bringing its own distinct emotion. Shock, sympathy, anger. Her matter-of-fact tone only upset him more. He pushed back the anger and tried to focus on Josie.

His arms tightened around her. "Oh, honey. Why didn't you ever tell me?"

"I was . . . ashamed, I guess."

His heart broke for her. For the little girl who'd been at some man's mercy. For the woman who still believed she was to blame.

"It wasn't your fault. You were just a child."

"It-it happened more than once. His name was Shark—that's what they called him anyway. He'd come in late at night and—"

"Shhh. It's okay." He didn't want to know. Already he wanted to hunt the man down and pummel him. Her stepfather, too, except he was already dead.

"G-guys used me, and after a while . . . I just decided to start using them right back."

Her words sank in, making sense in a way he hated. He'd known she'd been promiscuous. Even if he hadn't paid mind to the rumors about her life in Cartersville, he couldn't have missed the fact that his wife had been very accomplished in the bedroom.

He'd tried not to think too much about it. But now she'd shed a whole new light on it.

They sat in silence for a minute. Then five.

Noah couldn't get it out of his head. His heart was thumping a hundred miles an hour, and his breathing had grown shallow. He had so much adrenaline flooding through his veins he couldn't sit still another minute.

He loosened his hold on her. "I'm going to go find a stream and fill up our water bottles, okay?"

Josie turned, a flicker of alarm on her face.

"I'll be back soon, I promise. I think I heard running water when I was gathering branches. I'm going to need my boots back for a while though."

She leaned forward and began working the laces.

After watching her struggle a moment, he helped remove the boots and put the dry part of his socks on her feet, leaving the wet ends to hang off.

As worried as he was about frostbite, he was even more worried about her core temperature.

He shoved his feet into his boots, then shrugged out of his coat.

"What are you doing? You need that."

"I'll stay warm enough hiking, getting my blood circulating." He squatted down, wrapping it around her, arms and all. Then he zipped it up.

He pulled the hood up over her own and tightened the drawstrings, his fingers clumsy with cold. He took in her grayish pallor and trembling lips. Fear leached deep into his bones.

*Soon, Jesus. Before dark. Please.*

After he finished the tie he dredged up a smile. "Prettiest Eskimo I've ever seen."

It didn't even draw a smile. "Hurry b-back."

He grabbed the backpack and set off into the woods, Josie's admission echoing in his head. The emotions that had been roiling inside revealed themselves in the quickness of his footsteps, in the clenching of his muscles. He wanted to slam his fist into the nearest tree trunk. But he couldn't afford an injury. He had to think about survival now. His and Josie's.

Even so, he shook with excess energy. He thought of Josie's stepfather and couldn't imagine what kind of man wagered a young girl's body in a poker game.

He paced in place, a scream building inside him, one he couldn't release. So he stuffed it down with all the feelings. He remembered that the event had happened more than once and thought of the little girl. That helpless little girl.

He looked up into the heavens, past the snow-laden branches to the gray abyss, eyes burning. He swallowed against the knot in his throat, and his stomach turned.

*God!*

His prayer started and ended there. He wanted to weep for that little girl. She was still there inside Josie. He saw it now. In her guardedness. In her provocative nature. In her cynicism.

Why was she telling him this now? When there was nothing he could do? When she wasn't even his to protect? She'd held it close through their relationship when they'd shared an intimacy he'd only dreamed of. Why now?

The answer sprang up like the first spring crocus through the snow. She told him now because she had nothing to lose. Because she didn't think they'd be rescued.

She was giving up.

But he wasn't going to let her. He looked back where he'd come from, taking a step that direction. But no. They needed water.

He needed to remember his military training. Improvise. Adapt. Overcome. He hadn't survived a tour in Afghanistan to die on a mountain only miles from home.

He forced himself to take slow, even breaths so he could listen for the sound of running water. The wind cut through the branches, rubbing them together. They creaked as they swayed. A bird chattered from a nearby tree.

And then, in the background, he heard it. A faint rippling sound. He followed it, going another hundred yards down a hill, and found a trickling stream. He cleared the snow and ice, using the helmet visor. Then he pulled off his gloves and filled the bottles, careful to stay dry.

His hands were shaking, though with cold or some other emotion he wasn't sure. When he got back he was going to get Josie hydrated, then he was going to convince her help was on the way and work on another fire. He couldn't let her lose hope and give up. Despair was an enemy as dangerous as the cold.

# Chapter 27

*J*osie watched Noah rotating the stick between his palms, producing a *tch-tch-tch-tch* sound as it rubbed inside the stump's hole. A frown of concentration bunched his brows. He'd been at it for at least a couple hours. She didn't know where he got his patience.

He'd refused to take his coat back, and amazingly enough, his forehead was beaded with perspiration. He'd whittled more kindling from a dry stick he'd found beneath a rock overhang. His little nest remained hopelessly cold, though he'd managed a bit of smoke.

The *tch*-ing stopped as Noah paused to wipe the sweat from his forehead with the back of his hand.

She caught sight of his bare palm, red and raw. "Noah . . . your hands."

He spared her a glance. "I'm all right."

He wasn't all right. Neither of them was. But he wore that look of determination he'd had since he'd returned with water. He had insisted she drink a whole bottle and had broken out the last of the peanuts. It hadn't been near enough. Her stomach was already growling again. But that was the least of her worries.

He started again with the stick. Those palms needed tending to, though he was too mulish to admit it.

She changed tactics. "C-can you take a rest at least and come warm me up?"

He looked at her for a long moment, his eyes inscrutable. Then he set down his tools. "Yeah, sure." He tried the lighter a couple times, and when it didn't work, he set it on the lightweight nest of kindling so it'd stay put.

Stretching, he looked at the sky, his lips tightening.

"What time do you think it is?"

He rubbed his chin. "Probably around four or five. I'm going to go ahead and fire off those shots."

He didn't have to say what he was thinking. As much as he'd wanted a signal fire first, they needed someone to find them before dark.

Josie held her ears as he cracked off three shots, a steady distance apart. He paused afterward, staring off into the distance, probably breathing a heartfelt prayer.

"Someone'll notice," he said as he set the gun down. "Three shots earlier, three again now. It's clearly a signal."

"Come warm me up."

He regarded her closely as he approached. "Why don't we get you up first?" He began trading his boots for the socks on her feet. "You should walk around, get your blood circulating a bit."

"I'll t-try."

As he put his gloves back on, Josephine caught sight of his raw palms again.

"You should put something on your hands. There's some kind of cream in that kit."

"They'll be fine."

He squatted down, unzipped the coat he'd wrapped around her, and began directing her arms into the sleeves.

She pulled away. "No, you need it."

"Not right now. All that work kept me plenty warm. Look, I'm sweating."

She gave in. She was too tired to fight. Her movements were slow and clumsy even with his help, and she wondered if her legs would support her.

"Ready?" At her nod he took her hands and tugged her up. "Upsy-daisy."

Her muscles locked up under her weight, and her legs buckled.

"Whoa." He caught her around the waist, holding her until she steadied, his warm breath on her temple. "If you wanted to cuddle you should've just said so."

She breathed a laugh.

"I can't walk with you." He was only wearing socks and standing on the pine boughs to stay dry.

"I can do it."

He slowly released her, allowing her to adjust to her own weight. She took a step, and pain shot up her leg, making her waver. She bit back a groan and forced herself to take another. Walking hurt. It hurt like the dickens. Her feet were hardly working either. They felt like blocks of bloated wood. Her legs threatened to give out, and to top it all off, her head was spinning.

Five steps away she stopped. "I-I think I need to sit down."

Noah reached for her as she limped back to the bed of pine boughs. "What's hurting?"

*What isn't?* The worry on his face, however, tempered her

response. "I'm just a little lightheaded, that's all. I'll try again later."

He helped her down and settled behind her, wrapping his heat around her. The weight of his chin on her head comforted her.

She gazed out at the snowy landscape. At the clouds gathering on the horizon. "The sun will be setting soon."

They'd have no firelight tonight. No extra warmth. She could almost feel her body shutting down, inch by inch. She was already shaking uncontrollably.

"We'll be all right. I'll cut more boughs and make a snow shelter. The roads are probably cleared by now. Between the gunshots, my brother, and Mary Beth, someone'll come looking. Maybe even before dark."

She thought of something to say about that. Something about the snowmobile tracks, but the thought was gone before it could take shape. That was happening a lot.

Noah talked a long time. About his family, about the ranch, about his childhood. She listened, loving the deep hum of his voice against her back. The warmth of his arms around her. His musky cologne was long gone, leaving only the manly scent that was all Noah.

She turned her face into his arm. *This isn't such a bad way to go.*

Her eyes opened. She was in danger of freezing to death. He didn't have to tell her that. Her body was saying plenty. And clearly her mind was messing with her.

"Josie?"

She noticed belatedly that he'd gone quiet. Noticed also that the sky had gotten a fraction darker.

"Mmm?"

"How are you feeling? Is there anything I can do?"

"You're doing all you can, Noah."

He adjusted his coat around her, tightening his arms. "Help is on the way. I'm sure of it. They'll find us."

She wished she had his optimism. All she could think of was the long cold night ahead. Dread settled over her like an icy cape. She looked up into the darkening sky and thought of God. Thought of Noah's fervent prayers. Of her own, when she'd been a child. When she'd believed.

She still did. She just felt . . . unworthy, she supposed. Unworthy of God's attention. Of His love. With so many faithful people like Noah, why would He waste time on her?

And yet, here they were: Noah and Josephine, suffering the same experience. She deserved it, no doubt, but Noah didn't.

She didn't understand God. Didn't understand Him one bit.

"What are you thinking about?" The rough texture of Noah's voice scraped pleasantly over her.

"Hmm. God mostly."

"What about Him?"

"Do you think He's here? Right now?"

"Of course. He's omnipresent."

She'd thought of that many times. It made her think of the small dark room in that trailer. Of the little girl, desperate for help. She pushed the image into a dusty corner of her mind.

"If He loves us, why doesn't He help us?"

"He will. One way or another."

"What does that mean?" She didn't want a puzzle. Her brain was in no shape to piece it together. She wanted an answer to the question she'd struggled with all her adult life.

"Remember how much I loved my Grandma Mitchell?"

"The one I favor?"

"Yeah. I think I told you she died of pancreatic cancer."

"Uh-huh."

"I was twelve. I prayed and prayed for God to heal her. But she just got worse. The doctors stopped treatment, and she continued to go downhill, but still I prayed, and I believed too. One day I was visiting her, and she was barely coherent. I told her she was going to be healed because I was praying she would be."

He tipped his head down until his chin scraped her temple. "She said He'd heal her one way or another. I didn't understand what she meant until I was sitting at her funeral a week later. She was in heaven, whole and healthy. It wasn't what I wanted. And then I got to thinking about it. I'd wanted a miracle, and I felt cheated because I didn't get one. But which is more miraculous—healing a body here on earth, or taking that earthly soul and giving it a new body, an eternal body?"

Josephine understood what he was saying. Still. "But she suffered. If He loved her, why'd He let that happen?"

"She did suffer, and I hated it. But whatever God's reasons are for the things He allows, His love for me, or for Granny or anyone else, isn't something I question. He settled that one on the cross."

Josephine thought of everything she'd done. All the men she'd used. What she'd done to Noah. Unforgiveable. Shame crawled over her like a thousand ants over a morsel of food.

"He loves you, Josie. Don't ever doubt that. He's been with you all these years. He knows what happened to you. Your stepdad and that monster who did that to you won't get by unscathed. He cares about you. You just have to decide to believe it."

She didn't know what to say about that. She'd dealt with some of this in counseling. Her feelings of unworthiness. Maybe it was as simple as he said. A decision.

She was going to believe it. Maybe it didn't all make sense to her—how God could love someone like her. Or why He allowed some of the things that happened. Maybe she didn't have to understand everything.

She closed her eyes. *I'm just going to go ahead and believe, if that's all right by You, God.*

Somewhere deep inside, the brittle shell around her heart gave another hard crack. Peace settled around her, and she wondered what had taken her so long.

# Chapter 28

Josephine's heart had been racing since her little whispered prayer. She'd closed her eyes a dozen times, hoping to doze off, only to have them snap open moments later. She was like a shaken bottle of Coke. If she didn't release the pressure soon she was going to burst.

It was time to tell him. Maybe she was finally brave enough to explain. Maybe he needed closure, and what did she have to lose now? What did either of them have to lose? Maybe she couldn't give him anything else, but she could give him this.

She was sitting in the V of his legs, his arms still wrapped around her. She turned her head until her ear was against his chest. She was shivering so hard she was shaking him. Or maybe he was shivering too.

"Noah?"

"Yeah."

"Can we . . . can we talk about that night?" There was no need for clarification.

He was quiet for a long moment. "I s'pose so."

"We don't have to if you don't want." She clung to the hope

like a child to her blankie. He'd demanded she explain when he'd found out what she'd done. But how could she have explained what she hadn't understood? And once she finally understood, he wasn't part of her life anymore.

"No. I want to know."

She swallowed hard. She didn't know where to start. They'd had their share of arguments leading up to that night. Mostly her, pushing him, she knew now. She'd been pushing him away. Daring him to love her. She was a fighter.

And she'd fought him hard about that camping trip.

"Josie?"

*Just get it out there. What are you so afraid of?*

"I guess it started with your camping trip with Jack. You remember how I fought you on that?"

"I wasn't trying to get away from you, I promise."

She'd used every excuse in the book to get him to stay home. "It wasn't about that. It was—it was about Jack."

He went stiff against her. "Jack?"

"He—he knew everything about me. He'd been counseling me for weeks before you and I started dating. Well, not counseling really. I just kind of needed to confess to someone. And God seemed so far away. From the moment I realized he was your friend, I was so afraid he'd tell you everything. And then when that camping trip came up—I was just sure the other shoe was about to drop. I lived in fear of that very thing."

He was quiet for a long moment. Her body shuddered in the wake of her confession. Knowing the worst was yet to come didn't help.

"Noah?"

"Why did that scare you so much? You could've told me about your past. I would've understood."

"I was ashamed. There'd been so many men and I-I knew I didn't deserve you, okay?"

"No, it's not okay. I loved you. I didn't care about any of that. It was all in the past."

"But it wasn't. Not really."

He went quiet again for a long, tense moment. His arms slackened, and she instantly missed his warmth. "Were there others? Before that night?"

"No! No, that's not what I meant. I meant the things that happened to me in the past were still driving my behavior. I wasn't aware of it at the time. It took a year of therapy to finally get to the bottom of it."

"Therapy?"

"I—I've been seeing someone in Ellijay, trying to figure it all out. I didn't want to hurt anyone else like that ever again. It scared me, what I did to you. To us. I threw away everything we had, and I didn't understand why."

"Tell me."

She didn't even know if she could put it into words, much less make him understand. It was so messed up. She fought the shame that threatened to plow her over.

"You know how I was sometimes difficult after we married? How I pushed you away sometimes?"

He didn't answer for a moment. Probably surprised she was taking responsibility for that when she'd always denied it before.

"It was a test of sorts," she admitted.

"You were testing me?"

"Not intentionally. But deep down . . . Listen, Noah. Please understand. I'm not trying to excuse my behavior. I'm just trying to explain it." She needed him to know it wasn't his fault. That he'd done nothing to cause this.

She felt the deep pull of his lungs against her back. The warm puff of his breath against her temple as he exhaled.

"Who was he?"

Something twisted hard inside, like a rag wrung dry. "An old boyfriend from high school. Garrett."

"Did you seek him out?"

"No." She'd been such a wreck while Noah was away on that trip. So afraid he was going to leave her. "I hadn't heard from you for three days, and I was so sure Jack had told you everything about me."

"I told you I might not have cell service."

"I know but . . . the mind can play cruel tricks." When three days passed without word, the old worries had swooped in like vultures over a dead carcass.

"I was afraid and restless, and the house was so quiet without you. I just couldn't stand the thought of going home and facing another long night. So after work that Friday night I got in my car and started driving. I ended up in Cartersville."

"I thought you hated that place."

"I did. But I told myself I had to face my past. Be brave. I was hungry, so I stopped to eat at a bar. I ran into him there. I'd had a couple drinks. I wasn't drunk or anything. Just . . . a little loosened up, I guess. I'm sure that contributed, but it wasn't why I did it."

"Well, by all means, tell me why."

She couldn't blame him for his anger. Her mind flashed back in time to Garrett. In high school she'd fancied herself in love with him. He was from the right side of the tracks, and though his friends accused him of slumming it with her, he'd professed to love her too.

"Noah . . . you're not the first man I've stepped out on. I

cheated on Garrett in high school. With his best friend. And . . ." Her throat thickened. "There were others."

"That's supposed to make me feel better?"

A wave of shame washed over her, and her eyes burned. "I'm just saying it was a pattern. One I didn't care enough to explore until I lost you."

"I'm flattered."

She pressed her palm against the ache in her chest. She hurt all over from the cold, but nothing hurt as bad as that ache in the center of her chest. What had she expected? That he'd understand?

"Sorry." His voice strained with control. "Go on."

"I don't expect you to understand. It was inexcusable. You didn't deserve it. Back then I was just trying to—this sounds so selfish. It is selfish. But I needed to know you loved me."

"I did!"

She clutched his coat sleeve. "I know. I know you did, Noah."

In fact, he'd had her on a pedestal, and the thought of letting him down—the thought of losing him—was a crushing fear. How could Noah, the man who'd put his desires for her on hold until their wedding night, ever understand the way she'd gone through man after man? The way she'd been unfaithful so many times? She hadn't understood it herself.

"But . . . there was this hole in me, Noah. I'd never been loved unconditionally. Not even by my mom. And I so desperately needed to be loved like that. When I said I was testing you, that's what I meant. Deep down I needed to be loved *no matter what*."

"So I was supposed to just, what? Let you cheat on me?"

"No."

Although deep down that's what she'd longed for. When

he'd filed for divorce within days, it had devastated her. After she'd been served she'd spent the next three days in bed. Had told Callie she was down with the flu. She'd fallen into a deep, dark hole, and it had taken everything she had to climb out of it and go on.

Even though she'd known she deserved Noah's response. She'd proven herself right—she *was* unworthy of love. His or anyone else's. Those voices in her head telling her she was good for one thing. That she'd never keep a man. They played relentlessly. Sometimes she still fought to silence those voices.

"I needed something from you that my parents hadn't given me. And that wasn't fair."

"You didn't have feelings for this guy?"

"No. I didn't want him in any way." She hadn't made it five miles outside of Cartersville before she was emptying her stomach by the side of the road. "I was repulsed by what I did. So ashamed. And so scared. I knew you were going to find out. I knew I was going to lose you. That I deserved it."

And she had. His brother had been exiting the adjoining Mexican restaurant that night. She'd known he went there occasionally. Maybe subconsciously she'd wanted to be caught— she'd talked about that in counseling. That maybe she'd needed to see if Noah would love her anyway.

She'd gotten her answer right quick.

"I'm only telling you this because I want you to know it was nothing you did, okay? You—you were a great husband. The best."

She swallowed against the ache in her throat. She was suddenly so exhausted. Not just physically, but mentally. But she needed to say one more thing.

"Those things that happened when I was a child made me

feel so powerless. And later all those other men—it was just my way of taking back control. Men weren't going to use me anymore; I was going to use them first. I know it sounds horrible, and it is. But in my mind, sex was power. You didn't let me use that weapon when we were dating, and I didn't know what to think of that."

He was quiet so long, and she wondered what he was thinking. No doubt he was realizing just how messed up the woman he'd married was.

"Noah?"

"I was . . . thinking about, you know, after we were married. Was it . . . not good for you?"

She clutched his arm. "Oh, Noah. I felt so much with you. Things I'd never felt with anyone else, and it scared me silly. Before you, sex just made me . . . numb. It was like I was seeing through a dark tunnel. But with you I felt everything. You were different from the very first kiss.

"M-my past had such a hold on me. A death grip. You don't know what powerless is until you're twelve years old and trapped under a grown man who takes whatever he wants."

He exhaled and a long silence followed.

"And your only parent is in the next room, letting it happen. Oh, Josie. I've been such an idiot."

"I think you're due your pound of flesh, Noah."

His arms tightened around her. She felt the warmth of his breath on her temple. The delicious friction of his whiskers on her skin.

"How about if I just forgive you instead?" he whispered softly.

At his words peace spread through her, like the sweetest of nectars.

"Thank you." She heard the relief in her own voice.

She was tired. So tired. But she wasn't quite finished. "There's one more thing I need to tell you, Noah."

She felt him tense behind her, and she couldn't blame him. She'd dumped an awful lot on him.

"What's that?"

"There—there hasn't been anyone else since our separation. I don't know what rumors you may have heard, but . . . I haven't so much as looked twice at another man."

She felt him relax, muscle by muscle. Moment by moment. He said nothing else, just tightened his arms around her.

# Chapter 29

*A*while later Noah got up to cut more pine boughs. He needed time alone to work through everything Josie had said. It all made sense, in a twisted kind of way. It made him sorry for her childhood. Thankful for his own.

He brought the boughs back and carved out a spot big enough for them to lie down. He built the banks around the bed as a shelter against the wind and hoped it was enough.

It was almost dark by the time he was finished. After Josie lay down on the makeshift bed he settled in behind her, wrapping her tight, his knees tucked against the back of hers.

Awhile later he began shivering, and she tucked his hand inside her coat. A fist tightened around his heart. Something had shifted with her confession. With his forgiveness. He wanted to explore it, but he had other, more pressing concerns.

Her confession seemed to have sapped the last of her energy. She'd grown quiet, and he was so worried for her. Worried she wouldn't make it till morning.

The chances of help coming before then were slim to none. The night stretched ahead, long and cold, and fear settled like a rock in the pit of his stomach. It was now so dark he could barely make out the silhouettes of the trees against the starless sky.

"Noah?"

"Yeah, honey."

"J-just wanted to see if you were still awake."

He curled his gloved hands into the material of her shirt. "Want me to turn on the flashlight?"

"I'm okay."

He shifted his arm under Josie's head. She was shaking so hard, and her stomach felt like marble. Her words were slurred, and she was too apathetic for his liking. He should probably keep her awake, but that was unrealistic. He'd check on her through the night. Convince her help was on the way.

"Noah? You awake?"

A shiver of fear raced through him at the repetition. "Yeah. Just hang on, Josie. Help's coming."

He'd give anything to fix this. But he'd done everything he knew to do. Prayer was all that was left, and he had that covered too.

He was glad they'd talked about their faith earlier. She'd always shied away from those conversations. Now that he knew more about her past, he was beginning to understand how it all tied together.

He thought again of all she'd been through. What did he know about hardship? He'd grown up in a loving family—his biggest worry was who he'd play with at lunch. Josie'd been thrust into adulthood at a young age. No safety net.

He opened his eyes a few minutes later to pitch black. He wished again for a fire. Not only for the warmth but for the light.

He tightened his arms around her. "Sorry it's so dark."

"Never bothered me, long as you were near."

"Why's that?"

It took awhile for her answer. "You make me feel safe."

The words tightened his chest. He felt unworthy of her faith in him somehow. He wasn't the one who'd spoiled what they had. Yet he couldn't help but see it as his failure, at least to some extent. Regret settled inside, leaving a heaviness in his chest.

"I wish I could've made you happy," he said softly, the darkness somehow giving him courage.

"Oh, Noah. You did. Best thing that ever happened to me."

He didn't know how that could be true. But he wanted to believe it in the worst way.

"It was me. Not you. I'm sorry." Her voice was thick with tears. "I never wanted to hurt you."

"Shhh. I forgive you." She didn't need to waste energy on this.

What did any of it matter now, anyway? When they were lying here in the middle of nowhere, slowly freezing to death. If help didn't come soon, those documents back at the house wouldn't matter one iota.

*We're still married.* The thought wrapped around him like a warm blanket. Was it crazy that he was comforted by that somehow?

He suddenly needed to touch her, feel her skin against his own. He removed a glove and palmed her cheek. Her skin was so cold. Colder than his fingers. And wet.

He brushed away her tears and pressed a kiss to her temple. "Better stop that. Your tears will freeze on your face."

She turned in his arms to face him, her movements slow and clumsy. "You mind?" she asked as she snuggled into his chest.

"No." The words had been building up over the past couple

hours, ever since her confession. He had to say them. His heart hammered in his chest until he shook with the force.

"Josie?"

"Mmm."

He touched her face again, sliding his thumb along the curve of her cheek. "I never stopped loving you," he said softly, the words coming from the deepest reaches of his heart. The confession was like a release. Something inside him, something that had gone hard and tight, loosened, unfurled.

"You hear me, baby girl?"

She turned her face into his neck. "L-love you . . . too. Noah."

The words washed over him like warm water. He pressed a kiss to her forehead.

As relieved as he was to hear it, he didn't like the way her sentences had grown shorter, her words blending together. He threw a leg over her, pulling her closer. A pine branch dug into his side, but he couldn't think of anything but her warm breath on his neck.

Josie tucked her hands between their bodies and clamped her teeth against the chattering. And here she'd always thought the Georgia heat and humidity would be the death of her. She was so cold.

*Don't think about it.*

She focused instead on the night sounds that pressed in around them. On the roughness of Noah's stubbled jaw against her temple. His warm breath on her skin. She'd never dreamed she'd be back in his arms. Not for any reason. She had another thought—something about a ten-foot pole, but she couldn't assemble the words in her mind.

"This is crazy." Her words were slow and laborious. "That we're here, like this."

He pulled her closer. "Pretty crazy. Pretty amazing."

She was glad she'd gotten to say her piece earlier. Though she couldn't quite remember what she'd said just now. Didn't matter. Even the cold didn't seem to matter so much anymore.

She woke to a *tch-tch-tch*. A puddle of light in the darkness. Cold. Reality settled around her, in a distant kind of way. As if she were dreaming.

"Noah?" Her voice was a thready whisper.

The *tch*-ing stopped. "I'm here." He shuffled closer.

She felt the warmth of him as he settled behind her. Comforted by his presence, she closed her eyes and began sinking back under. It was better that way.

"Josie?"

Her lips parted, but she couldn't seem to form a response. Blackness closed in. So tired.

"*Josie?*"

The alarm in his tone gave her the determination to respond. "Mmm?"

A zipping sound. A weight settling over her shoulders. Oblivion beckoned.

"I know you're cold, baby girl. Just—just promise me you'll hang on. Don't give up. Help's on the way. I promise." His words came as if from afar.

"Josie?"

It took everything in her to push out the word. "'Kay."

Noah woke sometime later. It had grown colder. Or maybe it just felt like it since his coat was around Josie now.

Something felt wrong. He blinked against the fog in his brain, trying to figure out what it was.

Josie. She wasn't shivering anymore. She was still as death in his arms. Panic closed around his throat, suffocating.

*"Josie."*

He pushed up. "Josie."

He pulled his glove. Felt for a pulse.

*Please, God. Please.*

He tried to still his own shivering as he searched. Time slowed to a crawl. Fear washed in, flooding him from the inside out.

There it was. A pulse. It was weak. Slow. But it was there.

He pulled the coat tighter around her, trying to keep her core warm. "Help is coming. You hear me, baby girl? Help is coming."

He sank back down, his pulse racing now, his body suddenly drained of energy.

He made himself feel for the lighter in the pine boughs where he'd set it. He didn't want to leave Josie even long enough to find his little nest of kindling. Besides, he was too tired to get up. He fumbled with the lighter before he finally grasped it. He tried again to produce a flame. Once. Twice. Three times.

No use. He dropped the lighter and sank back down, exhausted from the effort.

He set his hand on Josie's back, reassured by the slow rise and fall. He couldn't rid himself of the notion that he was failing her. A lump swelled in his throat, and the back of his eyes burned.

*"Jesus!"* The raw plea ripped from his throat, full of so many things. Frustration. Anger. Love. Helplessness. The helplessness was a crushing weight.

"Hang on, Josie," he whispered into her ear. "Just hang on a little longer." He tightened his arms around her, as if he could hold her there by sheer will. It was all he could do.

# Chapter 30

His alarm was going off. The buzz tugged at his subconscious, but he couldn't get his brain in gear. Worse, he couldn't seem to open his eyes. They were dry—and cold, somehow. Everything was cold. Must've kicked off his blankets again.

He tried to reach for his alarm, but his arm lay immobile, as if weighted by a pile of bricks. His legs, too, seemed frozen to the bed.

He was paralyzed. Helpless. What was wrong with him? Why couldn't he move? Why couldn't he wake up? Was he dreaming? Was he in Afghanistan, injured, lying in the sand? Dying?

The buzz persisted, feeding the panic that had begun swirling in his head. His heart was a bass drum in his chest, pounding out a driving rhythm. His lungs struggled to keep pace. And still he couldn't move.

The buzzing grew louder.

*Wake up.*

He pried his eyes open. Bright. So bright. He blinked, disoriented. There was no sand. No alarm clock. No bed.

Only sunlight peering through skeletal branches. Snow. Cold.

*Josie!*

He rolled her onto her back, searched her neck frantically for a pulse. He couldn't find it. *Come on, come on!* Where was it? And then he realized he was still wearing gloves. He jerked one off and tried again.

Her skin was cold, a pale shade of gray. Her lips bleached of color. Her lashes lay still and lifeless against her ashen cheeks.

"Josie!" The cry ripped from a raw throat.

He'd slept too long. It must've been hours since he'd last checked on her.

*Idiot!*

His hand trembled uncontrollably, making it hard to feel anything. A moment ticked by. Two. His own heart stopped.

And then he felt it. A tiny flutter against his fingertip. Irregular and slow. But present. He breathed again.

*Thank You, God. Oh, thank You.*

He set his hand against her cheek. "Stay with me, baby girl. Hear me?"

And that's when he heard it. The buzz. It was real. And it was getting louder.

He looked up, listening, staring into the horizon where the sun glinted off the snow. It was real all right. It was the high-pitched whine of a snowmobile.

His heart hammered against his ribs. Adrenaline flooded through him, providing much-needed energy. He pushed up.

"Help!" he cried, the raspy word barely audible.

They were downhill from the road and further hidden from

view by the snow shelter he'd built. He struggled up, gathering Josie in his arms. He fumbled with her weight, hardly able to support his own.

"Help!"

The engine was getting louder. Surely coming this way. He had to get up the incline. His legs wobbled. His arms trembled. His muscles disobeyed him.

Halfway up he realized he should've left her behind. Flagged down help. But his brain was encased in fog, and he couldn't seem to clear it. Too late. He couldn't leave her in the snow.

He slipped on the slope, nearly dropping her. But he landed on his knees and pushed up again. Pressed on.

"Down here!" The drone of the engine swallowed his words. Just a few more feet. Just a few more.

He took a halting step, then another. By the time he crested the hill he was out of breath and nearly ready to drop her. He sank to his knees, then his haunches, cradling her, his eyes peeled on the peak of the hill. Was it getting louder?

*Please, God.*

He strained to listen over his ragged breaths. It was. It was coming this way. The sound continued for what seemed like forever with no sled in sight.

Could this be some kind of mind trick? A—what was the word? Not dream. *Hallucination.* He was pretty sure hypothermia caused them. And what a cruel joke that would be.

But he wouldn't be having such rational thoughts if he were hallucinating. Would he?

And then there it was. Cresting the hill.

Unless he was dreaming that up too.

*Let it be real. Please, God.*

The machine picked up speed, the whine louder and higher

pitched. He saw a blue sled. Red knit hat. Gray coat. Surely his imagination hadn't conjured up Mary Beth.

He'd just struggled to his feet, Josie in his arms, as the machine came to a quick stop beside him. A wave of dizziness made him waver.

"Please be real," he whispered.

"Noah!" Mary Beth slid off the sled. "Oh my gosh!"

Real. She was real.

His breath emptied. "T-take her . . . and go." He trudged toward the machine. Josie needed help and now.

But Mary Beth was messing with her phone.

"Take her to the hospital!"

"I'm calling for a medevac. It'll be quicker."

He blinked. Of course. Wasn't thinking straight.

"Are you okay?"

"Yeah, but she—she's not. Tell 'em to hurry." His teeth clattered together, making his words barely distinguishable.

Mary Beth started talking to someone on the phone.

His arm muscles burned. They were ready to give out. He lowered Josie onto the sled and fell onto the seat behind her, supporting her weight with his body.

"Josie." He lightly tapped her cheek. "Josie, honey . . . help is here. You hear me?" He felt for her pulse again, searching. Couldn't find it.

His chest went so tight he couldn't breathe. Blood rushed in his ears, whooshing. He leaned forward, feeling for her breath.

There. A soft puff of warmth against his cheek.

"Hang on . . . baby girl. Hang on."

His throat swelled shut and tears stung his eyes. "Help is here," he whispered. "Going to be all right."

Mary Beth approached. "Help is on the— Noah, your feet!"

She was off the phone. He must've zoned out a minute. She was pulling off her own boots, putting them on Josie and putting his boots back on his own feet. He couldn't feel them anymore. He fought to stay alert.

Mary Beth said something, but he couldn't process it. He blinked, trying to unscramble his thoughts.

"Where's your coat?" she asked.

Finally understanding, he looked down and wondered the same thing.

She touched his arm, grounding him. "Noah, where's your coat?"

He'd put it around Josie last night, hadn't he? It must've fallen off somewhere. Unable to form words, he gestured down the hill.

Mary Beth disappeared and returned what seemed like two seconds later with his coat. His arms wouldn't seem to work. She helped him into it, zipping it for him.

"They're sending a medevac from Chattanooga. It won't be long." She pulled her gloves and felt for Josie's pulse. "Hang on, honey." She wrapped her warm hands around Josie's neck and looked him in the eye. "Noah . . . you still with me?"

"Y-yeah."

"Make room on that seat, bud. Let's see if we can warm this girl up."

He heard a zipping sound. It was the last thing he remembered.

# Chapter 31

*Present day*

*F*rom somewhere far away, from the depths of an endless tunnel, Noah heard a quiet hum. The sound grew louder. An insistent beeping joined the mix. Light pressed against his eyelids. Warm. Glorious. He reached for it.

And found pain. A throbbing pain.

Tired. So tired. Exhaustion pulled him back into the tunnel, and he went willingly.

"Noah."

The word fell into the long tunnel, distant and faint. The hum was back. The beeping. Light and warmth washed over him like an ocean wave, and he gave himself over to it.

"Noah . . . can you hear me?"

He forced his eyes open. Lights glared. He squinted against them. Pain pricked his eyelids.

A face hovered nearby. A stranger, her skin the color of cocoa. "You're at CHI Memorial in Chattanooga. But you're going to be all right."

Hospital. He shut his eyes against the light, trying to remember. Everything was foggy.

The pain intruded, sharp, throbbing. He hurt everywhere. He tried to ask what happened but couldn't make his tongue move. It was dry, stuck to the roof of his mouth.

"You probably have a little amnesia, honey. You got lost in the mountains. You were hypothermic, but you're going to be all right. Sounds like you and your friend had quite the adventure."

Mountains . . . hypothermic . . . friend . . .

*Josie.*

His eyes flew open. He tried to sit up, but his muscles were slow and weak. He told his legs to swing out of bed. They barely budged. A cord tugged. Beeping filled the room.

The woman pushed against his chest. "Oh no you don't."

*Josie!* He fought back. But he was as weak as a kitten.

"Hey, you're going to rip out your IV. Settle down now."

"Josie," he rasped.

"Your friend?"

Another nurse appeared. He was helpless against the two of them. Flat on his back. He gasped for air. Tried to remember.

The buzzing sound. Mary Beth. He couldn't remember anything after.

He found the nurse's eyes. "Is Josie okay?"

"She's in surgery. They're working to get her body temperature up. Don't you worry; they're taking good care of her."

*Working to . . .* That was tricky business, wasn't it? He suddenly remembered a story he'd read. A bunch of fishermen rescued from the frigid North Sea. In the rescue ship they stepped below for a cup of hot tea. Every last one of them dropped dead from the shock to their systems.

Panic sliced through him. *Josie.* He struggled to sit up again.

"Now, now. None of that." The nurses pushed him back, held him down with a force that belied their size.

"If you don't settle down we can't check on her, now can we?"

"That's it. Just take it easy. I'll bring back word. You've been through an ordeal yourself, you know. You need to rest."

He was suddenly exhausted. His weight sagged into the bed, his body like a lead weight. He fought to stay conscious, but the tunnel beckoned him. Pulled at his eyelids. And then there was darkness.

"Noah? Are you awake?"

He opened his eyes. Blinked against the glaring light. Found Mary Beth standing over the bed rail, frowning.

"There you are. How are you feeling?"

He wetted his lips. "Josie . . . How's Josie?"

She squeezed his hand. "She's out of surgery. She's doing all right. How are you feeling?"

He hurt all over. He tried to move his fingers. They twitched. He tried to swallow and found his throat dry and swollen.

"Thirsty."

She produced a cup with a straw.

He forced his lips around it, swallowing greedily.

"Take it easy."

His head fell back against the pillow, his breath coming quickly. "Want to see Josie."

"Soon. I just checked with the nurse. She's not alert yet, but her body temperature is rising nicely."

He remembered what the nurse had said. "What was the . . . surgery for?"

Mary Beth set the drink on the rolling table. "They put a catheter into her abdomen to warm her organs with fluids. They also flushed her veins with warm saline through an IV. Same as you."

"She's going to be all right?"

"That's what they tell me. Seth's on his way. So are your parents. They're flying home."

He wouldn't feel settled until he saw Josie for himself. Until he saw her cheeks flushed with color, her skin warm with life, looking like his Josie again.

# Chapter 32

"M s. Mitchell?" A persistent tap beckoned from someplace far away.

"Josie, wake up."

She wanted it to go away. The voice. The tapping. She tried
to say so, but nothing happened.

The tapping brought a consciousness that made her aware of
her body. Of the pain. Heavens to Betsy, the pain. Her toes. Her
legs. Her stomach. She tried to move, and someone whimpered.

"That's it, open your eyes."

Brightness. Blinding.

"Someone's been asking after you."

The face floating over her came into focus. A dark-skinned
woman stared down at her with kind brown eyes. A nurse.

Josephine felt as if she'd been gone a long time. But she
didn't know where she'd been.

"What—" She cleared her throat, wincing against the
pain. "What happened? Where am I?"

"You're at CHI Memorial in Chattanooga. You've suffered
hypothermia, but you're going to be all right."

*Hypothermia?*

Tired. She was so tired. But she had to think. She remembered getting stuck at Noah's place. Looking for the horse. Memories marched in fast-forward. Running out of gas, falling through ice, pain and cold, lying under the starless night in Noah's arms.

*"Noah."*

The nurse placed a hand on Josephine's shoulder, weighing her down. "Noah's just fine. Settle down. We're taking good care of him. I'm afraid you got the brunt of it."

Josephine melted into the bed, her body limp and useless. The beeping on the monitor was fast and frantic. Her head was full of cotton.

The woman checked a bag hanging nearby. "That's some ex you got, honey. Heard tell he gave you his boots and coat. Mine would've left me to freeze to death."

Pain stabbed at her toes. She looked down at them, but they were covered by a mound of blankets.

"Your toes are going to be fine. No blisters yet. Just superficial damage, though I'm sure they hurt like the dickens. I'll see about getting something for the pain."

Josephine's eyes drifted shut. She worked to keep them open. But they were suddenly so heavy.


Her eyes opened. Her brain fought to acclimate. The insistent beeping nudged her memory. The hospital. She was at the hospital. Hypothermia.

It was darker now. And warmer. Oh glory, the warmth! Her eyes closed briefly in relief alone. Even the pain had faded to a dull ache.

She heard a movement close by.

A shadow hovered at her bedside. A hand squeezed hers through the railing.

"Hey, you," a voice whispered.

"Noah." Her voice was rusty.

He produced a drink, slipped the straw between her lips, holding her head up. Some of the liquid dribbled down her chin. When she was finished she fell back against the pillow. She was so tired. So groggy. Whatever they'd given her for the pain made her loopy.

Noah folded his arms on the rail and set his chin on them, his face shadowed. "You're going to be fine. You even get to keep all your fingers and toes."

"That's . . . handy."

He smiled at her. "Look at you, making jokes. You had surgery, so your stomach's probably sore, but you're going to be fine."

"Just like you promised." She tried for a smile, but her face muscles only twitched.

He squeezed her hand. "Just like I promised."

"You're—you're all right?"

"I'm fine. Or will be as soon as I can get out of this ridiculous gown. Looks much better on you, I have to say."

Her mind went back to those two long days and nights. The memories unfurled like a rolled-up map laid flat. The complete and utter cold. The closeness they'd shared. Her confession. His forgiveness. Everything after that turned fuzzy until the memories were buried under an avalanche of delirium.

And yet, here they were. "We—we really made it."

"God heard our prayers."

"He must've. That was . . . pretty intense."

"Sure was."

The stroke of his thumb on the back of her hand was the sweetest thing she'd ever felt. Something niggled at the frayed edges of her thoughts. A sadness. Bittersweet. Something she couldn't quite put her finger on.

She struggled to keep her eyes open. To focus.

"I've been so worried about you," he said softly.

"You . . . should be in bed."

"I had to check on you. Make sure you were—"

Light crept in as the door opened. Noah turned.

A silhouette stopped in the doorway. "*Mr.* Mitchell . . . what do you think you're doing?"

His grip tightened on Josephine's hand. "Checking on my—"

"Never you mind. Get on back to your own room."

"I want to stay awhile longer."

"This ain't about what you want. The lady needs her rest. Now, up you go." The nurse took his arm, helping him up as she tsked. "I suppose you just ripped out that IV. Not on my shift—no siree."

"Get some rest," Noah said over his shoulder as the nurse escorted him out. "I'll be back soon."

"You'll be back when I say so, young man . . ."

The woman's voice continued, chastising Noah all the way down the hall until it faded to nothingness. Josephine's lips turned up even as her eyelids drifted shut.

# Chapter 33

The squeeze of the automatic blood pressure cuff pulled Josephine to consciousness. The room was empty and quiet, save the rhythmic beeping and the hum of the cuff machine.

Her body ached, especially her toes. Her abdomen. But at least she was lucid this time.

A nurse entered the room as the cuff deflated. She looked to be in her thirties, had her dark hair pulled back in a messy bun, and amply filled out her Peanuts scrubs.

"You're awake. How are you feeling? It's time for more pain meds if you need them."

Josephine didn't want drugs again. They only made her loopy. "I'm okay. How's Noah?"

The nurse flashed her a look as she switched out the IV bag. "Your ex-husband is *not* a good patient. But I probably don't have to tell you that."

*Ex*-husband? Josephine blinked away the last of the fuzz. She'd been through an ordeal and a half, and her memory wasn't at its best. But she knew she hadn't dreamed up those papers.

"M-my ex-husband?"

The nurse gave her a funny look. "Noah . . . ?"

Josephine's face warmed. "Of course. I just . . ."

"I'll tell you this much. Most people get lost in the wilderness with their ex—one of them doesn't make it back alive. Know what I'm saying?"

"He's all right?"

"He's insisting on an early discharge, despite the doctor's recommendation. Maybe you can talk some sense into him. He could use another day."

Josephine responded halfheartedly to the nurse's questions, pretending she was tired. She wanted to be left alone. Needed to think. Those feelings that had been humming in her head when she'd woken earlier were now buzzing like a neon sign.

Once the nurse left, Josephine opened her eyes and stared out the window where the sun glistened off the treetops. Another day was underway, the sunlight a promise of warmth, the cloudless sky a promise of spring.

But a heaviness settled over her as a fist tightened around her heart. Somehow she'd felt more hopeful freezing to death in Noah's arms in the middle of the wilderness than she felt right now.

She had a vague recollection of waking earlier to find Noah in her room. Another snippet of memory—the other nurse referring to Noah as her ex. She and Noah shared the same last name. There's no way the nurses could've reached that conclusion unless Noah had told them it was so.

And he wouldn't have said it unless he intended for it to be true. It was all done but the paperwork, after all.

Her stomach twisted painfully. Was she the only one who had thought that, perhaps, things might've changed? The back of her eyes stung, and her throat thickened.

*Stupid, Josephine. You're a stupid, stupid girl. When will you ever learn?*

Just because they'd survived an ordeal together didn't mean they were bound for life. Just because she'd bared her soul didn't mean she deserved a second chance. Just because he'd forgiven her didn't mean he still loved her.

The voices returned, taunting her.

*You're only good for one thing, Jo. No man's ever gonna love a girl like you.*

*No man's ever gonna love a girl like you.*

*No man's ever gonna love a girl like you.*

She shook her head, hoping to shake the thought loose. Send it flying into the universe. She was so tired of it.

She closed her eyes, needing escape. She should be grateful just to be alive. She whispered a prayer of gratitude, not quite feeling as blessed as she ought. Words dried up in her mind as shame and hopelessness filled the hollows of her chest. The familiar pain overrode the ache of her recovering body.

She should've known better than to hope. Noah deserved better. Someone not messed up. Look what he'd done for her out there. Given her the boots off his feet, the coat off his back. And after all she'd done to him. She could never be worthy of someone like him. What could she do but release him?

A shuffle sounded nearby, and she opened her eyes.

He stood in the doorway in his street clothes. His hair was ruffled, his jaw scruffy, his shirt buttoned crookedly, one tail longer than the other. He'd never looked more handsome.

His lips lifted as he strode into the room. "How're you feeling?"

She clutched the bedsheets in her hand and forced a smile. "Fair to middling."

"Your color's a lot better."

"How'd you escape Nurse Ratched?"

"Her shift's over. 'Sides, I worked my charm on her. Had her eating out of my palm by the time she left."

Josephine's laugh sounded dry even to her own ears. "What day is it?"

"Wednesday. We've been here two days, one night." He slowly lowered himself into the chair beside her bed. "Have you eaten?"

At the very thought of food her stomach clamped down hard. "I'm not hungry."

"There've been people calling to check on you. Callie. Daisy. Ava."

"Nice of them."

"They're your friends."

She closed her eyes, feigning exhaustion. It was easier than looking him in the eye. Easier than keeping up a pretense.

The silence lengthened, and she realized he was going to let her rest. But instead of leaving, he settled deeper into the chair. She felt his scrutiny like a touch. She couldn't sleep with him staring at her.

She opened her eyes and pulled the sheets to her chin.

"Are you cold? I can scrounge up another blanket."

"I'm fine." She gave a thin smile. "I never want to be cold again."

"I hear you."

"How did—what happened? Who found us?"

"Mary Beth."

Of course. Who else would it be?

"She was plowing her drive and saw the gas can right off the side of the road. It had my name on it. She went to my place and realized the horses hadn't been tended to. I wasn't there, and Shadow's bowl was dry. She remembered the shots she'd heard and put it all together."

"She followed our tracks."

"The plows had come through already. But somehow she found the tracks on the service road." His voice had grown thick. He took a long blink. "I've never been so glad to see anyone in my life."

She steeled herself against the emotion in his voice, on his face. Her defenses kicked in. "Sorry I missed it."

His eyes searched hers until her cheeks warmed under his scrutiny.

"What—what happened next?"

It took him a moment to answer. He was too busy looking inside her soul. "She called medevac. We took a helicopter ride, though I'm afraid I missed that part too."

Noah's eyes traveled over Josie's face, taking in her creamy skin, her pinkened cheeks.

He'd come in here hoping to find her awake. He couldn't wait to tell her he loved her again and hear the words from lips that weren't bleached of color. Fading with life.

The memory of her skin, gray and marble-like, had haunted him every waking moment. Only when he was with her was there any sense of peace.

But now even that was fading. Was she embarrassed by what had transpired between them out there? She wasn't looking him in the eye. And when she did there was a guardedness he hadn't seen since—well, it had only been a few days. But somehow that seemed like forever ago.

He'd told her he loved her, and he'd meant it. She'd said it back. But sometimes people said things they didn't mean when they were in the middle of a trauma. Things they otherwise never would've said. This hadn't been one of those times.

At least, not for him.

He couldn't forget what it had felt like—almost losing her out there. The same desperation swelled in him again.

"You're probably eager to get home and check on your horses," she said.

"Mary Beth's taking care of them for me."

"Shadow's probably beside himself."

His chest tightened, and his extremities felt twitchy all of a sudden. He shifted in the chair. "I get the feeling you're ready to be rid of me."

Her cheeks flushed with color. Her eyes toggled around the room, finally settling on the IV on the back of her hand.

She fiddled with the tape. "Why, of course not. You're just . . . all dressed and ready to go. There's no reason for you to stick around here any longer."

"So you'll be fine—if I just leave you here."

She smiled. "Of course. I'll be out of here lickety-split and I'll, you know, get on with my life. We can both get on with our own lives."

"Get on with our own lives." His voice was as flat as a punctured tire.

Her smile faltered. "I mean, as terrifying as the past few days have been . . . it was good for us, don't you think? Healing. We—we're in a better place now. Each of us."

*Each of us.*

"I'm glad we talked. I feel better for telling you about my past, for having received your forgiveness. And you must feel better now that you're not . . . angry with me anymore. It was . . . good closure."

"Closure."

"Right."

"Right."

He didn't know what to say. Awkwardness hovered between them like a cloud of sawdust.

They'd shared awkward moments before; what couple didn't? Their first morning as husband and wife came flooding back, taunting him.

*He studied her as she slept. The morning light fell like a whisper on her creamy skin. When she opened her eyes and found him staring, her cheeks slowly colored—the night before, no doubt, flooding back. She wasn't shy or naïve. He had no doubt she'd awakened naked in bed with others before him. But he had a feeling she felt stripped bare this morning in other ways. More important ways.*

*And he suddenly wanted, more than anything else, to put her at ease.*

*In an abrupt move, he rolled on top of her and began planting sloppy kisses on her forehead, her cheeks, her nose, her eyelids, her neck, finding ticklish spots. He kept on until she was shaking with laughter.*

*Eventually his kisses wandered lower, to her shoulder, growing slower, softer, until she wasn't laughing anymore.*

Now he found himself wanting to break the tension again. Wanting to make her laugh. See her eyes curve into crescents, hear her smoky laughter ring out between them.

But he could think of nothing to do. Nothing to say. And the ache in his gut was no laughing matter.

"I thought I'd find you in here."

Noah turned as the nurse entered the room. She had him sign his early discharge papers and gave him take-home instructions. Noah gave back the signed paper mechanically, his mind still on Josie and their conversation and what would happen next.

When the nurse left, Noah looked at Josie. "Well . . . I guess that's that then."

She'd raised the head of her bed while he'd been distracted with the paperwork. Her hair was finger-combed, now artfully tousled around her face. In short, she was beautiful.

She gave him a saucy smile that seemed to come out of nowhere. "You know, I just can't let you leave like that, all buttoned up crooked."

His eyes dropped to his shirt.

"Cute as can be, but with all the scruff you've got going on, it's a bit derelict for you."

He blinked at her. She was flirting. Doing that thing she did. Keeping him at arm's length with that façade of hers. She'd found a way to deal with the awkwardness.

And darned if it didn't hurt like the dickens.

He cleared his throat. "I'll be back tonight after I check on things at the ranch."

She fussed with the sheets. "Oh, now, don't do that. It's much too far to drive. I'll probably be out of here in the morning anyway."

It was less than an hour's drive. And the whole reason he'd busted out early was so he could be with her without those nurses hovering. But Josie didn't want his company.

Everything they'd been through, everything she'd said—it

had only been the desperation of the moment. She'd been dependent on him. They'd been dependent on each other.

But that was over now, apparently.

His throat tightened painfully as the walls of his chest closed in. Maybe this was what she needed. Maybe he'd only been a brief stop on her way to being a healthier person.

An intern came into the room, a food tray clattering in her hands. "Here you are, Ms. Mitchell."

"Thanks, sweetie," Josie said as the intern left. She tore the wrapper off her straw and stuck it into the foil lid of her juice. "I'm suddenly ravenous."

Noah scratched the back of his head. "Well . . . I'll just . . . get out of your hair."

Before he could leave, Josie grabbed his hand. "Noah, wait."

Hope swelled at her touch. At the look in her eyes. An authenticity was there that hadn't been seconds before. He squeezed her hand, waiting.

Something shifted on her face. "I-I don't know if I even said thank you. For everything you did out there." Tears shimmered in her eyes even while her smile dazzled. "I don't know what I would've done without you, Noah. Frozen to death, no doubt."

Something inside shriveled up and died. His heart, perhaps. He didn't want her gratitude. He wanted her love.

He swallowed hard, took a second to compose himself. "It was my pleasure, Josie," he said. And realized he meant every word.

# Chapter 34

*Copper Creek*

The tall domed sanctuary stretched ahead like an ethereal passageway to another world. From the back pew of Messiah Lutheran Church Josephine stared up at the stained-glass windows behind the altar. Sunlight filtered through in jeweled tones, outshining the overhead pendants.

The stained glass depicted Jesus on the cross, His disciples grieving at His feet. A scripture scrolled across the heavens. *Greater love has no one than this, than to lay down one's life for his friends.*

The service had ended awhile ago. The parishioners were long since gone, and the throbbing organ had given way to a hushed silence. Josephine hadn't intended to stay, but the tranquility of the building comforted her.

And God knew, she needed comfort.

A lot had happened up there in the mountains. Some of it good, she'd realized over the past few days. She'd found peace about certain things. The deep-down kind that made sitting through a church service an act of worship rather than a form of torture.

It had been three days since her release from the hospital. Three long days. She was easing back into her work schedule. The flooding had, fortunately, been quickly resolved and limited to the mechanical room. The day of pampering had gone off without a hitch.

She had much to be thankful for. She was so glad for a warm bed. For food. Running water. And okay, makeup and hairspray. Folks had dropped by daily, arms laden with casseroles and cookies and homemade jams. Her body was recovering.

Her heart, not so much.

She hadn't heard from Noah since he'd left the hospital. Not that she expected to. On Friday, while she'd been at lunch, he'd dropped off the things she'd left at his house: her purse and her flats. He must've forgotten her phone or thought it was in her purse. She was going to have to call him eventually. Or go pick it up. She thought she'd left it on the sofa, but maybe it had fallen between the cushions or something.

Also noticeably absent were the divorce papers. He'd probably taken them straight to the attorney's office when he'd been in town on Friday. Any day now a judge would declare their marriage officially over.

Her chest squeezed tight, and she placed her palm over it, pressing against the familiar pain.

She'd heard through the grapevine that he was back on his feet. She tried to let that comfort her. But maybe there would always be that hollow spot inside—the spot that Noah used to fill.

The overhead lights flickered off, and she jumped. She

hadn't realized anyone was still here. She should leave. Go back to her quiet apartment and try to stay busy while she worked him out of her system. Her throat tightened against the emotion that gathered there.

"Josephine?" The low voice rumbled quietly through the empty space.

She turned in the pew and forced a smile. "Hi, Pastor Jack."

"Sorry, I didn't know anyone was in here," he said as he approached, all masculine grace in his Sunday clothes. His black hair shimmered under the lights. "Want me to turn them back on?"

"No, that's all right." She gathered her purse. "I should go. Let you get on out of here."

"You can stay as long as you want. The door will lock behind you."

A few heartbeats later she settled back in the pew, relieved. "Thanks. I think I just might."

"You had quite the week. What a blessing that help arrived when it did."

"An answered prayer, believe me."

"Oh, I believe. He always answers—sometimes just not in the way we want." The quiet hum of the furnace kicked off, and silence settled around them like a nest of feathers.

Jack shifted, tilting his head. "Is there anything I can help you with, Josephine?"

She drew in a long breath and let it out. She hadn't talked to him about anything personal since she'd found out he was Noah's best friend. And as much as she'd feared he would betray her confidences, she knew now that he never had.

"I don't know," she said finally. "I've been working through some things this week. Processing it all, I guess. What happened in the mountains. My relationship with God. With Noah . . . It's a lot to think on."

"Sounds like it."

"I managed to complicate both relationships. With Noah . . ." She swallowed hard and forced herself to say it aloud. "I guess I always doubted that someone like him could love me unconditionally."

"And then he went and proved you right."

Her spine lengthened even as the arrow hit its mark, leaving a ripple of pain. "He only did what I deserved."

"Human love has its limits, I guess." Jack's eyes softened. His hand landed lightly on her shoulder. "But if you're searching for a love that'll never let you down, you've come to the right place."

He smiled and gave her shoulder a final squeeze before he walked away.

He was a good listener. A good friend. He'd never judged her, never gossiped about her. She imagined he had his faults—he was only human. But she was suddenly very grateful Noah had him in his life.

"Pastor Jack . . . ?"

He turned, silhouetted by the light from the vestibule.

"Thanks for your . . . confidentiality. And for being such a good friend to Noah."

"Of course," he said. "Stay as long as you like, Josephine." And then he was gone.

## Chapter 35

*N*oah drew the brush across Sweetpea's withers. The bay quarter horse had gotten into some burrs and needed a good brushing. She put her head down and gave a deep, fluttering sigh as tension eased from her muscles.

"You did this on purpose, didn't you?"

The horse's eyes rolled toward him.

"Yeah, I got your number, little girl."

In the corner of the barn Shadow ceased his sniffing and regarded Noah, one ear pricked, the other flopping helplessly forward. Poor dog had hardly left Noah's side since he'd gotten home from the hospital. Being cooped up alone for two days and two nights had spooked him good.

"Wasn't talking to you, fella."

Shadow sniffed the air, then went back to his investigations.

Noah's hands worked mechanically over Sweetpea's lean muscles, then he set down the brush. He worked baby oil into the crest where the bulk of the burrs were located and began the tedious task of brushing them out.

He'd already fed the horses and turned them out, cleaned out the stalls. A couple of his friends had gone out while he was still in the hospital and tracked down Kismet. The horse had some nasty scratches on his foreleg and chest from busting through the fence. He was also malnourished and more anxious than ever. Noah had spent a lot of time with him since his return. Had spent a lot of time out here, period.

There was a lot to catch up on. The horses needed extra care from their neglect. Buffer Zone had signs of an infection, and Noah had called the vet in right away. He was going to be okay. They all were.

That's what he was telling himself anyway.

He had plenty to keep him busy out here. But he also needed to finish sanding the drywall seams in the attic, get a couple coats of paint on. He was almost finished. But he couldn't seem to work up the motivation. He'd found himself avoiding his own home.

The house held too many memories. Josie was everywhere he looked—standing over his stove, steam curling her hair. Sprawled on his rug with her Monopoly money, his socks bunched around her ankles. Tucked into her corner of the sofa, her red nose peeking out from his quilt.

He couldn't even escape her in his bedroom; his sheets still carried the sweet and spicy scent of her. He'd reminded himself a dozen times to run the bedding through the wash, but he hadn't found the time.

Either that or he was a glutton for punishment.

He missed her. There was no getting around it. He couldn't think of her without feeling all hollow inside. He told himself he'd survive this. He'd lost her once before and lived to tell about it. He could do it again. But in some ways this time was worse, because there was no anger to cushion the hurt.

It had been hard to stay away from her this week. To keep

from checking in on her. She didn't have family like he did. Didn't have parents calling, a brother stopping over to lend an extra hand, cousins ribbing her about running out of gas. She was alone in the world but for a handful of friends and a grandma she hadn't met until three years ago. One who didn't even remember her from one visit to the next.

He'd driven into town last Friday to return her things. Man, he'd gotten himself all worked up over that. First he'd grabbed coffee with Jack, then gone to the grocery, telling himself if he had cold food in the truck he wouldn't be tempted to make a nuisance of himself.

But when he finally made his way to the barbershop, she was gone for lunch. Waiting around seemed too pathetic, so he left her things with Callie and headed back up the mountain. He didn't know if that made him a saint or a coward.

Since he'd returned, his mind had been as active as his body, reliving all the things she'd said out there. Their final conversation at the hospital.

His thoughts spun back further too, rehashing everything from the past ad infinitum with the fresh perspective he'd gotten since learning about Josie's childhood.

A three-year-old conversation with Jack replayed like an annoying airport announcement in his head. It had happened a few days after Josie's betrayal. His wife had been staying in her old apartment over the barbershop, and Jack had come over to see him.

*"We're getting a divorce." Noah tossed back the last of his Coke, wishing for something stronger. Something to numb the pain.*

*"Is that your choice or hers?" Jack asked.*

*"Oh, it's mine. I'm filing tomorrow." He got up and paced*

*across the small space. His body had never housed this much anger. He didn't know what to do with it all. His wife stirred up anger and hurt with the same force she'd stirred up love and desire.*

*"Are you sure that's what you want?" Jack asked.*

*Noah gave him a hard look. "First you don't want me to marry her, and now you don't want me to divorce her? What's your problem?"*

*Obviously Noah had rushed into the marriage, just as Jack had warned. Obviously he'd made a huge mistake. He didn't need his friend rubbing his nose in it.*

*Noah clenched his fists. "You want to hear that you were right about her? Fine. You were right. Happy?"*

*"Don't be an idiot. Of course I'm not happy. I want what's best for you."*

*"And that's an unfaithful wife?" His eyes sharpened on Jack. "She cheated on me, Jack. That's grounds for divorce by anyone's standards, even God's."*

*Jack gave a slow nod. "That's true. You have every right."*

*"Darn right I do. And it'd be nice if my best friend was on my side."*

*"I'm on both your sides, Noah. You're angry, and that's perfectly understandable. I just think it might be a good idea to slow down a bit. Not make a rash decision. That's all."*

*"And I think it might be a good idea if you just butted out."*

Sweetpea nickered and shifted. Noah had been pulling too hard on a tangle of burrs. "Sorry about that, girl."

Just remembering that period of time, the anger had seeped under his skin all over again. He blew out a breath, reminding himself it was over. That he'd forgiven her.

He wasn't sure if he'd ever apologized to Jack for taking his anger out on him. He needed to; it was long overdue. And his friend had been right.

Noah *had* rushed into the marriage. But he'd also rushed into the divorce. Given what he'd learned about Josie in the mountains, her behavior was understandable, if not excusable. He wondered again why she'd never told him before. Why she had to be practically dying in his arms to tell him.

She'd been unsure of his love, obviously. She'd taken all the responsibility for that, but did some of the blame belong at his feet? He'd hardly let the door slam behind her, then he was filing for divorce.

Divorce.

He thought of those papers still sitting up at the house, hidden from sight by sections of newspaper he'd purposely laid there. He wasn't rushing this time. Maybe it was stupid. But he was going to let the dust settle a bit.

Josie's words came back to him. *There was this hole in me, Noah. I'd never been loved unconditionally. And I so desperately needed to be loved like that.*

Had that really been his job though? Wasn't that a parent's responsibility? His heart twisted as Josie's childhood—what he knew of it—played back in his mind. If so, her parents had failed miserably.

Was married love even supposed to be unconditional? He didn't think so. Otherwise there would be no "out" for infidelity. Besides, wouldn't that give people free rein to do anything they wanted? Basically a free pass to cheat or abuse?

A cold shiver passed over him, and his skin suddenly felt too tight. One heartbreak had been quite enough, thank you very much. Why would he willingly sign up for more? Such a love would require an abundance of either courage or insanity. He wasn't sure which.

But what if God was calling him to do just that?

A recent conversation with Jack buzzed in his head like a pesky mosquito. This one from last Friday at the coffee shop. Noah had told him at length about their ordeal in the mountains. He left out the specifics of their emotional connection and focused instead on the logistics. That was about all he could handle.

Jack listened patiently, no doubt hearing a lot more than Noah said. He ended the story with the rescue, giving only a brief recap of his time at the hospital. He purposely made it sound as if he and Josie had merrily gone their separate ways.

Jack took a slow sip of his coffee, his brown eyes reflective as he studied Noah. "Let me get this straight." He took his time setting his cup back on the saucer. "You were freezing to death out there, literally—and yet you gave Josephine your boots. Your coat."

Heat flushed into Noah's neck. His jaw clenched. He stared steadily into his friend's eyes, daring him to say more. He should've known Jack would dare.

"I guess," Jack said, "it's sometimes easier to give your life than your heart, huh?"

His buddy had a way of saying just the wrong thing. Or maybe it was the right thing. Noah wasn't so sure anymore. Maybe he was less afraid of dying than he was of getting hurt again. Did his friend ever think about that?

Noah sure did. Ever since Friday. And the thought was like a burr of his own, deep in the tangled mess of his heart.

# Chapter 36

*J*osephine couldn't put it off any longer. Her phone wasn't going to walk down the mountain on its own. She'd already missed a call from the nursing home about Nana, and multiple calls from Ava—and those were just the ones she knew of.

Ava had stopped by the barbershop on Josephine's first day back to work and wrapped her arms around Josephine mid-shampoo. "I was so worried about you!" she said with the drama only a teenaged girl could deliver. "Don't you ever get lost in the mountains again!"

Josephine took her for hot chocolate when she got off work. Ava told her all about spring fling night with Alex, and Josephine oohed and aahed as she scrolled through the photos on Ava's phone. The girl had looked lovely in a fitted pink dress, her hair in a half-up, half-down arrangement, and Alex looked handsome in his black tux.

Apparently the two had hit it off, and a second date had already been set. The girl's cheeks flushed as she told her about Alex holding her hand on the way home and the good-night kiss at her door.

Ah, young love. Josephine hoped it worked out for Ava.

Or at the very least, that Alex wouldn't break the girl's tender heart.

Josephine turned onto Noah's road. Her car was running fine now. He'd had it towed to the garage before she'd even left the hospital. Apparently he didn't want her coming back up here to fetch it. Well, too bad. If he hadn't wanted to see her, he should've returned her phone.

She pulled into Sweetbriar Ranch. All of the snow had melted off, leaving the grass bright green, and leaf buds proliferated on the trees. Pointy daffodil stems poked through the ground beneath the white fence that wound and curved alongside the drive. Spring had officially arrived. It was almost as if their wintry nightmare had never happened at all.

Blood whooshed in her ears as she pulled up to Noah's house. Her heart beat up into her throat, and her blood pressure shot up at the thought of seeing him again.

*Jeez o Pete, Josephine. Take it easy.*

She still wasn't quite up to speed. Her toes still hurt, and she tired easily. That's why her chest felt too tight to draw a breath.

She turned off the car and gave the steering wheel a squeeze, whispering a quick plea for help. Noah's truck wasn't in the drive, so maybe he wasn't here at all. Fingers crossed.

*Yeah, that's why you spent all that time on your hair and makeup this morning.* Her eyes flashed up to the mirror, checking her lipstick.

Disgusted with herself, she snapped the mirror shut and stepped from her car. She walked resolutely up the wooden steps to the porch. She could handle this. Never mind the thorny vine of hope that twined around her heart at the thought of seeing him again.

She lifted her hand and knocked on the door. There was no raucous barking or sound of claws clicking against the wood floors. If Shadow wasn't here, then neither was his master. He was tending to his horses or fixing a fence or something. Maybe he was even at Mary Beth's. She told herself the little twist in her stomach was relief.

She gave a second knock anyway, shifting on her feet, peering casually through the darkened living room window.

She fiddled with her purse strap, uncertain. She hadn't wanted to come back up here again. It had taken all morning just to work up her nerve. As most folks around here did, Noah left his doors unlocked. She'd just find her phone and go. He'd never even know she'd been here. Only Shadow would know, when he detected her scent, and it would be their little secret.

Yes, she was a big fat chicken.

She twisted the handle and stepped over the threshold into the quiet house, a perplexing mix of relief and disappointment filling her.

*Just find your phone and be grateful you avoided additional pain.*

When would she learn? She dropped her purse on the table and went to her corner of the sofa. Her corner. She scowled at the fanciful thought.

She stuck her hand into the crevice between the armrest and cushion and felt around, wincing at the feel of crumbs and whatnot. She pulled out a pencil. A black balled-up sock. A—she frowned, pulling out the round object—chewed-up golf ball?

She was setting aside the hodgepodge of objects when she saw something else lying there on the end table. Under a stack of newspapers. Just the corner peeking out.

The divorce papers.

Her breath caught. She slowly straightened, her eyes locked

on the document. Her heart played dead as her breath left in one long exhale. He hadn't taken them yet.

Maybe . . .

*No. Do not do that to yourself.* He'd only forgotten about them. Of course he had.

Their little trek in the mountains had no doubt set him behind. His horses had probably suffered for their neglect. He had his hands full, and like her, he was likely not quite recovered. Buried as the papers were under the newspapers . . . out of sight, out of mind. She wouldn't allow herself to think otherwise.

She'd take care of it herself. It was the least she could do. She'd brought him nothing but trouble, after all.

The end of their marriage—her fault.

The bungled divorce—her fault.

Their near-death experience—yeah.

She would definitely take this chore off his hands. She'd run the papers to the attorney's office today and get the thing finalized, as she'd promised to do a long time ago.

She lifted the sections of the *Gazette* and pulled out the papers. A pen sat nearby. Her heart worked overtime as she flipped to the last page.

Blank. His line remained blank. He hadn't signed.

She expelled a breath. Great. Just great. Now she was going to have to hunt him down. Have to don that fake smile and pretend it didn't hurt like the dickens to see him again.

She stuffed the papers into her bag. She'd handle it. Handle it all and with a smile. Just as soon as she found her stupid phone.

She rooted around between, behind, and under all the cushions, her hands now trembling at the thought of seeing Noah again. The façade she'd always worn was getting harder to hold in place.

*Don't be silly, Josephine. You can handle five measly minutes with the man.*

Coming up empty, she dropped to the floor and lifted the sofa skirt, peering underneath. Heavens, he really needed to sweep under here.

Her eyes lit on a familiar flat object. There. She reached for the phone and pulled it out just as the door snapped open.

Paws clicked quickly across the floor. Josephine sat up in time to intercept Shadow, who all but knocked her over in his excitement. She petted the dog, turning her face just as he swiped her cheek with his tongue.

"Hey, buddy." Her eyes shot to Noah, still standing on the threshold. He seemed like a giant from her place on the floor.

She extricated herself from Shadow and scrambled to her feet. "Hi, Noah."

His brows collided like thunderclouds. "What are you doing here?"

"I, uh, came for my phone." She held it up as if needing proof. "When you didn't answer the door, I thought I'd just . . ." *Let myself into your house, invade your privacy. Wreck your world.* She winced.

Shadow nudged her hand with his cold, wet nose, soliciting more attention. She ducked her head as she ruffled the dog's fur. "Sorry," she said to Noah. "Guess I shouldn't have barged in."

When she couldn't avoid it any longer she straightened, meeting his gaze.

His eyes were fixed on hers as if taking her in. She wished she could tell what he was thinking, but today his tawny eyes were keeping all their secrets. A long, tense moment stretched like an overinflated balloon.

She didn't breathe until he turned to shut the door. He faced her again, tucking his hands into his pockets. His eyes were tight at the corners, but his mouth lifted in a thin smile.

"Did you check the forecast before driving up?" he asked.

It took a moment for his meaning to sink in. When it did, her laugh held more air than humor. Hard to believe it had been less than two weeks ago that she'd shown up here with those stupid papers. Pathetic how suddenly desperate she was for an unexpected snowstorm.

"No worries." She smiled and tried to mean it. "Fifty-five and sunny. Zero chance of snow, and zero chance of getting stuck with an unwanted houseguest, you'll be happy to hear."

Shadow's sniffs were loud in the sudden quiet. He meandered over to her purse, nose twitching.

Noah's eyes followed the dog. Something registered in them as they locked onto her purse and, no doubt, the familiar document sticking out of it.

Her mouth went dry, and her bones melted a little. She strolled to her purse on wobbly legs, lengthening the distance between them. Needing space.

She grabbed the papers and held tight to her smile as she faced him. "Yeah. I, uh, found these on the table there and thought I'd run them back to town. I was going to come find you in the barn. Get your signature. You saved me the trouble though, so that's great."

*Stop babbling, Josephine.* She locked her lips down tight.

His face was inscrutable, his posture still and rigid. His head tipped back, narrowing his eyes ever so slightly.

She tore her gaze away, not wanting to get lost in those amber pools again. Next time she just might drown.

Her hands trembled as she rooted blindly through the newspapers on the table, finally coming up with the pen. She held both out to him, somehow unable to take a single step. To close the distance between them.

Her eyes made it as far as his top shirt button. "You, um . . . just need to sign it, and then I'll be out of your hair. I assume you had the chance to read it over."

Her arms grew heavy, gravity tugging. As if she held a five-pound weight in each hand instead of pen and paper.

"Oh, you want me to sign it, do you?" There was an edge to his voice.

Her eyes snapped to his. Got caught in his gaze where a storm seemed to be brewing. He took a step, then another. His eyes pierced hers as he closed the distance between them, all masculine grace.

She held her ground, her heart thrashing against her ribs, her smile faltering on her lips. She tried to dredge up something to say. Something light and sassy to break the tension.

Nothing. She had nothing.

He stopped an arm's length away. Snatched the document from her hand. Held it from the top with both hands.

The ripping sound was loud in the quiet of the house. An endless moment later the halves fluttered to the rug.

Her jaw slackened. Her eyes locked on his again. Speech seemed like an impossible task when she couldn't even breathe.

"I don't want a divorce," he said. "Got that?"

A chill swept through her from head to foot. Something fluttered in her belly. She couldn't seem to get control of her mind. Her mouth. Her muscles. In fact, her whole system seemed to be shutting down.

Something shifted in his face. A shadow moved across and his jaw muscle twitched. And then his eyes warmed. She couldn't have torn hers away if she'd tried.

"Something happened out there, Josie." The rough texture of his voice sent a wave of gooseflesh over her skin. He took another step closer. "And I don't even know if you remember, but . . . I told you I love you. And I meant it."

Her heart turned over in her chest. Her eyes burned. With hope.

He cradled her face. "I don't think I ever stopped."

Melting. She was melting.

But the voices came back, taunting her. Her past intruded, filling her with shame even as her eyes filled with tears.

She struggled to hold them in place. "But I don't . . ." She couldn't squeeze the rest past her constricted throat.

He drew his thumbs down her heated cheeks. "You don't what?" The tenderness in his voice was her undoing.

Her throat released a gurgle. A tear slipped out. "I don't deserve another chance."

His features softened. The intensity in his eyes unraveled her. He wiped the tears from her face. "But, oh, baby girl. I want to be that person . . . the one who loves you no matter what. Completely. Unreservedly. Unconditionally. I don't think I could stop even if I wanted to." His words choked off as his eyes filled with tears.

Something inside her, something tight and aching, unfurled like a fragile ribbon. There was no doubt she still loved this man. But somehow, knowing he loved her in spite of everything she'd done . . . It only made her love him more. Made her want to be the protector and guardian of his heart. If he was giving her another chance, she would be oh so careful with it this time.

"Oh, Noah." Such a love was a gift. One she had neither the desire nor the ability to refuse. "I love you too. So much."

He drew her close, a ghost of a smile in his dewy eyes. His

breath whispered across her lips before they met hers. He kissed her softly, reverently, his hooded eyes never leaving hers.

He slayed her. He always had. There was no numbness here. Only pure, sweet love. And a passion that left her breathless and aching.

He deepened the kiss, clutching her tightly as if never letting her go. Her heart skittered across her chest. Her lips parted on a breath, and he began a soft exploration, as if reacquainting himself with her.

She scarcely heard the *plunk* of the pen as it hit the floor.

She pressed against him, her hands trembling against his face. He tasted like Noah. Like heaven. The musky smell of him filled her senses, the familiarity of it leaving her raw and desperate for him.

*Noah*, her heart cried out in relief. In joy. It welled up in her, demanding release. A whimper caught in her throat.

Noah pulled back, his knowing eyes searching hers. He thumbed away her tears. "Don't cry, baby girl."

She prayed this wasn't a dream. That she wouldn't wake up in the hospital, brain fuzzy, to beeping monitors and fussy nurses, the word *ex-husband* rolling off their tongues.

*Please, God.*

She took a slow blink and swallowed hard. Got her emotions under control. Her heart was like a jackhammer in her chest. "You really still love me?"

"Is that so hard to believe?" His lips tilted in a tender smile, his eyes fastened on hers, filled with love and so much more. "I fell for you the moment we first met. You stole my heart. And I don't ever want it back, Josie."

She felt a pinch in her chest. Her lip trembled as her vision went blurry again.

He swept another tear away, smiling tenderly. "Stop that now. You're giving me a complex."

Shadow nudged between them, wanting in on the moment. Noah smiled at the dog's persistence, finally dropping a hand to appease him. Shadow wedged in closer, and the scattered papers crinkled under his paws.

The papers that had started all this. The papers Noah had resolutely rejected.

"We're still married," she said in wonder. Somehow it was only now sinking in.

"We're still married, Mrs. Mitchell." Noah's smile spread to his eyes, the emotion there making her insides melt. "For always."

She was Noah's wife. For better or for worse. It was a position she'd never take for granted again.

She cupped his face, reveling in the smoothness of his cheek. Then she rose on her toes and brushed her lips with his, savoring the softness of his kiss. The strength. Oh, how she'd missed him. Missed this. The very thought that he was hers again nearly made her come undone.

"For always, Noah Mitchell." As she drew away, the smile that curved her lips was neither planned nor calculated. It was merely impossible to restrain because it was born from the joy bubbling up from within.

# Epilogue

Sunlight filtered through the leaf-laden trees in a glorious golden haze, dappling the spring-green lawn. Josephine's eyes fastened on the object of her affection, standing in the middle of the yard—a little boy with black hair and tawny eyes.

He turned just then, and those eyes brightened as they lighted on her. "Mama!"

He came running, his pudgy little legs working hard, and she knelt down just in time. He barreled into her, all thirty pounds of baby-soft skin and rugged boy. She chuckled as she stood with him, so filled with love she was nearly bursting with it.

His round fists clutched at her shirt as other arms—thicker, stronger arms—wrapped around from behind, enveloping them both.

"Good morning, sleepyhead," he whispered in her ear.

Her eyes popped open, and a familiar pair of tawny eyes smiled down at her.

*Noah.*

He was lying beside her in their bed, propped up with his

elbow, his other arm curled around her waist. His hair was damp, one wet strand falling rebelliously over his forehead.

His smile made her besotted heart skip a beat. "Breakfast is getting cold."

She stretched, the remnants of her dream floating away. "Mmm. What time is it?"

"Almost ten." One brow hitched up. "And we even went to bed early, young lady. I waited as long as I could."

She smiled at his boyish impatience. He loved taking Mondays off with her and never wanted to waste a minute of them.

"Don't move," he said, pressing a kiss to her forehead. "You're getting breakfast in bed this morning."

The bed shook as he left it, and Josephine enjoyed the retreating masculine form of her husband.

She slipped into their bathroom to take care of business and returned a minute later. Sliding beneath the covers, she propped herself against the headboard with pillows. Noises came from the kitchen: the hum of the microwave and clatter of dishes, followed by a loud *clang*.

She winced. "Need some help, honey?"

"Nope. You stay right there."

A lot had happened in the four months since their reconciliation. They'd had a small ceremony to renew their vows. She'd wanted a fresh start, wanted their friends and his family to know she was serious about their new beginning.

His parents had taken time from their retirement travel to return for the informal ceremony. His family had been understandably skeptical about their reconciliation, but they were coming around. They were important to Noah, and she was determined to earn back their trust.

Noah had gone back to Mitchell Home Improvement. He'd missed working with his hands, and it seemed the attic renovation had sparked the idea of expanding the family business. His brother was happy to have him back, and now Noah was officially running the room-addition portion of the business.

He'd sold the ranch to Mary Beth, lock, stock, and barrel, and he and Josephine bought a house on Mulberry Lane just outside of town. It was a tidy bungalow with a lovely front porch and huge trees shading the property. Copper Creek rippled by, just beyond the fenced-in yard.

At the thought of their spacious yard her dream rushed back with startling clarity. The little boy with black hair and amber eyes. It was the second time she'd had the dream—the first time had been before she'd even suspected she was pregnant.

Her hand drifted over her flat belly, and she couldn't stop the smile that curled her lips. She'd intended to tell Noah last night after their late supper, but then he'd kissed her in the kitchen over a sink full of dishes, and one thing had led to another. By the time she'd caught her breath, her limbs were weighted with fatigue, her eyelids too heavy to hold open. That was happening a lot lately.

Noah entered the room, balancing a tray full of food in his hands. "Breakfast is served, m'lady."

Shadow followed on his heels, watching the tray with hopeful eyes. He let out a little whimper.

Noah gave him a look. "You had yours, Buster. Go lie down."

Shadow pouted a moment before skulking off to the foot of the bed, where he plopped down on the rug with a heavy sigh.

Josephine's stomach twisted with hunger at the savory and sweet scents of bacon and maple syrup. "Mmm. Smells delicious."

She'd been ravenous all week. She'd only taken the pregnancy test the day before, but it already felt as if she'd been sitting on the news for a month. She couldn't hold it back another minute.

Noah started to set the tray on her lap, but she laid a hand on his arm. "Wait. Can you set it on the nightstand for a minute?"

His eyes toggled to hers, questioning, but he did as she asked.

The bed sank as he lowered himself beside her, searching her face. "What's wrong? Are you feeling okay?"

"I'm fine. I just—"

What if Noah wasn't as happy about the baby as she was? Her hands tightened on the bedsheets, and her gaze fell to her lap, her old insecurities rising.

They hadn't planned for this. In fact, they'd talked about waiting a year or so until the new part of his business was more established and they were in better shape financially.

He took her hand. "What's wrong? You're scaring me."

She met his eyes, trying to wipe the worry from her expression. "Everything's fine. At least, I think it is."

"What is it then?"

She bit her lip, hoping against hope for a positive reaction. "Well, honey . . . it seems I'm . . . pregnant."

His eyes widened slightly. His lips parted. A long moment stretched between them as his mouth worked. "Pregnant?"

She nodded slowly, searching his eyes for some clue as to his feelings.

Then his lips began a slow, beautiful curve as happiness flashed in his eyes. His arms swallowed her in a hard, tight hug. "You're pregnant!" he all but yelled into her ear.

She laughed, filled with equal parts joy and relief. "That's the gist of it, mister."

"Wow." He pulled back. "How long have you known?"

"I took the test yesterday." She settled against the pillows and savored the pleasure on his face. Her own face was flushed with joy. It was so much more fun sharing the secret than it had been keeping it. Especially when it put such a big smile on Noah's face.

"*That's* why you've been sleeping so much." His gaze sharpened on her face. "Wait a minute, how are you feeling? Are you doing okay? I shouldn't have woken you up. Food. You need to eat." He reached for the tray.

She laughed. "This mother-hen side of you is mighty cute. But I'm perfectly fine. Just a bit tired at times."

He settled beside her, the worry fading as a look of wonder drifted over his face. "I'm going to be a daddy."

"You're going to be a great daddy."

"And you're going to be a great mama." His gaze raked over her face with such tenderness it made her eyes sting. Then his hand slid over her waist until his palm lay flat against her tummy.

"I hope it's a little girl," he whispered. "With blond hair and blue eyes and a great big heart."

She smiled. "Maybe next time. This one's all boy, Noah Mitchell."

"Oh yeah?" His gaze dropped to her mouth just before he drew his thumb over her lower lip. His eyelids lowered to half-mast, and he gave her that look that made her legs turn to jelly.

A hum started low and slow in her belly, spreading outward. He replaced his thumb with his mouth, and within moments she was lost in his kiss. By the time his lips left hers, her brain was foggy with want.

His kisses trailed down her jaw, her neck, pausing over the sensitive spot just under her ear.

"Is it too late to shoot for twins?" he whispered.

Her laugh was shaky. "Way too late."

"Can't blame a guy for trying."

Just as he went to pull down the sheets, her stomach gave a loud, hard growl.

Noah ended the kiss, reluctance evident in his slow, lingering withdrawal. A sheepish smile played at his lips. "I guess I'd better feed my girl."

As he reached for the tray, she caught his arm. "Your breakfast smells delicious, and I am very hungry . . . but maybe it might keep for a bit?" She lifted a brow.

Eagerness flickered in his eyes as he lowered his weight beside her. "Oh, it'll keep."

Her smile might have been a little smug. "I thought it just might."

# The Story Behind the Story

Dear friend,

*Sweetbriar Cottage* was initially conceived during a workshop at a writer's conference. Over the next few days the ideas just kept flowing. The characters arrived on the scene fully fleshed, scene ideas poured out, and dialogue came as fast as I could jot it down. This is my thirtieth book and, I assure you, that is not normally the case for me.

But by the time I was heading home from the conference I was starting to waffle about writing this story. I realized it would have to be a stand-alone novel. With the exception of one book, I had only written series for my current publisher, and I doubted they wanted to change that anytime soon.

Also, part of me was nervous about this particular story. I worried I wouldn't be able to quite pull it off the way I saw it in my head. Josephine has a pretty dark past, and though I already loved her and felt compassion toward her, I worried about making her likeable for readers. Self-doubt crept in (boy, did it), and I shoved the story on the back burner without telling a soul.

Months passed, and my publisher asked me for a four-book proposal. I was expecting this and had three stories already in mind for a series; I only needed one more. It occurred to me that I could water down my stand-alone idea and pitch it as the first story of the series. After all, I already had thirteen single-spaced pages of notes! The story I proposed to them was basically all of Josephine and Noah's backstory. Their meeting at the barbershop, their courtship, and (ta-da!) their happily ever after. No cheating. No divorce. No reconciliation. All the hard parts were gone now. Clever me.

Fast-forward a couple months. I was eagerly waiting to hear from my editor how the publishing team felt about my series proposal. I was especially anxious because I needed to start the first novel very soon in order to meet my deadline. And then I got the e-mail I'd been waiting for. They loved the series idea. But . . .

"Could you possibly write a stand-alone book before you start the series?"

I was shocked. They had their reasons—good ones—but inside I was panicking. Every story I had in my arsenal was already in my proposal. And since stories typically "brew" inside my head for months before I ever start writing . . . what on earth was I going to write? I needed an idea and *quick*!

I'm sorry to say it took two full days of panic to even remember my initial idea for *Sweetbriar Cottage*. And once I did, I knew it was the book I was supposed to write. It seemed Someone wanted me to write this story the way it had been given to me. It seemed Someone had vetoed my idea of watering it down. And Someone had told my publisher I needed to write something else.

I immediately scheduled a call with my publisher. My

throat tightened with tears as I explained all that had happened "behind the scenes." It was obvious that this story already had me by the heart, and I hadn't even written a word of it. They agreed I needed to write it as a stand-alone.

But I knew I needed help—the heavenly kind! I confided in my dad and stepmom, asking them to please pray me through this book. They were happy to oblige. Throughout the writing of this manuscript the words *Trust Me* remained in the header, in red ink, as a daily reminder. Believe me, I needed it.

I'd like to say the fear disappeared after I started the story. But to tell the truth, every day I sat down to write this book was an act of faith. And yet each time I placed my fingers on the keyboard, the words seemed to pour straight from my heart in a way they never had before.

I hope I did the story justice. I hope Josephine and Noah became as real to you as they are to me. I hope their struggles and pain changed you in some little way as they did me. I'm so grateful I got the chance to tell the story, just as it was meant to be told. And I'm grateful that you chose to come along on the journey with me.

Blessings!
Denise

# Discussion Questions

1. Who was your favorite character in the story and why?
2. Which scene was your favorite and why?
3. In what ways does the horse Kismet represent Josephine?
4. Did you get frustrated with either Josephine or Noah as the story progressed? Was their emotional upheaval realistic?
5. How is their journey in the mountains like their marriage?
6. Should love between a married couple be unconditional? Why or why not? Who loves you unconditionally? How does that kind of love make you feel?
7. Josephine, desperate for unconditional love, pushed Noah to the limits to test if it was real. What do you think made her so desperate for unconditional love? Did she deserve a second chance? Discuss a time when someone gave you a second chance.
8. Josephine felt powerless because of what she endured as

a child, and she used her sexuality to regain her power. Have you ever known anyone who did something similar?

9. Josephine had "voices" in her head—things her mother and stepfather had said that she'd convinced herself were true. Do you have any "voices" you need to eradicate from your mind?

10. Discuss the ways Noah's love for Josie might represent God's love for us.

# Acknowledgments

Writing a book is a team effort, and I'm so grateful for the fabulous team at HarperCollins Christian Fiction, led by publisher Daisy Hutton: Amanda Bostic, Karli Jackson, Paul Fisher, Kristen Golden, Jodi Hughes, Becky Monds, and Kristen Ingebretson.

Thanks especially to my editors, Becky Philpott and Karli Jackson, for their insight and inspiration. I'm infinitely grateful to editor LB Norton, who has saved me from countless errors and always makes me look so much better than I am.

Author Colleen Coble is my first reader. Thank you, friend! Writing wouldn't be nearly as much fun without you!

I'm grateful to my agent, Karen Solem, who's able to somehow make sense of the legal garble of contracts and, even more amazing, help me understand it.

Kevin, my husband of twenty-eight years, has been a wonderful support. Thank you, honey! I'm so glad to be doing life with you. To my kiddos, Justin and Hannah, Chad, and Trevor: You make life an adventure! It's so fun watching you step boldly into adulthood. Love you all!

Thank you to Barbara Hutson from Stillwater Farms in Dawsonville, Georgia, who took time out of her busy day to show this city slicker around her beautiful horse ranch. Her love of horses was truly inspiring. Any mistakes in the story are all mine.

Lastly, thank you, friend, for letting me share this story with you. I wouldn't be doing this without you! I enjoy connecting with friends on my Facebook page, www.facebook.com/authordenisehunter. Please pop over and say hello. Visit my website at the link www.DeniseHunterBooks.com or just drop me a note at Denise@DeniseHunterBooks.com. I'd love to hear from you!

RETURN TO COPPER CREEK

NOVEMBER 2017

WITH

*Blue Ridge Sunrise*

THOMAS NELSON
*Since 1798*

# About the Author

Denise Hunter is the internationally published bestselling author of more than twenty-five books, including *A December Bride* and *The Convenient Groom*, which have been adapted into original Hallmark Channel movies. She has won the Holt Medallion Award, the Reader's Choice Award, the Carol Award, and the Foreword Book of the Year Award and is a RITA finalist. When Denise isn't orchestrating love lives on the written page, she enjoys traveling with her family, drinking green tea, and playing drums. Denise makes her home in Indiana where she and her husband are rapidly approaching an empty nest.

DeniseHunterBooks.com
Facebook: authordenisehunter
Twitter: @DeniseAHunter